With her back to Baptiste, Vic sucked in a deep breath. He could make any woman fall head-over-heals in love before she knew what hit her, and that was the very reason she was hightailing it out of Oakland. She was on the verge of doing what she'd sworn eight years ago she'd never do again. With one bad marriage to her credit and enough heartache to last a lifetime, she'd learned one valuable lesson a long time ago—love and matrimony were as volatile as nitrate and glycerin combined.

"Honey . . ." A.J.'s voice faded as soon as his gaze landed on his favorite body part, her hips. With just enough curve to cause a man to go weak at the knees, they swayed gracefully. Willpower was the only thing that prevented him from going into full cardiac arrest at the sight of the thirty-eight double Ds beneath the sleeveless cream colored shell she wore.

Vic stopped, but didn't turn around.

"Baptiste . . ." she uttered the single word with exasperation. "What is it gonna take before you realize what you want will never happen?"

A.J. settled his back against the banister and went one better. "What has to happen before you realize that it will?"

WHEN A MAN LOVES A WOMAN

LA CONNIE TAYLOR-JONES

Genesis Press, Inc.

INDIGO

An imprint of Genesis Press, Inc.
Publishing Company

Genesis Press, Inc.
P.O. Box 101
Columbus, MS 39703

Copyright © 2008 by LaConnie Taylor-Jones

ISBN: 13 DIGIT : 978-1-58571-274-8
ISBN: 10 DIGIT : 1-58571-274-4
Manufactured in the United States of America

First Edition

Visit us at www.genesis-press.com
or call at 1-888-Indigo-1-4-0

DEDICATION

In memory of
Clara Anna Daniels Taylor
November 1927–June 2007

Mother:
Your wisdom, love, and guidance
will always be remembered.

ACKNOWLEDGMENTS

Thank you readers for once again re-visiting the Baptiste Clan with me. I hope you enjoy reading Vic and A.J.'s story as much as I did writing it.

My special thanks goes out to Dr. Catherine M. Waters and Captain William N. Hendricks (ret.) for providing their technical expertise.

Also, my heartfelt appreciation is extended to my author mentor and friend, Marilyn Tyner, for critiquing this story during the early stages.

Only time will tell what fate awaits the youngest Baptiste brother, Ray, so stay tuned.

In the meantime, be sure to visit my website at *www.laconnietaylorjones.com*.

I love to hear from you! Feel free to contact me via e-mail at: *lovestories@comcast.net*.

Until next time, stay strong, live well, and be blessed!!

Much love,
LaConnie

CHAPTER 1

"I'm gonna kill him!"

The words shot from Vic's mouth faster than a torpedo the second she spotted the white BMW belonging to A.J. Baptiste. She'd let the police decide if his death was due to voluntary or involuntary manslaughter.

With a vise grip on the steering wheel, Vic floored the accelerator as she sped up the driveway to the mansion of her close friends, Caitlyn and Marcel Baptiste. She left a trail of scorching rubber when she circled her black two-door Infiniti coupe so close to the X5 sports activity vehicle that she nearly took out the passenger-side door.

Today was supposed to be a joyous occasion, not a matchmaking spectacle. She and the man she'd always referred to as Baptiste were godparents to Etienne and Nicolas, Marcel and Caitlyn's two-month-old identical twin boys who'd made their arrival four weeks early. In a little over an hour, they would be christened. But her happiness immediately turned to fury after the phone call she'd received. That she was upset at Baptiste was putting it rather mildly.

She was livid.

Around eight that morning, she'd spoken with her realtor and learned the details of Baptiste's latest stunt in his effort to convince her to fall in love with him. During the entire drive over, the only thing Vic Bennett, who hated to be called Victoria under any circumstances, could think about was the unmitigated gall Baptiste had had to tell her realtor her condominium was no longer up for sale because her plans to relocate to Atlanta had been cancelled. Before she killed the engine, she thought about the telephone conversation some more. To hell with manslaughter.

She'd take Alcee Jules Baptiste out on murder in the first degree.

She got out of the car, not bothering to check her watch. Yes, she was running late even though tardiness was something she unequivocally loathed. With every ounce of strength in her arm, she slammed the door and raced toward the Mediterranean-style estate nestled within the Oakland Hills. She vowed to end Baptiste's interference in her life, to end it today.

July's blistering heat scaled up her back and plastered a sleeveless crème-colored top against her spine. Perspiration stains no doubt appeared at the back of her raw silk pantsuit, but she didn't care. All that mattered was finding a way to convince Baptiste she would never fall in love again, not with him or any other man.

Vic's fury catapulted up another notch when she scanned the words on a large, yellow post-it stuck to the double doors. What fraction of control she had, snapped. Crumpling the post-it inside her fist, she walked inside and slammed the door behind her.

All hell was about to break loose.

It seemed like the only thing she'd done the past year was fight off one life-altering attack after another. An organizational restructure at the outpatient medical clinic where she worked as nursing administrator had put her at odds with a bunch of fifty-year-old Dolce and Gabbana-wearing suits who only wanted to make money, money, and more money at the expense of her patients. So, she'd quit. And for the past ten months she'd been in outright combat, trying to convince Baptiste, her family, his family, their friends, and any stranger off the streets who'd listen that she wasn't budging from what she'd told them a zillion times over. She didn't want Baptiste's love and commitment.

And she'd never give in.

Silence surrounded Vic as she stood in the center of the marble-tiled foyer until Caitlyn's snow-white Bichon Frises puppies, Max and Kenji, darted down the dual staircase at breakneck speed and heeled at her feet.

Vic looked down with her hands planted against her hips. "Where is your mother?" Listening to the canines' rapid succession of barks, she figured they understood exactly to whom she was referring.

Max and Kenji merrily bounced halfway up the stairs before stopping to look back at Vic.

"Go on," she ordered, shooing them forward. "That's right. Take me to Caitlyn." Vic stomped up each step, grinding her teeth in frustration. "Doggone her little bitty soul. Nobody told her to play Cupid."

Once she made it to the top of the staircase, she spotted Max and Kenji with their tails wagging in front of a closed door two rooms away.

"Umm-hmm," Vic mumbled, slowly bobbing her head up and down. "She's in there, right?"

Max and Kenji barked again.

Squaring her shoulders, she tucked her clutch purse under her arm. In about two seconds, it was going to be show time with her best friend and Baptiste's sister-in-law, Caitlyn.

Afterward, she planned to introduce Baptiste to an early Armageddon.

"T-One . . ."

A.J. paced in a full circle, but stopped the second he heard the thunderous boom from downstairs. Hurricane Vic had just made landfall. From the loud thud of the door slamming shut, this Category Five storm would leave a path of total devastation before subsiding. All morning he'd prepared for her fury, but he hadn't counted on handling a dress crisis at the same time. At wit's end, he squatted again in front of one of his identical twin daughters. "Sweetheart, for the last time will you put your dress back on for Daddy?"

"Why?" Taylor, the older, questioned for the umpteenth time.

A.J. sighed softly. "Why not, baby?"

Taylor choked out her words between sobs. "It's ugly."

A.J. glanced over at her sister, Tyler. "What about you, T-Two?"

"Uh-uh," Tyler whimpered, shaking her head with adamant finality.

A.J. wrapped his muscular arms around his four-year-old adopted daughters and hoped the famous backdoor approach he'd practiced as a pediatrician for the past ten years would do the trick. "Don't you think the dresses are pretty?"

The ebony-skinned look-alikes silently conferred with each other via a teary-eyed glance before Tyler loudly voiced her opinion first. "No."

A.J. hung his head and sighed again. "Why not, pumpkin?"

Sniffing, Tyler wiped her nose with the back of her hand. "'Cause you not do the bows right."

"Yes, I did, princess." A.J. stood, walked to the bed, and lifted one of the dresses in front of him. "See, Daddy tied it right."

Taylor moved up closer to carefully examine the lop-sided ribbons and more tears welled in her eyes. "No, you didn't."

A.J. placed the dress back on the bed and focused on the wall straight ahead, contemplating his next move with the dynamic duo who were as fierce, prickly, and beautiful as Vic, the love of his life. The corners of his lips formed a smile once he decided a round-about approach was the only way to convince these pint-size divas to wear their outfits.

"Hmm." A.J. sat sideways on the edge of the bed, rubbing at his chin, as he glanced at the girls out the corner of his eye. "Well, I guess Daddy will just have to find some other little girls to give these dresses to. What a shame," he mockingly mumbled, then held two fingers up in front of his face. "Let's see now, how many little girls will I need to find to wear them?"

The twins were stymied for a moment. They had just learned to count, and two sets of doe-brown eyes focused intently on his hand. A.J. hid a grin behind a quiet cough at their quizzical expressions. Between Taylor's inquisitiveness and Tyler's vociferousness, he knew they'd figure out the answer before long.

Tyler cupped her hand next to Taylor's ear. "How many is that?"

Taylor shrugged and placed a chubby finger at her temple, pondering.

A.J.'s eyes twinkled with delight at how they always worked together to solve a dilemma. "Okay, let's figure it out." He scooted around to face them with his fingers still up and folded them down as he counted. "One . . . two."

Tyler lifted her right hand and replicated her father's movements. Suddenly her eyes widened. "My fingers are gone."

A.J.'s brow lifted with confidence. "That's right. Now what number is that called?" He clarified his question when they stared at him, baffled. "Remember when we practiced counting our numbers the other day?" He curved his thumb and index finger into the shape of an "O". "What did Daddy tell you this is called?"

Taylor shrugged. "Nothing."

The only thing A.J. could do was chuckle. He wanted to hear them say *zero*. However, mission accomplished. They got the concept.

A worrisome look crept over Taylor's face and she waggled her finger between herself and Tyler. "No, no, Daddy. Those our dresses."

A.J.'s eyes sparkled with victory. "Oh, they are?"

Their little heads bobbed up and down emphatically.

He reached behind him and picked up the white satin dresses accented with pastel petals at the hem. "Are you ready to put them back on and keep them on?"

"Umm-hmm," Taylor and Tyler agreed in unison.

A.J. smiled. "Okay. First, let's wash our hands," he insisted, remembering that Tyler had used the back of her hand instead of a tissue. He grimaced when he noticed their tousled mass of thick, black curls. "When we finish, Daddy will brush your hair again and we can get dressed."

He stood and followed the girls toward the bathroom, a full grin emerging. If he could slip a shot into a fearful three year-old, he could certainly find a way to get Vic to fall in love with him. And he knew exactly how to do it. Although he'd be swamped the next few days with the opening of the health clinic he'd founded in East Oakland, absolutely nothing was going to stand in the way of winning Vic's heart.

Vic burst through the door of Etienne and Nicolas's nursery to find her best friend, Caitlyn, along with two of their other friends, Tara Spencer and Chandler Perkins, calmly waiting.

"Caitlyn Renee Thompson Baptiste." Vic smoothed out the wrinkles from the balled-up post-it and waved it in front of her. "What's the meaning of this?" She read the note aloud. "We need to discuss you and A.J."

Caitlyn, who was nursing Etienne, giggled softly. "Oh, I see you got my little note."

Chandler glanced at her watch. "Vic, you're running late. Girl, that's a first." She tossed a sly wink at Caitlyn and Tara. "Let's put this one down in the record book, y'all."

"Hush, Chandler," Vic snapped. "Just as soon as I finish with missy here, I'm on you next." She looked at Caitlyn, again through narrowed eyes. "I would've been on time, if I hadn't had to try and undo what that crazy brother-in-law of yours did."

Caitlyn smiled. "Did you have a talk with your realtor this morning?"

Vic flashed a fake smile and mimicked, "Yes, I had a talk with my realtor this morning."

"Yeah, yeah, yeah." Chandler gestured at the empty rocker next to Caitlyn. "We'll discuss all of that later. Time's a wasting, so sit. We need to talk to you."

"Talk to me about what?" Vic glanced at the clock on the nightstand. "Is it just me or have you three forgotten we have a christening around here in an hour?"

"We know what time it is." Chandler pointed to the rocker again. "Sit."

Vic refused to comply. "Listen, ladies, Baptiste is not up for discussion, but the three of y'all playing match-maker is. This—"

"But you and A.J. belong together," Tara softly interrupted.

"Wrong," Vic quickly corrected. "That's your opinion, not mine." She stared a moment at the smiles on their faces. "And which one of ya spilled the beans and told Baptiste I was moving to Atlanta anyway?"

Chandler crisscrossed her arms above her head in defense. "Hold it there now. We're innocent. Louise and George Vincent committed *that* crime."

"My parents?" Vic shrieked so loudly that a sleeping Nicolas whimpered in his crib. "Hush now, sweet pea." Leaning over the crib, she gently rubbed the infant's back until he drifted back to sleep, then turned back around and whispered, "When?"

"Well," Chandler drawled, "Louise probably told A.J. over lunch. They have a standing date at least once a week. Wednesdays, you know."

"What?" The full impact of Chandler's statement hit her like a bolt of electricity, taking her breath away. Now she understood why for the last three months whenever she called her mother on Wednesdays to go shopping or have lunch she'd say she already had plans with a friend.

Tara chimed in. "And I'm pretty sure your dad told A.J. at one of the baseball games they've been going to."

Vic flung her head back and sighed in annoyance because another one of her suspicions had been confirmed. She knew Baptiste and her father, George Vincent, were diehard fans of the Oakland A's and had started going to the day games together. Instead of enjoying their little excursions, they were plotting against her. It was bad enough her friends had sided with Baptiste. Now her mother and father had committed treason and defected to the enemy's camp, too. She was putting a stop to everyone's matchmaking. Today.

"Where is he?" Vic hissed. Her words zoomed out so fast, she gasped for air.

Tara stifled a giggle with the back of her hand. "You mean A.J.?"

"Don't get cute with me, Tara." Vic narrowed her eyes. "Where is he?"

"Oh, I'm sure he's around somewhere," Chandler quipped with a mischievous chuckle, "waiting for you."

"Just wait until I find him. I'm gonna kill him!" Vic dashed out the nursery, mumbling something under her breath and ignoring the soft laughter of Caitlyn, Tara, and Chandler.

She reached the bottom of the staircase at the same time Baptiste came around the corner from the kitchen, and she headed straight toward him. The day she'd walked out on her ex-husband, Ron Evans, eight years ago, she'd vowed not to give another man the chance to stir her emotions, let alone get close to her heart.

Somehow, this man had managed to do both.

Getting too close to Baptiste was always a mistake. Her heart did a somersault, her legs buckled, and her palms broke out in a cold sweat. And Lord, she didn't even want to think about the activities erupting south of the border.

Sucking in a deep breath, she glared at the gorgeous hunk, who when she first met him had honestly believed a married woman couldn't manage a family and career at the same time. That warped mentality alone should have made her run, but it didn't. Baptiste was more handsome than any man had a right to be. Smooth café-au-lait skin, black wavy hair, and long, curly lashes a woman could spend hours on and never duplicate graced the most stubborn man she'd ever met in her life. It had been a couple of weeks since she'd last seen him, and she noticed that he'd cut the top of his hair. It layered nicely into his usual bound ponytail.

Angry with herself for losing control of her emotions, she ignored his caressing gaze.

"Baptiste, you got some nerve, you know that?" She planted her hands on her hips. "Why did you call my realtor and fire him?"

A.J.'s half-crooked grin lifted his moustache and deepened his double dimples. "Honey—"

Vic frowned. "Man, how many times do I have to tell you 'Honey' is not my name? Are you ever going to call me Vic?"

"As I was saying before you interrupted me . . ." He flashed a roguish grin and purred, "Honey . . ." He let his pet name for her roll slowly off his tongue. "I didn't fire him. I simply told him his services were no longer needed."

The only comeback Vic had was to shake her head at his annoying reference to her because he knew she hated it when he called her "Honey," but had given up hope he'd ever refer to her as anything else.

His eyes raked her without condemnation. "You look very nice today, but I much prefer to see you in a dress."

Goaded to fury, Vic retorted, "Baptiste, don't start with that dress mess today, pleassse."

He had some nerve, she thought, always telling her to wear a dress. She slowly perused his attire, starting feet first. Low-cut biker boots, faded jeans, and a well-worn Oakland A's T-shirt didn't exactly rank him as fashion model of the year.

A.J.'s appreciative gaze roamed her from head to toe. Despite his adamant belief that nothing was sexier than a good-looking woman in a dress, he had to admit she looked better than good. "Honey . . ." he said in a soothing, unhurried, bass-pitched tone. "I'm not starting anything. I'm just voicing my opinion. Really, you look very, *very* nice."

"Yeah, right," Vic mumbled as she arched her brow and bobbed her head. Oh, it had taken her a while, but she'd finally figured out his tactic of switching topics so she'd lose focus. Well, it wasn't going to work this time. "Listen, Alcee Jules Baptiste, your little tricks aren't going to stop me from moving to Atlanta."

A.J. folded his arms over his chest, enjoying the fire dancing around in her light-brown eyes. God, she was absolutely gorgeous when she got angry. "Really?"

"Yes, really."

He offered a friendly nod. If she wanted to think she was moving, it was okay by him. What she didn't know was that it would never happen, not on his watch. He was prepared to do whatever was necessary to make certain it didn't. "Everyone has a right to their own beliefs. But in this case, what you think you're going to do will never happen."

Vic gasped in disbelief. "Whatcha mean, will never happen?"

"Simply put, you're not moving."

"Man, you've got me mixed up with somebody else, telling me I can't do something."

"No, I don't." He palmed the side of his face and stared at the floor a second before settling his gaze on Vic again. "You know I'm curious about one thing. Why do you want to run away?"

"Who says I'm running away?"

"Me."

"Not."

"Are, too."

Vic released a nervous laugh. "Get serious."

She didn't exactly view her move as running away, as he called it. She preferred to think of it as choosing not to stay around to deal with his schemes to make her fall in love with him.

A.J. moved closer, the warmth of his breath fanning across her cheek. "Oh, I'm as serious as a terminal case of carcinoma. You've avoided me since the night we—"

"What are you talking about?"

"Don't play with me, woman."

Vic jerked her head away. "Baptiste, t-that was a mistake and you know it."

Her mind drifted down memory lane, recalling the hot, passionate kiss they'd shared four weeks ago at her condominium. The only excuse for allowing things to go as far as they had was temporary insanity. The mere recollection was causing a wet circle to form in the center of her panties so fast that she knew a trip to the laundry room was inevitable. And she silently conceded a stay at the psych ward wasn't a bad idea either, because this man had her going in circles.

A.J. closed the gap between them until their bellies touched. With his index finger, he angled her face back to his, and spoke in a voice so low he hardly heard his own words. "*That* was no mistake."

Vic didn't utter one word because she couldn't. Although quiet, his husky, sexy utterance was undeniably clear. And the conviction in those smoldering hazel eyes silently communicated that he meant every word.

"Now, why are you running?"

She didn't budge from the man who looked like a starting running back for the Oakland Raiders. With all of his six feet, four inches and 220 pounds of muscle next to her, she could smell the tangy scent of his aftershave, and her nostrils flared. Lord, he smelled so good. She discreetly inhaled again. She'd recognize the citrus blend of lavender and sweet spice anywhere. It was Swiss Army, her favorite.

"I'm moving, Baptiste. Period!" She stepped back and hoped the magnetic attraction between them would cease. She slipped her jacket off, flung it across her arm, and headed back up the stairs, determined to stay two steps ahead of the challenge behind her.

With her back to Baptiste, Vic sucked in a deep breath. He could make any woman fall head-over-heels in love before she knew what hit her, and that was the very reason she was hightailing it out of Oakland. She was on the verge of doing what she'd sworn eight years ago she'd never do again. With one bad marriage to her credit and enough heartache to last a lifetime, she'd learned one valuable lesson a long time ago—love and matrimony were as volatile as nitrate and glycerin combined.

"Honey . . ." A.J.'s voice faded as soon as his gaze landed on his favorite body part, her hips. With just enough curve to cause a man to go weak at the knees, they swayed gracefully. Willpower was the only thing that prevented him from going into full cardiac arrest at the sight of the thirty-eight double D's beneath the sleeveless crème shell.

Vic stopped, but didn't turn around. "Baptiste . . ." She uttered the single word with exasperation. "What is it gonna take before you realize what you want will never happen?"

A.J. settled his back against the banister and went one better. "What has to happen before you realize that it will?"

CHAPTER 2

"Hey, whatcha staring at, *mon frère*?" The voice belonged to A.J.'s youngest brother, Raphael, who only answered to Ray.

Smiling, A.J. stood at the bottom of the staircase with his head cocked sideways watching Vic ascend the stairs like an Egyptian goddess.

If he had an ounce of sense, he would've dismissed the golden-skinned, sassy-mouthed beauty the day they first met as mentors at the East Oakland Youth Center his sister-in-law Caitlyn once ran. A disagreement had ensued two seconds after introductions, and to hear Vic tell it, they had absolutely nothing in common.

She was as headstrong as she was beautiful, with more opinions than a hormone-raging teenager. It only took a millisecond after meeting her for him to realize that he could no more put Vic out of his mind than expect the sun to rise in the west.

Two days after they met, Caitlyn told him about Vic's agonizing divorce, and since then, he'd been careful not to broach the subject. Initially, he'd thought her resistance to him was because he believed married women shouldn't work outside the home. Until Vic, no other woman had managed to convince him otherwise. But the more he got to know this sista, the more he realized she was tough enough to juggle a family and bring home the bacon, too.

For months, she'd been dead set on ignoring the attraction between them. And it wasn't mere lust. He felt it and knew she felt it, too. No matter how much she ignored him, the way her lips parted, the silent beckoning in her eyes whenever they were together, made him even more determined to tear down every single wall she'd erected around her heart. But he needed to know the cause of her symptoms before his love could cure her.

Years of training to observe and assess kicked into gear as he watched her go up the stairs. He stared harder, longer, enthralled with her full figure and smooth, silky, honey-colored skin. Auburn-colored dreads sat atop her head, secured with two pearl-surfaced sticks, highlighting the teardrop diamonds hanging from her ears.

His gaze slid down and feasted on her pretty feet encased in open thin-strapped sandals. Each toe was polished the same as her French-manicured nails.

"*Mon frère*," Ray repeated, elbowing A.J. in the side.

"Hmm," A.J. absently answered.

"Don't tell me at thirty-seven ya hearing is shorting out." Ray looked up the staircase and whistled low. "Oooh, *daaayuuum*. Baby's got back."

"Yeah," A.J. lazily drawled. "She's got back all right."

Ray waited until Vic was out of sight. "She find out whatcha did yet?"

Smiling, A.J. nodded.

Marcel arrived in time to hear the answer and chuckled. "I'm surprised you're still in one piece, *petit frère*."

Ray looked at A.J. "She mad, huh?"

A.J.'s cheeks puffed out from the soft rush of air escaping his lips. "Oh, yes."

Ray sat on the bottom step and clasped his hands between his legs. "Well, what's your next move, *mon frère*? You ain't got but a few weeks left, you know."

A.J. had learned about Vic's plans to relocate to Atlanta the first day of August from her father, George Vincent, but gave his brother an unconcerned shrug. "Trust me, Honey isn't going anywhere. Besides, I learned a while ago you have to handle her with a little patience."

"Patience?" Ray yelled out, then broke into laughter so hard he almost choked. He glanced over his shoulder and lowered his voice. "Look here, that patience shit might work with T-One and T-Two and them baby patients of yours, but this is Honey ya dealing with. We talkin' straight-up sista, *mon frère*."

A.J. looked down at Ray and chuckled. "Honey's bark is much worse than her bite."

Ray snorted, settling back against the step. "Well, I'm surprised she ain't bit a plug outta ya."

"You know, Ray," A.J. said stiffly, "what little patience I do have, you're wearing on it."

Ray dismissed the look A.J. tossed him. "No, I'm not. Besides, ya got more patience than Job."

Marcel patted A.J.'s shoulder. "Listen, *petit frère*, I'm afraid Ray's right on this one. You're going to need more than patience this time. I'm not sure who's more stubborn, Vic or that little bitty wife of mine."

A.J. shrugged, totally unmoved by his brother's assessment because he'd already mapped out a strategic plan to prevent Vic's attempt to relocate. "So am I. Trust me, Honey's days as a single woman are numbered." He glanced between Marcel and Ray. "Has she told anyone the real reason she thinks she's moving to Atlanta?"

"When Vic first told Kitten," Marcel said, referring to his wife, Caitlyn, "she didn't offer a reason, and Kitten's upset. And when my baby's upset, I'm upset." Suddenly, he paused and narrowed his eyes. "What do you mean, *thinks*?"

A. J. smiled. "Tell Caitlyn not to worry. Honey's not moving to Atlanta."

"She's not?" Ray and Marcel asked simultaneously.

Confused, Marcel shook his head. "Listen, *petit frère*, your plan with Vic's realtor backfired. I don't know what more you can do to stop her from leaving."

Ray sided with Marcel. "I'm with *mon frère* on this one. It's the first of July." Blowing out a hard breath, he pursed his lips. "Thirty days and counting. That ain't a whole lot of time to snag a good woman."

A.J. chuckled at the renowned jazz musician. "Don't tell me this is coming from the man with women on call in half the cities around the world?"

Marcel narrowed his gaze on Ray, too. "Yeah, Ray. Exactly what do you know about getting a good woman, as you call it? What you need to do is settle your behind down, because everything out there that sparkles ain't gold."

Ray slid a pair of yellow-tinted lenses in Gucci frames down his nose, peering over the top. "Look it, I'm not searching for eternal light like y'all. Just need a small flicker or two from a woman until the break of dawn." He grinned. "She the one, huh, *mon frère?*"

A.J. stared up the staircase and silently pondered the question. Yes, Vic was the one, all right. Every woman from his past had become a fuzzy blur. Every single one of them had faded to a distant memory the moment he'd laid eyes on Victoria Louise Bennett.

Oh, yes, she was the one. She'd burst through the door of his serene life like an ocean wave, sweeping him so far out into the depths of desire that he didn't want to be saved. For months, nothing short of a cold morning shower staved off the guaranteed hard-on he got whenever he recalled the sound of her low, husky voice.

Marcel chuckled. "Well, I don't know what more you can do to Vic besides lock her up somewhere."

A.J. flashed a half-crooked grin and nodded in agreement. "My thoughts exactly."

Marcel and Ray quickly made the sign of the cross.

"*Mon frère,*" Ray uttered anxiously, "you ain't gonna pull the same stunt that almost got you and K-Mart kicked out of medical school—" he lifted his brow—"are ya?"

"I most certainly am," A.J. admitted without reservation. His mind flashed back, remembering every detail of the prank he and his best friend, Kevin Martin Bullock, better known as K-Mart, had pulled on a fellow student during their last year of medical school. "That's exactly what I plan to do—stage a quarantine."

"No," Marcel muttered below a whisper. "You wouldn't do that to her, would you?"

A.J. offered a wide grin. "Watch me. I've got to get Honey alone and onto my playing field. This is a sure way for me to win."

Ray grunted. "Well, just be sure to tell us what suit you wanna be buried in. *Mon frère*, you're as good as dead."

A.J. shrugged off his potentially dismal fate. "Well, at least I'll go a happy man."

Still stunned, the only thing Marcel could do was mouth the word *no* to himself.

Smiling, A.J. nodded at his brothers, then confidently strolled away whistling the wedding march.

Vic glanced through the crowd mingling in the living room after the christening and spotted Baptiste across the room. The designer suit molded to his bulky frame was flawless. Add the French-cuffed shirt, solid gold cufflinks, and a diamond stud in his right ear, and he looked good. She knew designer names as well as she knew her Social Security number. The suit was Prada all the way.

He winked and followed it with a sexy smile. Her ability to think rationally fled. His piercing gaze was compelling, challenging, and oozed with desire. The passion in his eyes was so potent that a sexual tension gripped her body in a way she'd never experienced before—not even with her ex-husband, Ron. It was that same look, and his demand for a commitment from her a few weeks ago, that had made her pull back. She'd almost given in that night, and vowed not to let it happen again.

Before she knew it, she raced out of the living room into the foyer, snatched her purse off a table, and headed for the door straight ahead. A hot flash hit her with such intensity, pea-size sweat beads surfaced along the bridge of her nose. At thirty-eight, the temporary body infraction had nothing to do with the change of life and everything to do with the man in the other room who had her hormones jumping like fleas.

She scurried inside the bathroom and braced her body against the door almost before she got it shut. Heaving, she was angry with herself more than with Baptiste. Why did she react to him this way? She pushed the question to the back of her mind and released a long weary sigh. *Don't let him get to you today.*

Saying the words out loud brought some measure of relief—until she glanced in the mirror. She cringed. Her face gleamed worse than the top layer of an oil spill. Mascara smudges had settled beneath her eyes, and her sable-colored lipstick was cracked and faded.

"Okay," she whispered, dabbing a makeup sponge across her face. She was determined to stay and get through the rest of the afternoon unaffected. "You can do this."

She tucked her dreads back in place, applied more lipstick, and snatched a tissue from the box on the counter to blot the excess from her lips. After one last mirror check, she declared herself ready and opened the door.

She froze and took two steps back inside the bathroom, her round face distorted with a scowl. He'd followed her to the john, of all places. She didn't believe any man existed who was as stubborn as Baptiste.

He never gave up.

"Running from me won't help." A.J. leaned against the doorframe with his arms folded across his chest, his thin lips pursed.

"Baptiste, why are you following me?" Vic half shouted through clenched teeth.

He ran a soft, assessing gaze over her before he answered. "We need to talk, Honey."

She sighed with frustration. "Man, you're wearing on my last raggedy nerve. What part of 'I'm moving' are you *not* getting?"

He stepped inside the bathroom and closed the door. "Why are you running away from me, Honey?"

Her brow rose. "You know, the last member of the male species I answered to was my father."

"Well, just pretend I'm him and answer the question, woman."

"Baptiste," she ground out, "I am not gonna discuss this with you any more. Case closed."

He shook his head. "What you've said so far is not what I want to hear."

"Well, that's just too bad."

"Honey—"

"Baptiste, don't make me jump to ABW in here."

He frowned and stared confused. "ABW?"

"Angry black woman," Vic bellowed.

He grinned. "You're angry?"

"Oh, Jesus, help me."

"I'm waiting, Honey."

Vic walked over to the bathroom vanity, splaying her fingers on the marble-covered top. "Job transfer. End of discussion."

"You're lying," A.J. countered and moved to stand behind her.

She looked up at him in the mirror. "Why do you say that?"

He grinned again. "You quit your job two weeks ago."

Vic's jaw tightened. Doggone his soul. He wasn't a pediatrician. He was a secret agent for the KGB. How did he find out she'd walked into the office of the wire-rimmed glasses-wearing, bean-counting nerd who was her boss and told him to kiss the upside crack of her high yellow behind?

"Who told you?"

Grinning, he shrugged. "My sources."

She stared at him, wondering if anything was sacred among her family and his, and made a mental note not to discuss a single detail with any of them until after she moved.

"Honey, listen, I admit I can be stubborn—"

"Finally," Vic shouted with joy and threw her hands in the air. "We're in complete agreement."

He shook his head. "You didn't let me finish, woman."

"Baptiste," she uttered loudly, with what little patience she had left.

"Yes?" he answered quietly and flashed another devastatingly bright smile.

Vic paused and sucked in a long breath. He was doing it again. Every time they disagreed about something, he'd lower his tone and then give her that sideways grin when she raised her voice.

"I'm moving to Atlanta."

He gave her a sympathetic nod. "I understand you *think* you're moving, but it's not going to happen."

Vic stared at him as if he'd just mistakenly been released from the nearest mental ward. "Baptiste, you don't have the sense God gave baby geese. Have you totally lost your mind?"

Ignoring the jab, he eyed her intently. "Why can't you accept the fact that we're going to be together?"

"I swear, man, you're U.S. certifiable, Grade-A," she paused, searching for the right word, then shouted out, "incorrigible."

He lifted his brow. "You really think so?"

"Dear God, help me," Vic muttered softly and dropped her head.

She silently counted to ten and looked back into the mirror. "Baptiste, there's not one good reason you can give me why I shouldn't move."

Observing their reflections, he shook his head in disagreement. "You're wrong, Honey. I can give you two. Number one, I love you. And number two, I intend to marry you."

"I'm *not* gonna marry you, Baptiste."

"You're wrong, Honey."

"Why can't we just enjoy the feelings we have for each other without any commitments?"

"No," he countered quickly, "I'm *not* going to settle for a casual affair."

"Why not?"

"Because you're worthy of more, and we deserve better."

Momentarily speechless, Vic took in a deep breath. Whatever response she'd expected, the one she'd just heard wasn't it. "Baptiste, I've always been honest with you. I've told you a thousand times, I don't do the love boat."

Reaching out, he turned her around to face him. "Is that why you're moving to Atlanta, because you've convinced yourself not to fall in love with me?"

"Boy, listen—"

"I'm not going to let it rest until you answer me."

"Baptiste, I told you shortly after we met that I wasn't going to let history repeat itself with you or any other man."

"What did Ron do to hurt you so badly that you can't learn to love again?"

Oblivious to where she stood, Vic recoiled, her hips colliding with the sink. For eight years, she'd been asked that very question more times than she cared to remember. Yet hearing it come from the man who stood in front of her packed the same force as a 200 mile-per-hour hurricane making landfall.

"I-I don't want to talk about it," Vic finally managed to say in a strangled voice.

At that moment, A.J. saw such profound pain surface in her eyes that he felt it, too. The question he'd just posed was the one he'd avoided asking for months. What could a man possibly do to cause a hurt so deep? He reached out and caressed her shoulders. "Honey, whatever Ron did, he was a fool."

"Y-You don't understand, Baptiste," she cried out, lowering her head to hide her tears.

With his index finger, he tilted her chin up. "Baby, if you tell me, perhaps I would."

"I-I can't tell you," she whispered, her words catching on a strangled sob.

"And I can't help you if you don't," he whispered back.

She wiped the tears from her face with both hands and glanced up at him. Maybe, just maybe if he knew, he'd understand there was no way they could ever be together. "You can't tell . . ."

"Tell what, baby?" He stroked his thumb along her brow, coaxing her into finishing her sentence. "Honey, I'm a lot of things, but I'd never share with anyone what you tell me in confidence. Understand?"

"H-He cheated on me . . ."

Finally, after ten, long agonizing months, he knew the cause of her hurt. He pulled her gently against his chest. "Honey, I'm sorry," he uttered softly, cajoling her face into the space between his neck and shoulder. "Whoever the other woman was, she doesn't measure up to you."

Vic's spine went rigid and she retreated to a private place inside where loneliness and pain resided, the place she never allowed anyone to enter.

The depth of the agony she'd borne alone made her pull back. She stared up blankly at him. Before her brain had time to consult with her mouth, she blurted out the rest of the secret she'd kept hidden for eight long years.

"It was a man."

With that, she bolted from the room.

CHAPTER 3

Upstairs, Ray skidded up to the railing of the stair-case. "*Mon frère*, T-One's wheezing bad. Get up here."

A.J. was just about to open the front door to see if Vic's car was still parked in the driveway when he heard his youngest brother frantically call out to him. After the shocking revelation from Vic, it had taken a couple of moments for his brain to realize that she had disappeared from the bathroom. He turned around, his voice shaky. "Did you see which way Honey went?"

Ray shook his head. "Naw. What's wrong?"

There was no way A.J. would ever reveal to a living soul what Vic had shared with him. "I-I just need to find her, that's all."

"Find her later. Upstairs."

"T-One's inhaler is in my medical bag in the cargo area." A.J. stopped and hurriedly fished his keys out his pocket and tossed them to his brother while passing him on the staircase. Vic had probably headed straight to her condominium. He bolted up the remainder of the stairs two at a time. Once he made sure his daughter was okay, he'd head over there and wouldn't leave until they'd talked things through.

Vic drove around and around Lake Merritt for what seemed like hours. After she'd rushed out of the bathroom, leaving a speechless Baptiste inside, she'd raced to her car and sped off.

Emotionally exhausted, she sat at a traffic light, waiting for it to turn green. With the radio turned off, a deafening silence engulfed her and magnified the raw emotions piercing her insides. A tear slipped down her check and she choked back a sob.

She'd been scared to get into a serious relationship because it meant putting her heart at risk again and possibly being subject to another man's betrayal. She couldn't go through another round of heartache, and especially not with Baptiste. She was half in love with him as it was. The more time they spent together, the more her thoughts gravitated to two-point-five *more* kids, a house with a white picket fence, family discussions at dinnertime, and kiddie carpools from one activity to the next in the mommy mobile.

Memories of Ron's infidelity with another man stabbed a deep hole in her heart and flooded her with so much pain that her stomach churned and she fought back the need to heave. Betrayal, not just by any man, but by her husband, and the hurt that followed were two things she'd never forget or forgive. Since then, she'd convinced herself it was better to walk away from love than relive that kind of pain again. Until tonight, she'd never revealed what she'd told Baptiste to a living soul. She firmly believed there were just some things you needed to keep between yourself and Jesus, and Ron's affair with another man was one of them.

Another tear appeared, then another, followed by a gut-wrenching sob. She reached for a tissue and sat motionless with her head against the steering wheel until the sound of screeching rubber from behind forced her to look up into her rearview mirror.

"Oh, Jesus . . ." She frantically lifted her foot off the clutch and floored the accelerator as beaming headlights barreled toward her. It wasn't fast enough. The impact from behind hurled her car into the middle of the inter-section and, a split second later, there was a loud thud against her front bumper. She was so frightened that she screamed at the top of her voice.

Somehow, she stumbled from her car in time to catch a glimpse of the rear of the other car as it sped away. Her cracked headlight illuminated the figure sprawled on the pavement and she knelt, rolling the inert body over.

Recognizing the person, she opened her mouth to scream, but nothing came out.

It was the last thing she remembered before everything went black.

"W-When I said what I said . . . I didn't mean it . . ." Vic's voice cracked and she wept hysterically outside the double doors leading to the trauma unit at Highland Hospital.

"Hush now, sweetheart." Caitlyn gently wiped away the tears that ran down Vic's face. "You've got to pull yourself together. A.J. is going to be just fine."

The entire Baptiste family was assembled inside the waiting room, along with Vic and her parents, George Vincent and Louise Bennett, awaiting word on A.J.'s condition.

Louise walked up and wrapped an arm around Vic's shoulder. "Come on, baby." She walked them to a row of cushioned seats against the wall.

"Try and calm down, sweetheart." George Vincent sat next to his daughter and patted her hands. "A.J. is going to be just fine."

Vic heard her parents' words of reassurance and stifled another sob. No matter what they or anyone said, she didn't feel any better because it was her car that had crashed into Baptiste's motorcycle. She didn't bother to hide the tears rolling down her face anymore. From the moment she and Baptiste arrived by ambulance at the trauma unit, she'd been out of her mind with worry. He had drifted in and out of consciousness the entire ride. Even though Alta Bates-Summit Hospital was closer to the crash site, she and the paramedics had feared he'd sustained a major head injury and decided it was best to transport him to Highland, which housed the county's designated trauma unit.

Vic looked between her mother and A.J.'s grandmother, Zamora Rousselle, whom everyone called Mama Z, and began to sob all over again.

Louise looked over at Mama Z, who was seated across from them, and mouthed, "You try."

Mama Z swapped seats with Louise and gently turned Vic by the shoulders to face her. "Ya listen to me here, child. Since I knows ya, ain't seen ya 'fraid of nothing. This here is no different. That man ya got in there needs ya to be strong. Hear me?"

Vic blinked back unshed tears and nodded. "Yes, ma'am."

A.J.'s brothers, Marcel and Ray, walked up and squatted in front of Vic to lend their comfort.

"It was an accident." Marcel reached out and folded Vic's hand inside of his. "No one is blaming you."

Vic was amazed at the understanding, compassion, and forgiveness Baptiste family showed even though they all knew the accident was her fault.

"Marcel," Vic's voice trembled, "w-what if . . ."

Ray placed his hand on Vic's shoulder. "Come on now, Honey. We ain't even going there. He'll be up and about in no time. *Mon frère* has you and the girls—"

"Oh, my God!" Vic's gaze darted wildly around the room. "T-One a-and T-Two. Oh, God, where are they?"

Brie, A.J.'s oldest sister, answered. "Vic, they're fine. They're with Mrs. Bradford."

Vic collapsed back against the seat, comforted with the knowledge that Taylor and Tyler were safe and being cared for by Marcel and Caitlyn's nanny.

Vic wiped her face with both hands, then asked Baptiste's father, Alcee, "Does Alex know?"

Alex Robinson, a close friend of the Baptiste family, had grown up with Marcel, A.J., and Ray, and was considered as much a part of the family if he'd been born a Baptiste.

Alcee Baptiste nodded. "Vic, he knows. Marcel called him as soon as we got here, and he's on his way."

"We got here as soon as we could." Harrison Bennett, Vic's oldest brother, rushed inside the waiting room with his younger brother, Lincoln, two steps behind.

Vic walked over to them, wrapping her arms tightly around their waists. "Thanks for coming."

Harrison placed a kiss on his sister's cheek, then his mother's. "How's he doing?"

"No word so far." Louise glanced up at the emergency room physician, who worked at Highland Hospital, stroking the side of his face. "You look tired, son."

"I am." Harrison ran his hand across the stubble on his face. "Pulling sixteen hours will do that to you. Cates took over for me when I left, so A.J.'s in good hands."

Lincoln, a federal prosecutor who'd just moved back to Oakland from Dallas, gently nudged his brother. "Does this Cates know his stuff?"

Harrison turned to his brother and nodded with confidence. "Absolutely. He's one of the best." He glanced back at Vic. "Have you been in yet?"

Vic grimaced. "Well . . . sort of."

Puzzled by his sister's evasive answer, Harrison was silent for a moment until A.J.'s middle sister, Moni, who stood nearby clarified Vic's statement. "They threw Vic out."

Lincoln chuckled. "Figures." He frowned, rubbing at his chin, and gave his mother a puzzled look. "Wait a minute. Mom, you work in ER. Why aren't you in there?"

Harrison wondered the same thing, too, and his gaze settled on their mother. "You're the head ER nurse. Why aren't you in there?"

Vic answered instead. "They threw Mom out first."

Embarrassed, Harrison flung his head back and sighed. "Mom . . ."

Louise glanced at her children with a sheepish look. "Well, they weren't moving fast enough for me."

"Oh, Harrison," Vic sobbed. Accepting the tissue Mama Z walked up and handed her, she dabbed at swollen, red eyes. "He's got to be okay."

Harrison took his sister's hands inside his and squeezed them tightly. "He will, Vic, but you've got to pull yourself together and be strong for him, all right?"

Vic slowly nodded. "'Kay." Blowing her nose softly, she pointed at the trauma unit doors. "Can you go and check on him for me?"

Leaning over, Harrison kissed his sister on the cheek. "I'm on my way."

Lincoln frowned at what he saw when he brushed back a dread that had fallen over Vic's forehead. "Have you gotten that checked out yet?"

Vic gently fingered the slight, tender bump and shook her head.

A few moments later, Zachary Tate, a lieutenant with the Oakland Police Department who was married to A.J.'s sister, Moni, walked into the waiting room. He spoke briefly with Marcel, Ray, and A.J.'s father, Alcee, for an update on his brother-in-law's condition, and then headed straight toward Vic. "Baby Girl, I need to ask ya a few more questions about the accident."

Vic's heart accelerated to a frantic pace and her eyes grew wide with alarm. "Please, Zach, you gotta believe me. It was an accident. I swear to God, I-I didn't mean to hit Baptiste."

With every member of the Baptiste and Bennett family surrounding him, Zach nodded. "Calm down, now. I believe ya." He walked Vic back over to the row of cushioned seats, letting her settle down first, then sat next to her. "But I don't believe this accident involves just you and brother-in-law."

Vic stared, confused. As far as she knew, only two cars were involved, hers and the one that hit her. "So, what are you saying, Zach?"

Zach leaned forward and placed his elbows atop his knees. "Baby Girl, there was another car that got broadsided less than a mile from where y'all were hit. No witnesses actually saw either crash, but from the evidence we've been able to gather, we suspect the same car's involved."

"Oh, Jesus." Vic wrung her hands together. "Who was in the first car? W-Were they hurt?"

Zach cleared his throat. "I understand it was a young family. The mother and father came out with a few scratches, but their daughter . . . well, uh . . . she's in critical condition." He paused for a second. "Baby Girl, she might not make it."

Vic covered her face with both hands and sobbed. After gaining her composure, she became blistering mad. "Whoever was in the car that hit me and the first car didn't stop and try to help any of us!"

Zach released a weary sigh. "Listen, I know how ya feel, but I promise ya . . . and brother-in-law, I'ma find the bastard who did this."

Vic nodded.

"Baby Girl, this might not be a simple case of hit-and-run anymore. We might be looking at vehicular manslaughter or homicide, depending on how things turn out." Zach reached inside his suit coat and pulled out a notepad and pen. "Is there anything—*anything*—ya recall that ya didn't tell the officers at the scene?"

Vic shook her head vigorously, even though it throbbed. "No. I told them everything I remembered."

Zach flipped his notepad shut and placed a soft kiss against Vic's cheek. "I want ya to take it easy, hear me? If ya think of somethin' else, let me know. Okay?"

Vic nodded and reached over to squeeze Zach's hand.

A few moments later, Alex Robinson, a close friend of the Baptiste family, walked into the waiting room. He spoke to Marcel, Ray, and Alcee first, then squatted in front of Vic. "Hi there. How you holding up?"

Vic answered by bursting into tears.

Alex pulled a clean handkerchief from his back pocket. "The man in there is my brother," he declared proudly, wiping Vic's face, "and he would kill me if I didn't take care of his lady in his absence."

Vic offered a weak smile when Alex finished. "Thank you."

The next ten minutes passed in absolute silence, and the agonizing wait rattled Vic's nerves. She noticed her brother Lincoln inconspicuously beckon Marcel, Ray, Alex, Zach, and Alcee outside into the hallway. She couldn't help noticing the stoic expression on his face. After a few seconds, a frightening thought crossed her mind. What if Harrison had shared something awful with Lincoln about Baptiste's condition on the drive over to the hospital and they'd decided to conceal it in an effort to protect her? She didn't want to eavesdrop, but if there was something terrible going on with him, she needed to know. She eased over to the doorway, being careful to remain out of view, and listened.

"I *never* thought I'd live to see the day those two weren't battling with each other," Marcel said.

Alcee released a half chuckle. "Well, you know what they say. The Lord works in mysterious ways."

Marcel glanced over at Lincoln, Alex, and Ray. "How in the world did they end up crashing into each other anyway?" Marcel asked.

"Ain't got the faintest idea." Ray shrugged. "All I know is the last time I saw *mon frère*, he was in a panic to find Honey."

"Why?" Lincoln questioned. "They're always fighting."

Zach nodded. "Yeah. Did somethin' really bad happen this time?"

"Beats me," Ray responded. "Now I wish I had let him bolt on out the door when I first saw him."

Marcel frowned. "Why do you say that?"

"Timing, *mon frère*, timing," Ray offered. "If I'd let him go then, he wouldn't be banged up now."

Vic placed her hand against her stomach as tears streaked down her face. Oh, God, if Baptiste hadn't tried to go after her, he wouldn't be lying on a gurney in the emergency room. With her back to the wall, she squeezed her eyes shut and offered up a prayer on his behalf. Suddenly, she heard the familiar sound of the double doors to the trauma unit open, and her eyes flew open. "Edmond!" She bolted toward him and shook him hard by the shoulders. "How's Baptiste?"

Edmond Cates placed his hands on top of Vic's. "He's okay, Vic. He got banged up pretty good, but he's stable."

"You're sure?" Vic's voice was shaky. She'd known Edmond since the day he and her brother Harrison began working together in the ER, six years earlier. "You wouldn't lie to me, would you?"

With a smile, Edmond lowered Vic's hands to her side. "You know I wouldn't. A.J.'s one lucky man, I can tell you that much."

Louise stood next to Vic. "What's the diagnosis, Edmond?"

"Bruised ribs, a complex concussion—"

"CT scan?" Vic and Louise asked simultaneously.

"Yes, you Bennett nurses. I did one," Edmond answered with a chuckle. "Negative."

"No puncture to his lungs, right?" Vic questioned.

Edmond shook his head and smiled. "Negative again."

"Thank you, Jesus," Vic uttered with a sigh of relief and turned to hug her mother.

Edmond announced his orders for A.J.'s post-injury care. "Listen, I want him off his feet and on complete bed rest, at least for the first week. If he does that, he should be as good as new."

"I need to see him," Vic said anxiously.

Edmond nodded. "All right, but give us a few moments. He's being transferred up to a room. With that concussion, I want to keep him overnight, just for observation." He gave Vic a quick hug. "Gotta run, kiddo. I'll check on him again before my shift ends."

"Edmond, wait." Vic followed him outside the waiting room into the hallway. "Zach told us a young girl was injured, too."

Edmond nodded. "She's in surgery now."

"Will she be okay?"

Edmond palmed the back of his neck. "It doesn't look good for her."

A second later, a nurse from the trauma unit walked past Edmond and Vic and stopped at the entrance of the waiting room. "Is this the Baptiste family?"

"Yes," they all replied in unison.

Somewhat startled by the onslaught of people rushing toward her, the nurse clutched A.J.'s medical chart close to her chest. "I-I see. Well, I need to speak with his next of kin."

"There she is," they all answered together and pointed to Vic, who'd just walked back inside.

The nurse turned to Vic and flipped open A.J.'s chart. "Okay. Your name and relationship to the patient, uh—"

A.J.'s sister, Moni slid up in front of the nurse and answered without hesitation. "Mrs. Victoria Baptiste."

The nurse looked up from the chart and glanced at everyone with a puzzled look. "Hmm, I worked with Dr. Baptiste over at Children's Hospital when he was chief of pediatrics. I don't recall him being married."

Brie, Moni, Aimee, and Caitlyn converged on the nurse like a pack of pit bulls ready to attack.

"Things change," Brie hissed.

"Didn't you just hear us say she's his wife?" Aimee announced curtly.

"Uh-uh. That's okay. I got this." Louise pushed her way through the huddle until she stood in front of the nurse and gave her a glaring look. "Darlene, this is a family affair. Besides, I ain't but a half step off you anyway, having me thrown out the emergency room like that."

"Now, Louise, you know and I know you were being disruptive. It wasn't good for Dr. Baptiste," the nurse said defensively.

Louise looked at the women around her. "Did she just say what I thought I heard her say?"

The women all nodded at the same time.

Louise dragged the nurse off to a nearby corner, hemming her between the wall and herself. "Darlene, I'ma wax you regular, then turn you around and buff you to a high-gloss sheen if you don't come up with a room number for my child—and quick. Feeling me?"

"Uh . . . Mrs. Baptiste," the nurse stuttered over Louise's shoulder, nervously flipping through the pages inside of A.J.'s chart. "Y-Your husband is in Room 505."

Once the nurse exited, Vic turned to everyone. "I-I don't know what to say."

Marcel smiled and beckoned Ray and Alex. "Come on, guys. Let's get down to admissions and try to cover up this lie we just stood here and told."

Mama Z chuckled softly. "No need to rush, son. We told the truth. Just ain't come to pass—yet."

Vic stared speechless at Mama Z. "But—"

"No buts." Alcee gently shoved Vic by the shoulders. "Go."

Vic nodded, and a second later, raced out of the waiting room.

Vic tiptoed inside Baptiste's room a few moments later and eased back the partially drawn curtain around his bed. Though she was shaking from fear and racked with guilt, somehow her feet carried her closer to his bed.

"Oh, my God," she gasped, covering her mouth with both hands as she peered down at Baptiste.

The entire left side of his face was swollen and bruised, and the broken blood vessels caused a purplish hue that markedly discolored his complexion. When she noticed the wide strips of white tape wrapped around his chest, her heart pounded, and an intense emotion welled up inside her until she thought she'd explode trying to control it. When she finally found her voice, it was faint and hoarse. "Baptiste, baby, it's me . . . Honey."

"Hmm . . ." A.J. grunted, too dazed to recognize the voice. *Who's calling me?* Balls of cotton had been stuffed inside his mouth, his head pounded mercilessly, and he felt as if a steel blanket had been draped over him. His eyes fluttered and struggled to stay open. Jumbled thoughts swirled through his head as he slowly abandoned the world of unconsciousness. Pain so intense that it knotted his muscles invaded him, and he groaned in agony.

"Baptiste."

"H-Honey," he drawled in a faint tone.

Vic pushed the bedrail down and sat on the edge of the bed, gently running her fingers along his temple, carefully avoiding the injured side. "Hush now, and don't try and talk anymore."

He tried to shift his body and follow the sound of her voice, but immediately ditched his efforts when a searing pain zigzagged along his left side. A bubbling sensation erupted inside his stomach, and he heaved.

Vic registered the retching sounds right away and quickly grabbed a plastic kidney-shaped pan off the table and held it to his mouth. "That's right. Let it come on out." Afterward, she cleansed his face and mouth with a cool, wet cloth.

"Sorry," he slurred a short while later, embarrassed he couldn't prevent everything he'd eaten today from coming forth.

"It's okay," she whispered back.

He winced. "W-What . . . happened?"

Hesitating, Vic knew at some point she had to tell him the truth. However, the place wasn't in a hospital room, and the time wasn't when he was half-conscious from morphine. "Y-You had an accident on your motorcycle."

"Car," he moaned, remembering the impact.

Another wave of tears formed and she struggled to swallow her sob. "Y-Yes."

"Hurts . . . a lot."

"I know, baby. I know."

"Girls . . . where . . . are—"

"Man, stop asking so many questions," she half joked, hoping it would take his mind off his pain. She smoothed back the sweat-drenched hair matted at his temple. "Don't worry now. They're with Mrs. Bradford, and they're fine."

He ran his tongue along parched, cracked lips. "Had to find . . . you."

Her heart lurched and she bit down so hard on her bottom lip to keep her anguished wail at bay that she tasted the coppery flavor of her own blood. Guilt assailed her because she knew if he hadn't tried to follow her after what she'd told him, he wouldn't be lying there. "I'm so sorry."

He nodded faintly to communicate he understood. His head throbbed painfully and his tongue was heavy and stiff. Somehow, though, he managed to slowly move his bruised lips to weakly utter, "Pushed too . . . hard."

Vic's eyes filled with more tears, and her trembling was worse than before. "Hush now. We'll talk later."

His mouth moved again, doing its best to sound out the one word that remained soundless: *Stay*. His breathing slowed and finally evened out to a faint whistle. He blinked once, twice, before his eyelids gradually drifted shut.

Vic listened to his steady breathing and finally let the hot, scalding tears escape without restriction. Squeezing her eyelids shut, she desperately tried to block the memory of that split second when she thought she'd lost him.

Lifting his hand to her mouth, she kissed the back of it, wondering what he had tried to say two seconds earlier.

CHAPTER 4

"Oh, God, be careful with him now."

Vic nervously held the front door open late Sunday afternoon as Marcel, Ray, and Alex helped Baptiste inside the refurbished Victorian-style home he'd purchased in East Oakland, two blocks away from the health clinic, which was scheduled to open Tuesday morning.

Ray blew out a hard breath and wiped a bead of sweat from his forehead. "All right, Honey, where ya want him?"

Vic closed the door and pointed down the hallway. "Bedroom."

"Uh-uh," A.J. sluggishly drawled, undraping his arms from around his brothers' necks. With unsteady steps, he used the wall for support to slowly guide himself toward the living room.

Vic stepped in front of him. "Baptiste, don't go in there."

Alex placed his palm at the small of A.J.'s back to keep his wobbly frame upright and whispered, "Man, I'm telling you, don't argue with her right now."

A.J. closed his eyes and winced. Alex's soft murmur sounded like a sonic explosion going off inside his head. "Why not?"

"Because there's a new sheriff in town: me," Vic answered. "Until I can get you back on your feet, I give the orders around here."

Despite his swollen face, A.J. managed a half-crooked smile. "That's all I get, a few lousy days?"

Vic fought back the grin working at her jaw and peered around Baptiste to give Marcel, Ray, and Alex a hard look. "Well, what are y'all standing there for?" The authority in her tone left no doubt as to who was in charge. "Baptiste needs to be off his feet."

A.J. patted Vic on the shoulder. "Can't I go to bed later, Honey?"

"No! Baptiste, you and them sidekicks of yours got three seconds to start moving down that hall or it's gonna get real dangerous up in here." Vic glanced at her watch. "You've already used one."

"All right." Louise Bennett entered through the front door with a white bag containing A.J.'s medication. She tossed a sharp look at everyone. "Why is he not in bed?"

Vic snorted. "Stubborn and hardheaded." She stood in front of Baptiste with both hands at her hips and gave him an I-just-told-on-you look. "Maybe he'll listen to you, Mom."

"Well," Louise drawled, her gaze roaming over A.J. from top to bottom, "get to moving, son."

A.J pleaded, pouting. "But Louise—"

"Uh-uh. Don't even go there with me." Louise turned to Vic. "When Harrison gets off he's coming by to check him out."

"Wait, I'm a doctor." A.J. couldn't quite decipher why everyone stopped talking to stare at him with an incredulous look, then turned back around and resumed their conversation concerning his care.

Marcel tried to disguise his laugh by clearing his throat, but came up short. "Come on, *petit frère*. I think your lady and her *mère* mean business."

"Yeah, let's go," Ray huffed, lifting A.J.'s arm around his neck again. He blew out a hard breath. "Daaayuuum, *mon frère,* you heavy."

Later that evening, Vic knocked softly on Baptiste's bedroom door, which she'd left partially open, just in case he called out to her. "Got a couple of folks I think you'd like to see."

"Daddy, Daddy," Taylor and Tyler happily shrieked and took off at a dead run toward the custom-made king-size bed, ready to pounce.

"No, no, no." Vic's warning was gentle. "Remember what Honey said . . . no jumping. We have to take it easy with Daddy for a few days."

The twins heeded Vic's instructions and skidded to a stop at the bedside.

A.J. planted sloppy, wet kisses on Taylor and Tyler's foreheads when they stretched to reach him. "Missed my babies."

Taylor grinned. "Missed you, too, Daddy."

"Me, too." Tyler lightly touched the left side of A.J.'s face with her index finger. "Honey say you got a *big* old raspberry," she exclaimed, stretching her arms open as wide as they would go.

Vic chuckled at the reference Tyler used to describe their father's injuries.

Taylor peered over at her father's battered face from the right side. "Yep. It's big, all right."

A.J. chuckled. "Are you two being good for Honey?"

"Umm-hmm," both girls answered, bobbing their heads.

Vic moved to the foot of the bed and saw the yawn Baptiste tried to hide with the back of his hand. She also noticed the droopiness in his eyes. "Okay, ladies. It's time to get in the tub, say your prayers, and go night-night. Give Daddy some love so he can get some rest."

As Taylor and Tyler kissed the right side of their father's face, Vic chuckled.

A.J. was out cold.

Vic became frantic the moment she walked into Baptiste's bedroom the next morning after dropping Taylor and Tyler at preschool. The bed was empty.

"Baptiste?"

She scurried to the other side of the four-poster bed and found him sprawled atop a sisal area rug, moaning in pain. Her heart skipped two beats, and she immediately dropped to her knees.

"Oh, my God. Baptiste, what's wrong?"

Breathless, A.J. tried to sit up and almost made it before toppling onto his right side. "I need a shower," he said, gasping for air. "I stink."

At that moment, his personal hygiene was the least of her concerns. She needed to be sure he hadn't caused more injury to himself, and sighed with relief when he told her he hadn't fallen on his left side.

"Man, you don't stink."

"Look, woman, I haven't had a shower since Saturday." He lifted his right arm slightly. "Wanna smell?"

She chuckled. "No, I don't wanna smell."

"Well, I may not stink," he refuted and sniffed, "but I certainly smell bad."

"Didn't I tell you last night that after I dropped the girls off at school I'd give you a sponge bath?"

"Yeah, I know, but I wanted to be clean when your mother stopped by."

"Baptiste, Mom is a nurse, for heaven's sake."

"Nurse or not, I don't want her to smell me like this." He paused and scooted on his rear, trying without success to focus on the clock on the nightstand. "By the way, what time is it?"

"It's eight."

"And what time is Louise coming over?"

"She called right before I got ready to walk out the door to drop the girls off and said there's been an accident on Interstate 580 that's causing a major backup. That's the reason she's not here now."

Bracing his weight on his right palm, he attempted to sit up again. "Okay," he panted. "That gives me a little more time."

Vic's eyes widened. "A little more time for what?"

"To take a shower, woman."

She noticed that he was clutching his left side. "Don't even think about moving. Stay right there."

She raced to the bathroom and back, squatting in front of him with a glass of water and a container of pills. "Come on, open your mouth for me."

A.J. started to shake his head, but the pounding at his temples convinced him otherwise. "No more drugs."

"Baptiste . . ."

"Honey, I said no."

"You're in pain."

"I'll live."

Vic scooted up a little closer and swung the medicine bottle back and forth in front of his face. "If you take these, they'll make you feel better," she sweetly coaxed.

"No, they won't," he grumbled. "They'll make me sleepy."

She bit her bottom lip to keep from chuckling out loud. She knew doctors made the worst patients, and he was proving to be no exception.

"Morphine usually does that. Come on, man, open your mouth for me."

"No."

"You're making it harder on yourself."

He pursed his lips.

Vic discreetly took out two pills and placed them, along with the glass of water, on the nightstand. Gently cupping Baptiste's chin to steady his head with one hand, she grabbed the end of his nose with the other. When he was forced to open his mouth to breathe, she quickly slipped the medication into the back of his mouth, grabbed the cup off the nightstand, and placed it to his lips. "Drink and swallow."

"You play dirty," he said, his voice strangled from water traveling in the wrong direction down his windpipe.

"And I fight even harder." She pulled him into a sitting position, bracing his back against the bottom of the bed. "Open your mouth for me."

"Why?"

"I want to be sure you swallowed those pills."

He chuckled. "Woman, you're crazy."

"I know. Now open your mouth."

He complied.

She peeked inside. "Stick it out."

"What?"

"Baptiste, don't go there with me. Stick it out."

When he stuck out his tongue, she swept her finger underneath his tongue, and along the space between the gums and teeth. She wanted to be certain he hadn't hidden the medication.

He chuckled again. "Where did you learn that little trick?"

"When I worked in pediatric oncology." She sat back on her haunches. "Boy, I swear I don't know what I'm going to do with you. You got dizzy, didn't you?"

He nodded and immediately groaned.

"Umm-hmm. And your head hurts?"

He winced.

"Baptiste, you sustained a complex concussion, busted ribs—"

"And I stink."

"You *do not* stink. God, you're the most stubborn man I've ever met in my life."

"Look who's talking. If I opened a dictionary and looked up the word stubborn, your picture would be next to it."

"Boy, hush. Tell me, how many of me do you see?"

"Three."

"Well, the real me is in the middle." She stood and leaned over slightly, locking her knees. "Okay, arms around my neck."

"I'm too heavy for you to try and lift."

"No, you're not. We just gotta work together."

He wrapped his arms around her neck and locked his fingers together for added leverage.

"All right, move with me on three." She planted her feet firmly apart. "Ready?"

"Yes."

She bore most of his weight, and after a couple of tries, managed to pull him up until his hips were on the edge of the bed. Slowly, she guided him down to the mattress and slid a pillow beneath his head. Moving down a fraction, she swung his legs up on the bed, then pulled the sheet up to the middle of his chest.

"Baptiste, if you get out this bed one more time, I'll kill you. Do you hear me?"

He chuckled. "Yes, Honey."

After folding back the covers, she sat on the edge of the bed and smiled. "Got the clinic covered for you."

About a week after they met, Vic learned of A.J.'s efforts for the past eighteen months to set up a free health clinic for the residents of East Oakland.

He smiled back. "*Merci, mon amour.*"

Thank you, my love. Every time he uttered those words to her, she melted. "Okay, what else is on your agenda for the rest of this week?"

Now that the cobwebs had finally cleared from his head, he closed his eyes and sighed softly. Even though his family's corporation, BF Automotive, the top-ranked black-owned dealership in the country, had given a multi-million-dollar donation from their corporate philanthropic foundation, there was still a funding shortfall.

"I had meetings scheduled with a couple of foundations today to secure more money for the clinic."

He reached for the phone.

She caught his wrist. "And just what do you think you're doing?"

"I need—"

"You need to stay right where you are and get well," she reminded him, tucking his arm under the comforter. "I'll take care of it. Just tell me who your contacts are."

"The information is in my office," he slurred.

She nodded. "Anything else?"

His medication had kicked in, and he yawned. "We need to talk."

She stood and adjusted his pillows. "Later. Right now, I want you to go to sleep and rest."

Fifteen minutes later, Baptiste was in a deep slumber. Vic decided it was a perfect time for a sponge bath. After returning from the bathroom with a basin and towels, she methodically dipped the cloth into the water and carefully cleaned his face, mindful to avoid the left side. She used another towel, wringing the excess water out, to cleanse his neck, arms, and upper torso, which was covered with thick, black curly hair at the center.

Even though her touch was professional, Vic openly admired the magnificent male specimen lying before her. His body was well toned, and she knew that type of conditioning resulted from a rigorous exercise regime. Before she knew it, her fingertips ran lightly over the tattoo on his right bicep, trailed down the flat surface of his stomach, and even farther to stroke up and down powerful thighs and legs. His manicured hands and feet garnered her full attention. Caressing the softness of his palms, she could envision the calmness babies felt in his care. Then she wondered how they would feel on her.

Vic taped the left side of his chest, and then pulled the sheet up to cover his body. Once she drew the drapes to dim the brightness, she quietly closed the door and headed to his office downstairs.

Seated behind an antique wooden roll-up desk, she searched through every file neatly stacked inside a desk organizer to locate the information for the health clinic, but she couldn't find it. She sighed, wondering where it could be. Suddenly, she remembered a few months back overhearing Marcel tease Baptiste about writing the things he felt really passionate about in a diary. She knew his clinic was as fervent as they came. Thirty minutes later, she located the diary in a bottom drawer. Shifting through the pages, she quickly discovered not only had he journalized the information about the clinic, he'd also documented every detail of their relationship from the day they'd first met. Pleasure rippled through her body despite the faint alarm going off inside her head. All these months, he'd known exactly what he was doing in his effort to break down the barriers she'd placed between them. When she read his last entry from two days ago, the day of the christening, she knew she was in trouble. He wanted her and was coming after her with the full intention of winning her love. Tears blurred her vision as she read what he'd written again:

When a man loves a woman, he will stop at absolutely nothing to win her heart, her trust, but most of all, her love.

Later in the afternoon, around two, Vic knocked on Baptiste's bedroom door and entered, along with his best friend, Kevin Martin Bullock, who everyone referred to as K-Mart.

"K-Mart, don't let Baptiste get out of this bed while I'm gone," she said, walking over to hand Baptiste a bottle of Perrier. She leaned down and softly whispered next to his ear. "I'ma run a few errands, then pick up the girls. I won't be gone long."

A.J. smiled. "You promise to come back to me."

She smiled back. "I promise. Remember what I said, Baptiste."

K-Mart drew a glass of iced tea to his mouth. "Don't worry, Vic. Even if I have to sit on his big behind the entire time, I won't let him out this bed."

A.J. and K-Mart watched Vic walk out the room.

"Doc," K-Mart said with a chuckle, turning back around to face his best friend, "I told you years ago you needed to give up your Hell's Angel's ways." He set his glass on the table next to his chair and peeled out of his suit coat. "Damn near took you out of here this time, huh?"

"Shut up, K-Mart," A.J. replied, his voice full of humor. "Good to see you. I wasn't at fault this go-round. Whoever hit me came out of nowhere. I didn't even see them coming."

A.J. knew K-Mart would rib him for the passion he'd developed for motorcycle riding, which began when they were roommates back in medical school at Howard University. Slowly, he pulled to an upright position in the middle of the bed while K-Mart adjusted the pillows at his back. "All right, who called you?"

"Everyone," K-Mart answered matter-of-factly, loosening his tie. "Of course, you know Moni got to me first. After that, the rest of your clan started blowing my phone up every thirty minutes. Even talked to Cates the night you were admitted."

A.J. chuckled. "I'll say. He told me when I checked out that you called every hour for an update."

"Absolutely. Listen, doc, we go back a long way. I needed to know what was going on with you."

A.J. was thrilled K-Mart had finally accepted the top spot as the health officer for the Alameda County

Department of Public Health and would be relocating to Oakland from Atlanta. Suddenly, he frowned, and a puzzled look fanned over his features. "Wait a minute. Your flight to Oakland was for next—"

"I know, I know. When I talked with Marcel, he offered to send the corporate jet down to fly me out, so here I am."

A.J. nodded. He knew Russ Jenkins, the pilot for BF Automotive's corporate jet, had no doubt flown out immediately. "*Merci, mon frère.*"

Stretching his legs in front of him, K-Mart smiled. "Listen, doc, you didn't do justice with your description of Vic. You are one lucky dog. Man, she's gorgeous."

A.J. beamed proudly. "I told you."

K-Mart shook his head in amazement. "How in the world did you luck up and find a woman who loves your girls as much as you do, is a public health nurse, has a master's in public health on top of that, and heads up a clinic?" He lifted his brow. "Think she'd come work for me?"

A.J. didn't hear most of K-Mart's accolades because he was too busy trying to figure out which one of his five gossiping siblings had provided K-Mart with Vic's life story.

"Moni told you all of this, right?" Before he got a response, he added, "You would think since Little Zach has been born she wouldn't have so much time to spend running her mouth."

K-Mart shook his head and chuckled. "Wasn't Moni this time, doc. Zach spilled the beans on this one."

"When?" A.J. asked, stunned.

"When he picked me up from the airport."

"What?" A.J. exclaimed. "You mean Marcel forgot his manners and didn't send a limo over for you?"

K-Mart snorted. "A limo? For what? Listen, we're family, right?" He tossed A.J. a sly wink. "Besides, I got the latest update on the entire clan from Zach. That's better than a limo ride any day of the week."

A.J. laughed out loud. "Zach's been living with Moni too long."

K-Mart chuckled. "Listen, Zach also said your woman can burn."

A.J. patted his stomach and released a sigh of contentment. "Yes, she can."

"Hey, doc, thanks for downloading the last set of pictures you took of the girls and e-mailing them. I tell everyone my goddaughters are cuties. But I'm just a tad bit biased, you know."

"I know, and so am I."

K-Mart took another sip of tea and slowly shook his head. "You know, it's just like you to do the daddy thing without benefit of a wife."

"What's wrong with that?" A.J. asked, giving his friend a nonchalant shrug.

"I didn't say there was anything wrong with it. It's just in line with all of your other unconventional ways, that's all."

"So," A.J. drawled slowly, "I do things a little differently, unlike you. There's more excitement in my way. Your behind is as straight-laced as they come. You're always playing strictly by the rules."

"That's all right. At least I didn't have three quarters of the medical faculty happy to see me graduate."

"Stop lying, K-Mart," A.J. said, chuckling.

"Doc, I'm not lying. You were one scary, *brilliant* medical student and put all of us to shame. But trust me, darn near all of the professors lit candles when you strolled across the stage at graduation."

"K-Mart, man, you should stop lying," A.J. repeated, laughing so hard he had to brace his hand against his left side to ease the throbbing.

"You know I'm telling the truth," K-Mart said, snickering just as much. "You caused Dr. Wilson to turn in his resignation the same day."

A.J. snorted. "Come on, K-Mart. He was past seventy. He needed to retire anyway."

"Never ran across anyone who could miss three quarters of a class lecture and still ace the course."

"It was only a couple of times, and you know it. Besides, why sleep in a chair in a classroom at eight in the morning when I could be snoozing in bed?"

"I'm feeling you, but come on, doc, admit it. You can come up with some strange stuff. Who else would show up wearing shorts, no shirt, and sandals at graduation?"

"K-Mart," A.J. mildly protested, "we lived in D.C., and graduated in the middle of August, with a heat index close to a hundred that day. There was no way I was going to wear a suit and tie under a thick, black robe."

K-Mart nodded in agreement. "I almost roasted my damn self. So, when's the wedding?"

A.J. explained Vic's reluctance to marry him, leaving out the reason why and how his plan to quarantine her had been interrupted by the car accident.

"What?" K-Mart shouted and was on his feet in an instant, remembering the repercussions from the dean for his role in the quarantine prank he and A.J. concocted in medical school. "Doc, I want to look at your CT scan, personally. I think you sustained permanent brain damage *before* the concussion."

"Sit down, K-Mart. You've been in public health so long you wouldn't know what an X ray looked like if it slapped you." After sharing a long laugh, A.J. probed, taunting his friend. "What about you? Who's the lucky woman in your life?"

With his focus on his glass, K-Mart's face grew somber. "What are you talking about?"

"What am I talking about? You know exactly what I'm talking about, Doctor Workaholic. If a woman isn't sitting on top of your desk, you'll never see her."

K-Mart shrugged. "Look, I just haven't found her yet. But trust me, a man knows what he knows when he knows. You understand what I'm saying?"

A.J. nodded. He truly understood what his friend meant about finding the right woman because he'd found Vic. Despite the accident, which had interfered with his plans to win her love, he took it all in stride. The recent turn of events was much better than anything that he could have come up with.

With a confident smile, he settled back deeper onto the pillows. His only goal from here on out was to use the circumstances to his advantage.

And the results would be well worth the effort.

CHAPTER 5

"Yes, lawd." Zach closed his eyes and inhaled the tantalizing aroma of barbecue ribs, baked beans, and peach cobbler as soon as he walked inside A.J.'s house Friday afternoon to check on his brother-in-law's recovery.

A.J. chuckled and stepped aside to let Zach enter.

"Oh yeah, Baby Girl got it smelling real right up in here." He tapped his watch. "Know it's almost lunchtime, don't ya, brother-in-law?" He glanced around. "Where's Baby Girl at?"

"She had to run a few errands." A.J. headed toward the kitchen while Zach followed. He pointed to the overhead cabinets. "Grab a plate and help yourself." Suddenly, he frowned. "Has Moni stopped feeding you?"

Zach threw back his head and roared with laughter while washing his hands at the sink. "Come on now, brother-in-law. Everybody knows I love my baby, but cooking ain't exactly one of her strong points."

Zach fixed a plate for A.J. as well. Afterward, they headed back toward the dining room.

Once they had settled at a huge polished table, A.J. glanced over at Zach. "Any leads on the accident yet?"

Zach leaned back in a rattan chair with a frown etched on his face. "Not a one. This is one of those cases where things went down without any witnesses. The only person who could even remotely help us crack the case is Baby Girl. The problem is, she can't recall anything more than what she's already told us."

A.J.'s eyes narrowed and his fork clattered against his plate. "Wait. Back up here. What do you mean, Honey can't recall anything?"

Zach shook his head. "Uh . . . nothing. Better finish eating before ya food gets cold."

"Zach," A.J. uttered somewhat impatiently.

"Brother-in-law, I'm sorry. I-I thought she'd told ya by now."

"Told me what?"

"It was Baby Girl's car that hit ya."

A.J. stared at Zach, stunned. "It was?"

Zach pushed his plate away and put his hand up in defense. "Listen, now, don't be mad at her. She couldn't help it. Another car rear-ended her and caused her to hit ya."

A.J. was silent for a moment. Then a wide grin stretched across his face.

Zach lifted his brow. "So that means you ain't mad at her, right?"

"Elated is more like it."

Zach's mouth dropped open. "Whatcha mean, elated? Man, ya got tossed around last Saturday like a rag doll, and ya sitting here telling me ya happy about it?"

A.J. shifted in his chair to take some of the pressure off his side. He didn't need Zach to tell him what he already knew, because the dull ache was reminder enough. "Zach, you know when it comes to Honey, I'm an opportunist. Now you wouldn't want me to miss out on the chance to have her here with me for a while." He smiled and waggled his brow. "Would you?"

Relaxing in his chair, Zach chuckled. "So, ya gonna take full advantage of the situation?"

A.J. shook his head. "No. I'm going to use the situation to my advantage and convince Honey to see things my way. There's a big difference between the two."

"Whatcha got up ya sleeve here, brother-in-law?"

A.J. grinned. "Nothing."

"Yeah, right," Zach drawled with reservation.

A.J.'s carefree demeanor quickly shifted to concern. "Listen, back to the accident. If you don't have any witnesses, what happens now?"

Zach sighed, releasing his pent-up frustration. "Got the boys from the lab analyzing the paint chips left on the cars, but it's a long shot at best." He wiped his mouth with a napkin and reached over to pick up a glass of iced tea. "Ya know, I've been a cop for over fifteen years, and a hit-and-run ranks right up there with child molestation. Both burn the crap out of me. I want to nab the bastard who did this. *Bad.*"

A.J. was puzzled by the fierceness of Zach's last word. "Why?"

"Remember the car I told ya that hit Baby Girl?"

A.J. nodded.

"Well, we believe it might have also hit another car driven by a young family. Nice, hardworking couple, too. Their daughter, Nicole Broussard, got the worst of it. When I got off duty, I stopped by the hospital to check on her and see if the parents could provide any information." Zach hung his head sadly. "Brother-in-law, that baby's hanging on by a thread."

"Oh, man," A.J. uttered sadly.

Neither A.J. nor Zach spoke for a long time. It was as if their professions had trained them to the harsh reality of death, each of them understanding the difficult fate from two different perspectives. A.J. had witnessed it time and again trying to save young patients' lives. Zach, on the other hand, had become acquainted with it after he shot and killed an armed suspect in an effort to save his own life.

Zach sighed wearily. "It's a shame innocent folks gotta have their lives turned upside down like this."

A.J. shook his head, confused. "I'm not following you."

"From what I've been able to gather, the parents were headed to the emergency room anyway because Nicole was having bad headaches and they wanted to get things checked out. On top of all of that, they're like half the working folks in America—no health insurance."

A.J. released a long sigh of regret and his thoughts drifted to Taylor and Tyler. As a parent, he knew the agony Nicole's mother and father were going through. Just the thought of having to experience something even remotely similar with his own girls made his stomach plummet as if he'd taken a fifty-foot dive off a cliff.

Zach shook his head before running his hand down the front of his face. "The good guys got a raw deal, know what I'm saying? Ya got a young girl probably no mo' than a year or two older than T-One and T-Two, and her life might be cut short because some bastard was driving through the streets like a bat out of hell. Y'all had some angels watching over ya the other night."

A.J. made the sign of the cross. "Tell me something I don't already know." He lifted a bottle of Perrier to his lips. After a few moments, he glanced over at his brother-in-law. "Do you think offering a reward would help identify the person responsible?"

Zach shrugged. "Certainly won't hurt. Somebody out there knows something, and money always seems to bring 'em out the woodwork and cause diarrhea of the mouth." His eyes narrowed. "Why?"

For A.J., the answer to Zach's question was simple. Someone hurt his woman and didn't bother to stop and help her. That reason alone was enough, as far as he was concerned, to bring whoever was responsible to justice. Besides, from what Zach just told him about Nicole's injuries, her life could very well end before it even began. "Put the word out that there's a $250,000 reward for anyone with information that will help identify whoever is responsible."

Zach nodded. Closing his eyes, he slid down in his chair and slipped his suspenders off his shoulders with one hand atop a full stomach. "Ya gonna tell Baby Girl about the reward?"

"Eventually."

Zach opened one eye. "Brother-in-law, best not keep her in the dark too long."

"I won't."

Zach closed the eye and chuckled. "Ray and Marcel told me about ya plan to quarantine Baby Girl."

A.J. sighed softly. He'd learned years ago nothing was sacred with his family. If one of them, especially Moni, knew something, everyone would get wind of it before sundown. "You didn't tell that wife of yours, did you?"

"Heck, naw," Zach drawled as his eyes flew open. "You know once Moni gets information, it's like giving it to the AP wire."

"God, that's the truth."

Zach put up his hand. "Listen, don't tell me nothin' else. Don't wanna accidentally up and say something that'll get ya into trouble."

A.J. chuckled. "You mean you talk in your sleep?"

Zach shook his head. "Listen, when a brother's in a uh . . . compromising position, he's likely to say anything."

A.J. smiled; he knew exactly what Zach meant. He sighed with satisfaction because soon he planned to be in the same situation with Vic. He touched the tenderness in his left side. If he could just get his ribs to cooperate with him, he was good to go. He settled his gaze on the huge African painting on the wall in front of him and lifted the bottle of Perrier to his lips again.

"Brother-in-law, ya know Baby Girl told Caitlyn she's relocating the first of August, right?"

"Don't worry, Zach. The only relocating Honey will be doing is to this house."

Vic pulled Baptiste's BMW X5 into the garage at his home with Taylor and Tyler in tow after picking them up from school. Once she parked, she spotted a brand—new black BMW X5 off to the side. Why would he purchase another car? She had to put her query on hold because there were two demanding four-year-olds in the backseat asking her about dinner every two seconds.

Vic suspected Baptiste wasn't being totally honest when he told her he was tired and needed a quick respite before his dinner. His usual humor had disappeared, and she couldn't help noticing his sullenness. Once she got the girls settled down for the night, she figured if she brought his meal to him in bed, he'd feel better.

"Dinner," she cheerfully announced, pushing the bedroom door forward with her hip as she maneuvered the dinner tray in front of her. Suddenly, she stopped. His expression was totally unreadable. "Baptiste, what's wrong?"

A.J. adjusted two pillows at his back. "I talked with Zach this afternoon."

"Is everything all right?"

"We discussed the night of the accident."

Vic swallowed hard. "You did?"

"Umm-hmm."

"Uh . . . what did Zach tell you?"

"Would you like to take a guess?"

The moment of truth caused her hands to shake and the dishes rattled on the tray. "Uh . . . take a guess at what?"

"Don't play with me, woman."

Vic sighed softly and opened her mouth to respond, but his next question silenced her.

"Exactly when were you planning to tell me that it was *your* car that hit me, Honey?"

"I-I was going to tell you, Baptiste, honest to God I was. I-I was just trying to let you get a little stronger, that's all."

A.J. patted the copper-colored silk comforter. "Come on over here. We've needed to talk since last Saturday anyway."

Vic set the tray on the dresser. With the back of her hand, she swiped away the tears running down her cheeks. "No, we'll talk later," she said with her back to him. "You need to—"

"Eating can wait. Come on, Honey."

With her hands hanging limply at her sides, she glanced over her shoulder.

He held open his arms. "Come, *mon amour.*"

"Baptiste, I'm so sorry," she uttered faintly, her words catching on a soft sob the moment she placed her hand in his.

When she approached, he pulled her against his right side, the sheet dropping to his waist, exposing the wide expanse of his chest. "There's nothing for you to be sorry about," he whispered softly, breathing the intoxicating scent of her fragrance and kissing her forehead. "It was an accident, and you don't need to apologize."

"It's my fault," Vic cried out. "If I hadn't told you about Ron that night, you wouldn't have gotten on your motorcycle—"

A.J. covered her mouth with a tender kiss, silencing her explanation, which as far as he was concerned wasn't needed. Afterward, he lifted his head and stared into her eyes, which were shimmering with tears. "Finally."

"What?"

"I've found a way to keep that mouth of yours closed for a minute," he teased.

With her head resting on his right shoulder, she brushed the wetness from her face. "Why were you driving your motorcycle the night of the accident?"

"Whenever I'm upset about something, I usually hop on my bike to help clear my head. Besides, I could get to you faster on it than in my car."

Vic sniffed. "Did Zach tell you a young girl was critically injured, too?"

"Yes," he answered softly, "he did."

"I'm going to try and stop by soon and check on her."

"I think that's a good idea."

"Baptiste, you're not mad at me for hitting you, are you?"

He hugged her tighter. "No, I'm not mad." He chuckled. "Now, other things you do, that's an entirely different story."

"And you forgive me?" she asked a long time later, her fingers splayed against the triangle of hair at the center of his chest.

"Absolutely."

She lifted her head and gazed at him. "Baptiste, I swear to you, if I could take back that night, I would. I-I never meant to hurt you."

"I know you didn't. I'm glad it happened the way it did."

"You like being all banged up?"

He chuckled. "No, woman, I don't like being banged up and living on morphine." With the pad of his thumb, he wiped away a tear running along the side of her nose. "But if that's what it took for you to open up to me, I'll take it, pain and all." He brushed away another tear. "Did you notice the car in the driveway?"

She nodded. "Whose is it?"

"Yours."

As soon as Zach left, A.J. had phoned his brother Marcel, who was the CEO of the family's twelve automotive dealerships, and instructed him to have a new X5 delivered before the end of the day.

"Thank you," she managed to say through a weak smile.

She was amazed at his generosity. He wasn't angry and didn't fault her for the accident. He simply offered what she had struggled with her entire life—forgiveness. She lightly traced her finger over the heart-shaped tattoo on his right arm with the letters *AT&T* on the inside, which she'd noticed the day she had given him his bath.

"When did you get this?"

He glanced at his arm and smiled. "About two and a half years ago."

"What do the letters stand for?"

He patted the mattress. "Scoot over here, and I'll tell you." With her snuggled next to him, he wrapped an arm around her. "It stands for Alcee, Taylor, and Tyler."

She smiled. "That's kinda cute."

He leaned back and his eyes locked with hers. "Thank you, Honey, for trusting me with the pain you've carried inside for so long."

"Baptiste, please don't tell—"

"I'm only going to say this once more, okay?"

She nodded and closed her eyes.

"I will never *ever* abuse or misuse anything you share with me in private. I love you too much to do that. Understand?"

Slowly lifting her head, she nodded.

He kissed the right corner of her mouth. "That's Taylor's thanks." He repeated the gesture on the left side. "And that's from Tyler." He ran his tongue along the wet seam of her parted lips, probing, searching for entrance inside the warmth of her mouth. "And mine is . . ."

With agonizing precision and exquisite slowness, his tongue mated with hers, causing her to shiver from an onslaught of buried passion. She desperately tried not to press her body against his. He teased and tantalized until she opened fully. She nearly exploded when his hand closed over her breast, kneading the soft flesh, his thumb circling her nipple until it was taut.

"What are we doing?" Vic breathed faintly, her chin almost touching her chest.

"What we should've been doing months ago instead of fighting." He released one button on her blouse, then another. "Baby, tell me something."

She stared at his hands for what seemed like a lifetime. This was crazy, she was insane, and he was nuts. From the time of the accident, she'd promised to stay with him and do whatever needed to be done—no matter how long it took—until he recuperated. Nothing more. Their eyes met, hers dilated with desire and need, his narrow and burning. It was her undoing. Like always, his kiss, his touch opened a floodgate of longing, and before she knew it, she'd placed her hand atop his, imploring him to continue.

Unbuttoning the blouse all the way, he released the front clasp of her bra, burying his face in the space between her lush breasts, inhaling. "God, you smell good." Nuzzling his mouth across one breast, he drew a swollen nipple inside and sucked hard.

"Baptiste," she moaned in ecstasy.

"Yes, *mon amour*," he whispered roughly. He loved the thin, pleading way her husky voice called out to him, something she only did in the throes of passion.

She whimpered softly into his mouth. "We can't. The girls might—"

"You want more?" he rasped, the words coming from deep in his throat. He took her hand and moved it between them to where his erection strained against his pajama bottom.

She softly moaned, stunned at how passion always managed to detonate whenever they where together. "More . . ."

He pleasured the other nipple with the same adoration.

Her body quivered, and a second later she tried desperately to control the pounding inside her chest. Her hand explored the length of his arousal. It was useless to try and resist this man any longer. The need to be released from an eight-year-long hiatus had her body bubbling with anticipation. Large, strong hands palmed her face, and her mouth was devoured once more with a kiss that produced sheer delirium.

He caught his breath and groaned. No words could ever describe how he loved his woman. He needed to show her. "Go lock the door."

"Honey, where you?" Tyler called out from her bedroom down the hall.

Vic quickly pulled back and stared at A.J. before her eyes went to the door.

"Oh, Jesus." Vic scooted away from A.J. "Uh . . . T-Two, wait right there, baby." She turned her back to Baptiste, nervously fumbling to right her clothes.

"Gotta feed Harry and Sally, Honey," Tyler advised.

"Okay, sweetheart. Honey's coming."

"Turn around, woman," A.J. said, chuckling as he scooted toward her. He made a tsking sound, brushing her hands away to take over the task at which she was failing miserably. "You're doing it wrong, anyway. Didn't Louise teach you how to dress yourself?"

"Hush, Baptiste."

His brows bunched together as he wondered why the girls were still up. It was well past eight, and they were usually asleep by seven-thirty. "Who are Harry and Sally?"

"The newest members of the family. I brought them two goldfish this afternoon."

"Honey?" Taylor called out this time.

A.J. sighed. "T-One, is it an emergency?"

Taylor shouted back. "What's 'mergency, Daddy?" When she didn't get an immediate response, she hollered, "That Honey's new name?"

"Honey will be right there," he broke off and chuckled before adding, "and you, young lady, should be asleep. You too, T-Two."

"Honey gotta help feed 'em, Daddy," Taylor countered.

"I'm coming, pumpkin," Vic said tensely over her shoulder and swatted Baptiste's hand away as it inched upward to button her blouse.

"Wait." He pulled her back to him and swiped her mouth with a kiss. "This discussion isn't over."

She nodded and hurried out.

Thirty minutes later, A.J. stood at the threshold of Taylor and Tyler's bedroom watching Vic softly sing a lullaby to them as they finally drifted off to sleep. He turned and eased down the hallway, angry with himself. His plan to win Vic's heart had veered off course earlier. Now wasn't the time for lust to overrule love. He'd waited too long, had come too far for passion to win out over patience. Yes, he wanted her body, but more than anything, he craved her unconditional love. He'd seriously considered abandoning Zach's advice about telling Vic he'd offered a reward, but couldn't take the chance his brother-in-law would inadvertently tell his sister, Moni and . . . There was no way he'd risk losing her trust. He threw his head back, sighing softly. How was he going to tell her? Vic was a woman who didn't mince words, and the best way to tell her something was to just come right out and say it.

"Baptiste, what's wrong?" Vic walked into the dining room ten minutes later and stood behind Baptiste, placing her hands on top of his shoulders.

Looking solemn, A.J. reached to cover her left hand with his. "Sit down, Honey."

Vic felt his muscles knot beneath her fingers. Concerned, she pulled a chair next to him. "Is everything okay?"

"Honey, I told Zach to offer a reward. Hopefully, if someone knows any information about the person who caused the two accidents, they'll come forth."

"A reward?" Vic stared baffled for a moment. "How much did you offer?"

A.J. shook his head. "That's not important."

"How much did you offer, Baptiste?"

"Two hundred and fifty."

It took a moment for her comprehension to kick into gear and suddenly her eyes flared. "You don't mean thousand, do you, Baptiste?"

He nodded.

"No," she cried out and shot to her feet. "The accident was my fault. You shouldn't have to put up that kind of money."

"Wrong. You didn't cause the other car to broadside someone else and then rear-end you."

"I-I need to at least chip in something—"

"No," he said emphatically.

"Baptiste—"

"Honey, I said no. End of discussion. There's nothing you can say to make me change my mind."

"But—"

He stood and walked toward her. With her face cupped between his hands, he gently voiced his refusal again. "No."

With a warm smile, she wrapped her arms carefully around his waist. "Why not?"

"Three reasons."

She stared into his eyes, confused. "Three?"

He nodded. "First, somebody hurt you, and whether intentional or not, they didn't stop to help. Two, Nicole is fighting to stay alive. And three . . ."

She swallowed hard because she couldn't fathom what the third reason could be. "And?"

"*Je t'aime,*" he confessed without hesitation.

She turned her head away to hide the tears forming in her eyes and thought she would scream. God, she wanted to find the courage to tell him her greatest fear, but the words simply wouldn't come. "Please don't say you love me."

"*Je t'aime,*" he repeated slowly, nudging her face back around with his mouth.

She quivered when he bent his head, his mouth lowering to hers, lightly touching her lips. When he pulled back, her heart pounded, despite the reasons her mind offered to keep their relationship from going any further. "Baptiste . . ."

He looked at her, his gaze assessing. "Victoria Louise Bennett, will you let me love you?"

CHAPTER 6

The moment Baptiste led Vic into his bedroom, she conceded a bitter truth. Her libido had overruled what little logic she had. A shudder raced down her spine, and a chill swept over her despite the seventy-degree heat outside. Goose bumps surfaced on her arms the moment the door closed and the lock clicked.

"This room is our space, Honey," he said quietly, braced against the door. "Whenever we come in here, the past doesn't matter."

Running away from a challenge was something she'd never done in her life—until she met Baptiste. For six days, she'd been in and out of his room so much she could walk through it blindfolded. Now she was ready to bolt, knowing her vulnerability. The defenses she'd erected long ago to protect her heart from another man's betrayal were in jeopardy of being stripped away one by one.

She didn't want to fall in love again, yet it was too nerve-wracking to teeter back and forth with the physical attraction that had crackled between them for months. Why not enjoy the moment? When things were over, he could move on, and her heart would remain unscathed. Without saying a word, she turned and looped her arms around his neck. "What's right is you and me . . . tonight."

He placed his hands atop hers. "I beg to differ."

She whispered in his mouth, "Baptiste, enjoy this moment with me and what we feel for each other without any commitments, okay?"

"I can't do that, Honey." He lifted her hands and placed them at her side.

She stepped away, confused. "I-I don't understand."

"For the first time since I've known you, I'm going to love you. And just so you'll know, I'm not going to simply enjoy the moment. Never."

She shook her head. "What are you saying here, Baptiste?"

He moved closer, but didn't touch her. "I told you before, Honey, I'm not going to settle for a casual affair with you and then go our separate ways afterward."

"B-But you just said a moment ago you were in love with me, right?"

Smiling, he nodded.

"Well, if a person loves someone, they usually show it physically, right?"

"Usually," he concurred, lightly stroking his finger along her cheek. "The only problem is that it doesn't hold true in our case."

Frustrated, her hands landed on her hips. "And just why not?"

"Because you don't love me. If I simply wanted a booty call, I could get that anywhere. You're too precious to me to settle for anything less than your complete love."

Vic was more baffled now than she was earlier. "B-But you asked if you could love me, right?"

He nodded. "Precisely. I asked if I could love you, not make love. There's a world of difference."

"Difference," she cried out in bewilderment. "How?"

His hand fused with the back of her head. "Let me show you."

Before she knew what hit her, he wrapped her in his embrace, his mouth swooping down on hers. The feel of his lips was strong, yet ever so gentle. A voice inside her head screamed this was another one of his ploys to make her fall in love with him. The whisper from her heart confirmed he might succeed before all was said and done. The tiny flicks of his tongue against the corners of her mouth caused her arms to inch their way back around his neck. His fingers toyed with her skull, causing her lips to part, and he probed further, sucking away her senses and resistance until she released a moan of pure, unadulterated pleasure.

He stepped back, kicked his slippers off, and tugged at the tail of his tank top.

Vic swallowed hard. "W-What are you doing?"

"Getting ready to go to bed." He walked over and sat on the edge of the mattress and removed all his clothes except his underwear, then stood again.

Vic's eyes widened. She blinked once, twice, and a third time before it finally registered. *Oh, Jesus. Black silk bikini briefs?* She didn't even know such a design existed; she'd been out of circulation too long.

"Are you coming?"

"C-Coming where?" she stuttered in a strangled voice.

Didn't he just tell her two seconds ago they weren't going to have sex? She continued to stare, but this time, with appreciation. Muscular, toned, and powerful, his massive physique towered over her. She closed her eyes and held the image. Lord, the man looked good.

"To bed," he answered softly.

She shook her head to try and clear the confusion and looked down at her clothes before glancing back at him. "Take them off?"

"You can leave them on or off. It doesn't matter."

She sucked in a deep breath and tried to steady the trembling of her hands while she undressed down to her underwear. His gaze never left hers.

Their eyes met, and with slow, deliberate steps, he closed the gap between them.

"You're about to experience what it feels like to be loved by a man. Do you understand?"

Did she understand? He couldn't be serious? She hadn't been able to grasp the meaning of anything they'd done or said the last ten minutes, let alone comprehend the two of them together in his bedroom half-dressed. From the moment they'd laid eyes on each other, they'd fought worst than foes on a battlefield. Yet a bond existed between them that went far beyond the physical. She'd been sucked into a vortex of emotions she hadn't felt for any man, not even Ron, and would fight to the bitter end not to feel for Baptiste, if it meant protecting her heart.

When he held his hand out to her, she accepted it and followed him around to the right side of the bed. With her mouth ajar, she watched him push back the covers.

"Go on, get in."

"Whoa, back up here a minute, Baptiste. You just said you didn't want us to have sex."

He cleared his throat. "I'm going to set the record straight for you, Honey. We'll never have sex. And to clarify what I said, earlier, we won't make love—not tonight, at least."

Vic simply stared. Did he really expect for them to get in bed together, half-naked, and not wake up in the morning in tangled sheets?

She released a nervous chuckle. "You're not going to even try to . . . you know—"

"Nope. I told you what I was going to do. Remember?"

"L-Love me?" she finally managed to say, taking in a deep, shuddering breath, forcing her voice to remain calm.

"Yes. Now go on, woman, climb in."

A.J. went to the opposite side of the bed and got in. Once he settled his back against a pillow, he held his arms open, and waited.

After a few moments, she cuddled snugly against his right side. "Baptiste, what you said a few moments ago about loving me. W-What did you mean by that?"

"This . . ."

He devoured her mouth again with a kiss more urgent and scalding than the one they'd just shared. Once she caught her breath, she gazed into his eyes, which smoldered with desire. And he expected her not to go stone-cold crazy after this? No way.

"Now maybe you can relax and go to sleep," he whispered against her mouth.

Vic started to say something, but suddenly her throat tightened, and her words lodged somewhere in the middle.

Even though she hadn't uttered a word, he saw the play of emotions skirting across her face and tilted her head back a fraction. "Don't ever be afraid to share anything with me. What's discussed between us stays between us. Understand?"

She nodded, blinking back tears. Settling next to him, she thought about the irony of this whole situation. Here she was lying next to the man she'd tried for months to elude in an effort not to fall in love with him. And right now he was the one person in the entire universe who fiercely guarded her worst misery. Anguished emotions seeped down into the marrow in her bones, destroying her vow to never let anyone witness her pain.

She cried long and hard. Years of trying to remain strong and not crack under the pressure, of suffering in silence, of clinging to a painful memory, of trying to heal a broken heart alone, washed down her face in moments.

"B-Baptiste, it was the most painful experience in my life," she faintly whimpered in a hoarse voice an hour later.

He pulled her closer to the warmth of his body and felt her heart thud wildly against his chest. The tormented anguish in her voice pierced his very soul. "I can't imagine it would be anything less." He hesitated for a moment. "Listen, you don't have to tell me anything else. I realize what you've already shared was difficult enough."

Her head rested next to his heart and she shook it because she'd held the hurt inside long enough, simply too embarrassed to tell anyone.

"Ron and I met right after he'd finished up his residency. I'd wrapped up my nursing clinicals, and we ended up working at the same hospital." She released a half chuckle. "We actually hit it off from the beginning, and about a year later we got married."

"Did you ever suspect anything?" he whispered softly, reaching down and lacing their fingers together.

"Nothing that would make me think he was . . ." After all these years, Vic still couldn't say the word aloud, and blew out a hard breath. "We'd even talked about starting a family and buying a home. But right after our first anniversary, things started to change."

"How?"

"He became distant. I-I figured he was stressed because of our financial situation."

"Your financial situation? I don't understand."

Vic shifted to an upright position and faced him. "Ron was trying to get his practice off the ground, so we'd taken out loans for that. Plus, we both had student loans from school, and money was tight. I tried to work as much overtime as I could. I figured it would take some of the pressure off him," she choked out between sobs.

A.J. reached for her hand again and softly squeezed it. "It's okay. Settle down, *mon amour,* and take your time."

"One day," she managed to say as fine tremors shook her body, "I came home from work and found him in our bed with . . ." Even after eight years, it was still difficult for her to say out loud that she'd found her husband in bed with another man. "At first, I was so stunned, I didn't feel anything. Baptiste, I-I just stood there." Tears appeared again, and this time, she didn't bother to wipe them away. "I didn't even go inside. I didn't yell, I didn't scream, I didn't curse. I just turned and ran." Bowing her head, she gasped for air. "I-I was so hurt . . . and humiliated." Scooting backwards, she settled on her haunches. "You know, as close as my mother and I are, I couldn't even bring myself to tell her."

"So no one knows the real reason for your divorce?"

She shook her head. "Not even Caitlyn. You're the only person I've ever told. At first, I was too ashamed to tell anybody. Then after some time passed, I didn't know *what* to tell 'em."

He shook his head. "I'm not following you, *mon amour.*"

She accepted the tissue A.J. handed her and wiped her face. "What was I supposed to say, Baptiste? That Ron turned to a man because I was working a lot and wasn't around?"

"What?" A.J.'s voice was perplexed.

"At first, I-I thought it was because I wasn't there to satisfy him." Wearily, she shook her head. "To be perfectly honest, I'm still not sure what the real reason was, and that's what hurts the most. You know, you can accept things better if you understand them."

He nodded. "Did you ever sit down and talk to Ron after what you saw?"

"Why?" she shouted, focusing on the wall in front of her. "Everything I needed to say to Ron, I said through my divorce attorney."

"And since then?"

She released a contemptuous chuckle, and pure hate replaced her pain. "As a matter of fact, he called about six months ago. Ain't that a bitch?" She tore the tissue into shreds. "The no-good son-of-a-bitch. There's not a whole lot he can say to me at this point." She lowered her head, embarrassed because she'd never known Baptiste to use profanity. Even in the most stressful situations, she'd never heard him raise his voice or lose his temper. "I'm sorry. I-I didn't mean to say that."

"Listen, under the circumstances, I think you have the right to say that and more."

She sucked in a long breath, and then slowly released it. "Even though we'd always used protection, I was worried sick. For two years," she emphasized, holding up two fingers, "I got an AIDS test every three months. I didn't want to take any chances." Fury burst inside her again. "Nobody should have to go through that. Nobody." Tears leaked from the corners of her eyes and she screamed, "I should be a mother by now, but instead I got screwed, Baptiste. You hear me? Screwed!"

He shifted to an upright position and held her until her trembling ceased. "I understand that, and you're right." He leaned back, cupping her chin until she slowly lifted her head. "Let me ask you something."

"What?"

"Do you think I'd do what Ron did to you?"

"Baptiste—"

"Yes or no, Honey. Do you?"

"No," she whispered honestly.

He pulled her to his chest. "Good answer, because that's one thing you'd never have to worry about."

"I believe you, Baptiste. I'm just not willing to take the chance of having another man break my heart again for any reason," she admitted truthfully.

"And that's why you won't let yourself fall in love with me?"

She sighed with frustration and pulled away from his embrace. He just wasn't getting it. She simply couldn't gamble on believing whispered words of love a second time, the possibility of going through more heartache. This was the closest she'd been to a man's bed in eight years. Whenever she got desperate, she could always count on a well-made electrical device and six strong Duracells to take the edge off. Even now, she was struggling with releasing the raging pent-up sexual desire inside her while trying to hang on to her heart. And he wanted more? It would never happen.

"Listen, Baptiste—"

"Honey, the answer is simple. Yes or no?"

Vic lowered her head.

He smiled tenderly. "Well?"

"I-I can't."

"Why not?"

"Because I'm scared, Baptiste. I'm scared!"

His smile was shadowed by the darkness of the room. This was more than progress. It was absolute victory.

Whether she knew it or not, she'd just let him slip past her safety zone, the invisible boundary she'd established to guard her from hurt, pain, and disappointment. She'd just let down the defenses around her heart and allowed him to touch it. "Look at me and tell me what it is you see."

She obeyed. "The most bullheaded man I've ever met in my life." She sucked in a deep breath and offered a slight smile. "And one I wouldn't mind wrecking this bed with."

"I want that more than you'll ever know, but I want it predicated on love, not lust. And the only way we'll get there is for you to do two things."

She took the tissue he handed her and softly blew her nose. "What's that?"

"First, let go of the past. As hard as it may sound, find a way to forgive Ron. And second, take a chance with me. I want your heart, *mon amour*. Completely."

"Baptiste—"

"Honey, I'm not backing down on this. You can call me stubborn or any other name you can come up with, but nothing—and I mean nothing—will make me change my mind."

She glared at him a moment. "Those are the rules, huh?"

He nodded. "Those are the rules."

"Well, guess what?" she huffed, scooting to the center of the bed. "I'm not gonna play this game with you."

Evidently he didn't understand what she'd just said because he simply gave her a sympathetic nod, releasing a gentle smile at the same time that almost lit up the room. "Baptiste, I haven't seen or talked to Ron in eight years, and I don't plan on starting now."

"I didn't say anything to you about talking to him, now did I?"

"Man, you haven't heard a thing I've said, have you? He was wrong to do what he did to me." She shook her head. "I can't forgive him. I won't do it."

A.J. shifted and rested his weight on his right elbow. "I agree totally with your first argument, but let me ask you a question."

"What?"

"You've carried a tremendous burden inside of you for a long time, right?"

Vic stared and wondered where his line of questioning was going. "Baptiste—"

He inched up closer to her. "And for a long time, you've never allowed another man to get close to you, right?"

Vic was silent and turned her head to hide the new wave of tears stinging her eyes.

He moved a littler farther. "Right?"

"Yes," she whispered.

"It's been a long time since you've been loved by a man, right?"

Vic's emotions were too fragile to do anything else but nod.

"Yet you're in my bed and you just poured your soul out to me. You weren't scared to do that, right?"

She held her breath before releasing it, her eyes connecting to his. "No."

"Then falling in love with me will be much easier."

He didn't give her a chance to answer because he stretched out and patted the mattress. "Come on, lie down."

Vic simply stared at him. He'd asked her—no correction, told her she needed to do two things she had no intention of doing. He opened his arms to her and waited. Taking another deep breath, she pushed aside the roller-coaster emotions bombarding her and went to him.

Once she settled next to him with her back against his chest, she whispered over her shoulder, "Baptiste?"

"Yes, *mon amour?*"

"I-I don't know if I can get past the hurt," she uttered in a stifled voice.

He tightened his arms around her waist. "Yes, you can."

"How?"

"Stay with me for the next three weeks, and let's figure it out together."

She swallowed hard and offered up one last defense. "I-I'm still going to Atlanta."

He kissed the back of her head, but knew from the slight inflection in her voice she didn't mean a word she'd just said. "But not for another three weeks, right?"

She stared into the darkness, listening to silence. At that moment she was absolutely exhausted. In the past hour, her strength and determination had been zapped.

"Baptiste, come on, work with me here."

"That's exactly what I'm doing. And it's what I plan on continuing to do. Honey, I'm going to love you tonight."

"How?" she whispered.

He tightened his arms around her. "I'm going to hold you all night long. I'm going to be the man you dream about. And when you wake up in the morning, I'm going to be the man who starts the day with you."

"But Baptiste—"

He flipped her onto her back and kissed her with such thoroughness it removed any doubt in her mind of his love for her, and she was left breathless.

"Stay?"

"'Kay," she uttered quietly.

Afterward, he settled his chest to her back and wrapped his arms back around her waist. "Now, close your eyes for me and go to sleep."

"*Je t'aime*," he whispered, hearing Vic's deep breathing a while later. He smiled. She was exactly where she should be, in his bed, wrapped securely in his arms, and he drifted off to sleep knowing his prescription of a little patience when needed and a whole lot of love once per day had just about put her on the path to recovery.

CHAPTER 7

Saturday marked exactly one week since the hit-and-run. Around ten that morning, Vic walked into the intensive care unit at Highland Hospital to visit the other accident victim, Nicole Broussard.

Since she wasn't family, she figured it would be an uphill battle getting clearance to visit Nicole. Thankfully, one of her nursing colleagues, Pam Matthews, was the charge nurse on duty and made an exception.

The front area was quiet except for the occasional concentrated movements of nurses who vigilantly monitored the life-support systems. Vic walked through the unit, which had a strong, familiar aroma of antiseptic, and stepped inside Nicole's room. For a split second, her lung capacity short-circuited and her heart skipped before lurching back into rhythm again. Through labored breaths she struggled to breathe, and tears sprang to her eyes as she stared at the small, motionless body lying in the bed.

Nicole looked like a mummy. Wide strips of gauze were uniformly wrapped around her head and face. Only her lips, which were swollen and discolored, were visible. A clear plastic tube had been inserted down her throat to aid her breathing and the tiny stream of air that passed through whistled quietly in beat with the other machines softly beeping to record her body functions.

Vic's throat was so tight it was almost too painful to swallow. Slowly shuffling forward, she reached the bed and observed what she'd seen countless times before. A steady stream of tears trickled down her face, and she wondered how anyone injured this badly could still be alive.

Vic's fingers were stiff and cold, but the warmth generating from Nicole's body, indicated that life still existed for her, but just barely. Tears continued to slide down her cheeks, and she couldn't help thinking it could have so easily been her or Baptiste lying here. Yet, for some reason, they'd been spared. Why hadn't Nicole?

With fifteen years of training to her credit, Vic knew Nicole needed something medical science could never offer. She needed a miracle.

Vic did the only thing she knew to make that miracle happen.

She knelt next to Nicole's bed and prayed.

"So, Vic," Chandler said, with a hint of amusement after she noticed Vic trying to inconspicuously slip her cell phone back inside her purse. "How's the patient?"

Vic, Tara, and Chandler were enjoying Sunday brunch at Scott's in Jack London Square in downtown Oakland.

Vic tossed her friend one of those if-you-say-one-more-word-I'll-kill-you glances. The phone landed on the floor.

"Let's see . . ." With her laughter escalating, Chandler lifted her wrist to study her Rolex. "We've been here an hour and that's the fourth time you've snuck out to check on him. That's a call every—"

"Hush, Chandler," Vic interjected. "I know how to divide."

A broad smile graced Tara's chocolate-brown face. "Oh, now see there, Vic. That's not right. Are you trying to pull the code of silence on us?"

Even though the restaurant's air conditioning system was running at full blast, Vic was about to roast from the body heat generated inside the crowded building and removed the short matching jacket to her dress. "Back off, all of ya. Because of me, Baptiste is flat on his back. It's the least I can do."

Chandler leaned over, running her finger along Vic's neck, and snickered. "Well, it looks like you found the time to do a few other things."

Tara looked at Vic and gasped softly.

"What?" Vic inquired, her confused gaze darting back and forth between her friends.

Tara pointed to the space just below Vic's collarbone. "Oh, my . . . he got that spot, too."

Suddenly, Vic's hands inched up to her throat to cover the passion marks she'd momentarily forgotten were there. She released a soft, shivering breath at the memory of when and how she'd gotten them. Just before dawn that morning, she remembered how Baptiste had quietly slipped inside the guest room where she'd decided to stay for the next three weeks, and she'd awakened to the feel of his mouth moving sensually along her shoulders, leaving his brand in its wake.

"Take your hand down, heifer, you're busted," Chandler quipped, picking up her water glass and taking a sip. "Tell you what. If I was locked up with the man, you'd be seeing more than a few bite marks."

"Being on lockdown . . . oooh, how romantic," Tara crooned softly.

Vic glanced at Chandler. "Don't you have men to gloat over in San Francisco?" Before she got the answer to her question, she looked over at Tara. "And as for you, hush. Watching reruns of *Lassie Come Home* is romantic to you."

Chandler giggled. "Now leave our friend alone. You know how sentimental she gets. Girl, I can't wait until Caitlyn gets back from Paris to tell her about this."

Vic snorted. "See, that's the very reason I don't tell y'all any more than I do. Every single one of you talks too much."

"That's all right," Chandler defended. "Betcha Mrs. Baptiste will have a story worse than this one to tell us when she arrives home."

Vic threw her head back and laughed. "Yeah, she's no doubt making more babies with Marcel on the corporate jet over the Atlantic as we speak." After she settled down, she glanced over at Chandler again. "Don't tell me you're solo these days?"

Chandler snorted loudly. "Child, how about three years, okay?"

"But why?" Puzzled, Vic stared at the woman who looked like a runway model, dressed immaculately, had a career that was better than good, and swapped out her Mercedes every six months.

"The ones out there fall into three categories," Chandler explained, bending her fingers back. "They either one, don't know what they want to be when the grow up; two, don't have a clue on how to be with one woman at a time; or three, are of a different persuasion, and I ain't talkin' lighter either."

Chandler's last reference made the hairs on the back of Vic's neck stand at full attention.

"Chandler's right," Tara agreed with a nod. "D.C. was just as bad. I figured once I moved back home to Oakland I would have better luck finding relief for my drought."

Vic angrily tossed her thumb at the window behind her. "The world's largest ocean is just over the bridge. Both of ya go jump in it."

"My, my, my, we are testy here this afternoon," Chandler said, lifting her brow. "Girl, what's wrong?"

"N-Nothing." Vic was immediately mortified at her reaction to Chandler and Tara's innocent reference to homosexuality. When she noticed how her two friends glanced at each other with a baffled look, she shrugged. They had no way of knowing her situation with Ron, something she was still having trouble accepting herself, and she felt bad she'd yelled at them. "Listen, I'm sorry. I didn't mean to snap at you guys. Baptiste is doing fine. Hopefully, he can get down to the clinic—"

"Yeah, yeah, yeah," Chandler butted in. "Listen, that's more information than we need to know." Scooting her chair closer to Vic's, she braced her hands under her chin. "We want to know what it's like taking care of a home, you know, with a man, kids, goldfish . . . whatever."

Vic eyed the caramel-skinned epidemiologist skeptically. "You serious?"

Chandler nodded. "Like a drive-by shooting. Now, start talkin'."

"Well . . ." Vic couldn't stop her enthusiasm from dancing in her eyes. "It's kinda fun. You know, when you're raising two kids, you got to stay on a schedule."

Tara's doe-brown eyes widened. "Schedule? But Vic, you've always been organized and on time. You plan things out almost to the second."

"Sweetie, that's the only way I can do the mommy thing. You see, we have a nighttime ritual. We do our bubble bath, put on our lotion, then lay out our clothes for the next morning—"

"Why do all of that stuff at night?" Chandler asked, confused.

"Chandler," Vic quipped, "I have two heads to do in the morning. I spend forty-five minutes making ponytails—per child—thank you very much. But I put them in braids the other day."

"Oooh, I bet they look so cute," Tara said merrily.

"They do." Vic grinned proudly from ear-to-ear as she reached inside her purse for the picture she'd taken of them. "Just look at my babies."

Tara covered her open mouth with both hands while Chandler hailed the waiter.

"Your best champagne," Chandler instructed the waiter after he hurried to their table. "Ladies, Vic's conversion calls for a celebration."

Vic's eyes widened. "What conversion? Wait a minute. It's not even two o'clock. It's too early to be drinking champagne. And besides, we just left church."

"You're right," Chandler said, gleefully. Looking at the waiter's order pad, she amended her request. "Make that three VO and sevens, sir."

"We can't." Vic shirked at Chandler's request for her favorite drink—whiskey with a 7-Up chaser.

"Why not?" Chandler asked innocently and shrugged. "Listen, Vic, we've known you going on eighteen years and ain't never seen you glow over a man like this. Listen to yourself and the way you talk about A.J." She flicked her wrist back. "And his babies, too. Oh, pleassse."

"Forget you, Chandler," Vic replied, chuckling.

"Vic, come on, girl," Chandler chided. "Stop kidding yourself. You are so hooked on A.J. and those girls it ain't even funny. And the killing part in all of this is they feel the same way about you."

Vic glanced down at the picture in her hand and knew Chandler was right. A week ago, nothing in the world could have landed her inside Baptiste's home, let alone his bed.

Her hands began to tremble, and she knew Baptiste, Taylor, and Tyler had captured her heart without even trying. There wasn't a shred of doubt in her mind that she'd kill first and not even bother to ask questions later to protect them. Choking back tears, she tried to rationalize why she'd agreed to stay with Baptiste for the next three weeks. The answer was clear—because she wanted to be there. Plain and simple. Releasing a long sigh, she finally accepted hardcore reality.

Before the next twenty-one days were over, her life would be forever changed.

A week later, A.J. braced his muscular frame next to the bar at his brother Marcel's estate and sipped a Perrier at a fundraising event for his clinic. Shortly after he and Vic arrived, he'd gone up to check on his nephews, Etienne and Nicolas, after Caitlyn told him she thought they were coming down with a cold. He'd spoken with the boys' pediatrician by phone and provided his assessment. Then he reassured Caitlyn that Etienne and Nicolas would be fine. He didn't argue with her, though, after Caitlyn decided to skip the evening's event to stay with the twins.

Amazement slapped A.J. upside the head as he looked over the guests and wondered how Vic had managed to pull off the night's activities in a little over two weeks. Even after she'd told him she'd set up a meeting with several foundations, never in million years did he expect all of them to be assembled under one roof. She'd orchestrated the catered black-tie affair and invited the CEOs at the top ten philanthropic foundations in California. And how she ever convinced Ray and his jazz band to provide the musical entertainment was beyond comprehension.

Chuckling as a waiter passed by, K-Mart snatched a glass of champagne from his tray. "Doc, can't you wait until you're behind closed doors to catch your woman's eye?"

"What?" A.J. absently answered, pulling a pen from inside the jacket of his tailor-made black tuxedo and scribbling something on a napkin after noticing Vic's nod.

"I've been watching you and Vic winking back and forth at each other for most of the evening," K-Mart teased.

Ray rallied to A.J.'s defense. "Look here, K-Mart, whatcha seeing is *mon frère* and Honey's coding system."

K-Mart looked confused. "Coding system?"

"Yeah," Zach drawled, downing a shot of Crown Royal. "Every time Baby Girl gets a funding commitment, she tosses brother-in-law a wink." He nudged A.J. in the side. "Ya see that? Baby Girl just signaled in another pledge."

K-Mart whistled low and moved closer to A.J. "How much has Vic raked in so far?"

A.J. scanned the napkin before he placed it back inside his jacket. "That last donation puts us at nine."

K-Mart nodded. "That's pretty good. Nine hundred thousand is not a bad take for a couple of hours of work."

"Oh, hell naw," Zach protested mildly. "Brother-in-law can come up with that much from his petty cash. He's talking seven digits. Ain't that right, brother-in-law?"

K-Mart muttered a string of incoherent words in a strangled voice and ran his index finger along the inside of his wing-tip collar. "V-Vic raised nine million dollars in just two hours?"

A.J. nodded proudly. "Her goal is ten, and she still has thirty minutes left."

"I'm tellin' y'all, Baby Girl's handling business in here tonight," Zach boasted. "Moni told me when she made the invite to the big-wigs for them not to even show up if they weren't prepared to offer at least a mil."

Ray chuckled. "Oh, I can believe it. Got her whole family working the suits, too." He tossed his thumb over his shoulder. "On my way back in here, saw Louise with one of 'em pinned in a corner. Humph. When she got through with friend, on top of what his foundation gave, he pulled out his checkbook and handed over a *personal* check for fifty Gs."

"*Nine million dollars*," K-Mart mumbled under his breath. He grabbed another glass of champagne, gulped it down, and wiped his mouth with the back of his hand. "Doc, I need Vic on my staff, pronto. I'll pay her top dollar."

Ray patted K-Mart's shoulder. "Look here, K-Mart, *mon frère's* woman don't need to work now. He's got her back."

A.J. missed most of the exchange because his focus was solely on Vic. She looked absolutely stunning in a black lace-and-silk chiffon halter-top dress with a deep v-neck front, open-toed sandals, and a pair of gold chain earrings that hung from a square diamond mount. He chuckled to himself at the thought of how when they first met, Vic would call him chauvinistic whenever he asked her to wear a dress. There really was a method to his madness. If she wore a dress, he wouldn't have any trouble looking at her shapely legs.

K-Mart nudged A.J in the side. "Doc, come on and let me hire Vic to head up my public health department."

A.J. polished off the rest of his Perrier. "You ask her. If she wants to work for you, it's her call."

They all stood and chatted for a few more moments until K-Mart looked across the room, which was filled to capacity, and spewed out the champagne he'd just taken a sip of. "Doc, doc . . . nine o'clock to your right."

A.J. looked over to see Vic, Tara, Chandler, and another woman he assumed was with one of the foundations standing near the entrance to the living room. "What's wrong?"

"Who's the one standing on Vic's left who looks like Tyra Banks's twin?" K-Mart whispered.

"Uh, what did you say?" A.J. muttered under his breath, his eyes locked on Vic.

"Come on, doc," K-Mart whined. "Who is she?" Frustrated, he turned to Ray as he straightened his tie and brushed the lapels of his tuxedo jacket. "Do you know who she is?"

Ray glanced in the direction K-Mart pointed out. "Oh, man, that's just Chandler. She and Honey went to

Columbia together." He curved his hands to form the shape of an hourglass. "I'm trying to check out J. Lo's baby sister standing next to her. *Daaayuuum*, she's fine."

A.J. cleared his throat. "Ray, don't mess up what Honey's doing tonight with your womanizing."

"Settle down, *mon frère*," Ray answered, grinning. "I'll keep everything on the DL if the sista is with one of the foundations. And if she is, betcha I talk her into giving that last million Honey needs." Then he opened up his arms. "But now if girlfriend there wanna tack a little somethin', somethin' on the end, you know, what can I say?"

"Ray, I'm warning you," A.J. chided.

Ray inclined his head. "Come on, man." He beckoned K-Mart with his hand. "I suggest we move on over to the feeding trough." Peering over a pair of rose-tinted Dior glasses, he stepped forward and stopped mid-stride. "*Daaayuuum*, J. Lo is fine."

"Vic, Vic," Chandler uttered breathlessly. "Twelve o'clock coming in for a landing."

Vic looked up and saw Ray and K-Mart heading toward them. "Down, girl. It's just Baptiste's best friend, K-Mart. They went to medical school together."

"K-who?" Chandler smoothed down the front of her dress.

Vic chuckled. "Kevin Martin Bullock, but we call him K-Mart."

Chandler cupped both hands to her mouth and released two quick breaths. "A-okay." She tossed her hair over her shoulder and waited. "Midnight black, tall, fine . . . oh, sweet Jesus. Houston, we have landed." She grabbed Vic's arm. "Girl, I need an all-aboard announcement."

Vic reached up and gently closed Chandler's mouth. "Pull up your landing gear, child, you're drooling down the front of your dress."

"Ladies." K-Mart approached first and nodded at Vic and Tara. His gaze quickly shifted to Chandler.

Vic held her hand out to Chandler. "K-Mart, Chandler Perkins, Ph.D." Glancing back over at Chandler, who was running her tongue along her lips, she said, "Chandler, Kevin—"

In a sultry tone, Chandler slid up to K-Mart, extending her hand. "Well, how *do* you do?"

Smiling, Vic turned to tell Tara something, but she'd disappeared. She had to rotate a full circle before she saw her friend by the bar wrapped around Lincoln's arm like a rubber band. The hushed snickering from behind made her glance over her shoulder to find the tall, long-legged CEO who'd had a stoic expression all evening standing in a corner with Ray, grinning from ear-to-ear at whatever he was whispering to her.

A.J. walked up behind Vic unnoticed and snuggled his lips next to her ear. "You did a fantastic job tonight, Honey." He kissed the side of her neck. "*Merci, mon amour.*"

Vic turned to face him, pleased he was happy with her efforts. "Baptiste, thank you for letting me do this for you. I know how much the clinic means to you." She placed her hand over her mouth to hide her yawn.

"Tired?" He wrapped his arms around her waist and fluttered his lips along the space between her neck and shoulder.

Vic was exhausted, but not so much that she was unaffected by his touch. At that moment, she knew they probably looked scandalous to anyone who happened to walk by. Baptiste had pulled her in front of him, his hardness rubbing against her belly. The sensations of his moustache lightly scraping against her skin sent sparks of carnal pleasure from her head to her toes. With her head thrown back, she released a moan of pure contentment.

He slid his hands down her arm, and laced their fingers together. "Since you're the hostess, the sooner we can get everyone out of here, the sooner we can go home."

"You work the right side of the room. I'll get the left."

CHAPTER 8

On Monday morning, Vic walked through the waiting area at the East Oakland Health Clinic and noticed a young woman slumped over in a chair groaning in pain.

"Somebody better come up with a real good explanation for why a patient needing medical services hasn't been seen yet."

Rushing over, Vic gently tilted the slender girl's head back. "Jesus, have mercy," she uttered softly, staring at the badly battered face that looked like someone had mistaken it for a punching bag.

The girl groaned weakly. "Help . . . me . . . please."

"Easy now, sweetie." Vic rested the girl's head against the back of the chair. "Have you been here long?"

The swelling around the young woman's mouth made it difficult for her to say any more than what she'd already managed to utter.

"Harrison . . . Louise," Vic yelled over her shoulder.

Vic continued to hold the girl's hand, assuring her everything was going to be fine. Since Baptiste was attending a medical conference in San Francisco, she was grateful Harrison and Louise, who'd agreed to volunteer one day a week at the clinic, were there.

Harrison and Louise raced down the hallway, and after Harrison quickly assessed the girl's injuries, he lifted her slender body in his arms.

Harrison turned to his mother. "What exam room is empty?"

Louise pointed down the hall. "Just cleared Room Two."

"Let's go, people," Harrison ordered without hesitation.

Louise scurried down the corridor behind Harrison just as Vic looked up to see another nurse round the corner. "Cover me for a minute."

Vic bolted to the front desk. "Chanta, have you seen Jenkins and Goldberg?"

Chanta, the clinic's part-time receptionist, was a high school student whom Vic had met at the after-school program at the East Oakland Youth Center where she and Baptiste worked as mentors.

Chanta nodded and pointed straight ahead. "I saw them head to the lounge about ten minutes ago."

Vic raced off to the room at the rear of the clinic. She flung the door open and found the nurses who were supposed to be covering the patient intake station with their feet propped up on a table, sipping coffee. "Jenkins . . . Goldberg, why is there a patient who obviously needs emergency medical treatment sitting in the waiting area?"

Jenkins, the blonde-haired nurse, shrugged nonchalantly. "She should've gone to a hospital. This is a clinic."

Vic narrowed her eyes in fury and slammed the door. "Oh, now I know you didn't just say that."

Jenkins nodded. "Oh, but I did."

Vic walked closer to the couch where the two nurses sat. "Let me tell you one thing. Everybody who walks through our doors is a human being and deserves the best we can give them. Are we clear?"

Goldberg glanced over at Jenkins and tried to offer an explanation. "V-Vic, we're sorry. But it's like Jenkins said, we don't offer emergency services here—"

"I know that, but you stabilize them and get them *to* emergency, Goldberg. That's Nursing 101."

Jenkins glanced at her watch. "It was time for our break anyway."

"Break?" Vic bellowed. "A break is for folks who work, and from what I'm seeing, the two of y'all ain't doing a good job at that."

Goldberg stood to her feet. "Now, you wait—"

"Wait?" Vic cried out incredulously. "Oh, no, I'm not waiting for anything. I'm about two seconds from throwing both of your behinds outta here *and* reporting ya to the State Board of Nursing."

"You wouldn't do that, now would you?" Jenkins taunted, settling more comfortably on the couch.

Vic rolled her head on her shoulders, walked over to an empty desk, and picked up the phone. "You know what? I can show you better than I can tell you."

Goldberg raced over to Vic. "W-Who are you calling?"

"I told you who I was gonna call." It wasn't the first time in Vic's career as a nursing administrator that she'd had to make the call, and she knew the number from memory. She turned her back the two nurses and listened to the first ring of the state agency located in Sacramento.

"W-We could lose our licenses," Goldberg angrily blurted.

Vic nodded without turning around. "Exactly."

After reporting the incident, Vic placed the phone back on the base, walked to the door, and whirled around. "Break's over, and so are the two of you. You're fired."

"Bitch," Jenkins whispered under her breath just as Vic placed her hand on the doorknob.

Vic heard the comment and pivoted back around. She took in a deep, shuddering breath to control her anger. "That's right, Jenkins. I'm the *bitch* who's running this nursing staff right now. I'm also the *bitch* who'll decide if you ever draw another paycheck as a nurse to pay the rent and car note when it rolls due. But most of all, I'm the *bitch* who's spent the last fifteen years taking care of patients, not dumping 'em like you two just did." She tossed her thumb over her shoulder. "This clinic is open to serve folks, and that child deserved better than what she got from the two of you. I want both of you outta here. Now!"

Without another word, Vic stormed out, slamming the door.

It was around two in the afternoon and A.J. had decided to leave the conference early. He sat behind his desk at the health clinic with the phone cradle between his neck and shoulder. "Ray, I need a favor from you."

"Talk to me," Ray chuckled, then rushed on to add, "don't tell me you and Honey are fighting again? Do ya'll need to go somewhere and make up?"

A.J. smiled to himself. He liked making Vic lose her temper. In a basic way, it was electrifying to watch those pretty light-brown eyes narrow and her back arch like a hissing feline poised to fight. In the past ten months, he'd learned much about her personality that way. He'd also figured out exactly what someone would have to do to bring the volatility in her personality to the forefront. One day soon, he planned to provoke her to anger and then love her out of her rage. "Soon, *mon frère*, soon."

Then, he explained to Ray the medical emergency involving the injured girl who came to the clinic earlier that morning. If Ray could pick up Taylor and Tyler from preschool at four o'clock, after the clinic closed he and Vic could head over to Highland Hospital to check on her condition before heading home.

"Look here, *mon frère*," Ray teased. "How long will I be on kiddie lockdown with them future residents at San Quentin?"

A.J. chuckled out loud. "What's wrong, Ray? Don't tell me you're scared of two four-year-olds."

"Scared?" Ray mocked. "Ya damn skippy I'm scared. Them hellions might be only four, but I'm telling ya, *mon frère*, they were career criminals in their other life." He chuckled. "Last time I ended up babysitting 'em, they called 911 and told the dispatcher they needed help."

"Well, did they?"

"Hell naw. I sent those two convicts we claim as family to their room for a time-out. How was I supposed to know you'd taught them what 911 was?"

The only thing A.J. could do was smile. Taylor and Tyler were geniuses at finding cracks to slip through, and the family was always on guard around them. "Well, now you know."

"Yeah, right, after my name's been placed on the FBI's most wanted list." Ray chuckled again. "Listen, *mon frère*, you and Honey take ya time. I got 'em covered."

A.J. smiled. "*Merci.*"

"How long have you been using, Valerie?" Vic asked.

Racked with fear, the young woman jerked her head up. "H-How you know my name?"

It was a little past five in the evening. Vic and A.J. stood next to Valerie's hospital bed.

"Looked at your chart," Vic answered. "Also saw the results of your lab report. You got traces of crack in your system. Now when's the last time you used?"

Valerie wrung her hands together. "T-Two weeks. It's been two long weeks. I-I been clean since then, though."

Vic hitched her brow. "You sure?"

"I swear," Valerie answered truthfully and suddenly stared back with a panic-stricken look. "You the police?"

"No, sweetie. I'm a nurse." Vic smiled softly and sat on the edge of the bed, taking Valerie's hand inside of hers. "Do you remember me?"

Valerie focused through swollen eyelids and smiled slightly. "The lady at the clinic?"

Vic nodded. "That's right."

"What about him?" Valerie lifted a shaky finger and pointed at A.J. "H-He the police?"

"No, no, Valerie," A.J. answered in a soothing voice. He walked over to the opposite side of the hospital bed. "I'm not the police."

Valerie slowly raised her battered body to an upright position. "Who you, then?"

"My name is Dr. Baptiste, sweetheart." A.J. flashed a bright smile and pulled his stethoscope from the pocket of a long, white lab coat. "But most of my patients call me Dr. B." He knew he had to gain her trust, so he placed his hand on her shoulder to get her to lie back. "I want to listen to your lungs and make sure they're clear. Will you allow me to do that?"

Valerie gave Vic a hesitant stare.

Vic patted the top of Valerie's hand. "He's good people, baby. Lie back for him, okay?"

A.J. quickly examined Valerie's injuries and checked her vital signs, then placed his stethoscope around his neck. "Lungs sound great. Perhaps we can get you out of here soon."

"Y'all the only people who done helped me in a long time."

Vic smoothed back a strand of tangled reddish hair that had scattered across Valerie's face. "Who did this to you, sweetie?"

Valerie tried to pull her swollen bottom lip between her teeth and failed. "Nobody."

"Oh, so your face had an attack with a couple of fists all by itself, huh? Is that what you want us to believe?" Vic saw the fear in the young girl's eyes and a deep sense of sadness filled her. "Come on, now. We can't help you if you don't talk to us."

Tears rolled down Valerie's bruised cheeks. "I-I can't tell. He might hurt my babies if I talk."

"Where are your babies now?" A.J. asked. When he noticed Valerie's hesitation, he added, "Vic and I can't help you if you don't tell us the truth."

"At the house . . . I think," Valerie whispered.

"You're not sure?" Vic asked softly.

"I ran out to get away from Tony . . . uh . . . I mean Scooter."

Vic looked over and held Baptiste's gaze because she figured Valerie was trying to protect the identity of this Tony, Scooter, or whatever his name was.

A.J. picked up on Vic's clue and sat on the edge of Valerie's bed. "Did Scooter do this to you?"

Valerie didn't confirm or deny the question. "I-I'm tired of living like this."

A.J. cleared his throat. "Valerie, what made Scooter so angry?"

Valerie remained silent.

A.J. paused in his questioning for a moment and studied the fearful expression on Valerie's face. "Usually something happens that causes a person to become angry enough to hurt someone this way. Do you know what it might have been?"

Valerie brushed back a tear and swallowed the lump in her throat. "H-He heard me calling about the reward."

Vic and A.J. stared at each other, stunned.

A.J. returned his attention to Valerie and continued to gently coax the remaining information out of her. "What reward, sweetheart?"

"About that hit-and-run accident," Valerie admitted after a pregnant pause.

Vic's throat tightened and she silently counted to ten in order to regain her composure. She noticed how Baptiste lifted his brow, his eyes connecting with hers, an indication for her not to utter a word, at least for now. She was anxious to know more, but followed his lead not to let Valerie know they were two of the victims involved.

A.J. cleared his throat. "Why did you call, Valerie?"

"I-I figured if I got the money . . ."

"Go on, sweetheart," A.J. uttered gently. "If you got the money . . ."

"I-I . . ." Valerie hedged and began to cry.

Patting her hand, A.J. softly urged her on. "Go ahead, sweetheart, and finish what you were about to say so that we can help you."

Valerie sobbed. "So I could leave him."

A.J. sighed softly. "Valerie, do you know anything about the accident?"

Valerie nodded. "I-I was in the car with him when he hit them people."

Vic placed a trembling hand against her chest.

"Do you remember what kind of car Scooter was driving?" A.J. asked.

Valerie nodded. "I don't know the kinda of car, but it was red."

"Valerie," A.J. said, "think hard for me. Did the car have two doors or four doors?"

Deep in concentration, Valerie thought for a moment and gently wiped the tears running along her cheeks. "Two doors."

A.J. shifted so his vision was better aligned with Valerie's. "Okay, you said you were trying to get the money. What were you going to do with it?"

Valerie shrugged. "I-I need to turn my life around 'cause I got two babies. I figured I could go somewhere and start over. Y-You know what I mean?" She heaved and wiped her face with her hands again. "I'm tired."

Vic had remained silent long enough. "Sweetie, you're so young. How did you get messed up like this?"

Valerie sighed and shrugged. "Hard-headed. Wouldn't listen to nobody and started hanging out with the wrong crowd. I got caught up."

Vic had glanced over the young girl's hospital chart and knew she'd just turned eighteen. "You finish high school yet?"

"Had to drop out when I got pregnant with my babies."

"What about your family, Valerie? Are they willing to help you?" A.J. asked.

Valerie shook her head.

A.J. glanced at Vic, and then looked back at Valerie. "Is Scooter the father of your babies?"

Valerie nodded.

"Valerie," A.J said softly, "do you have a job?"

Valerie bowed her head with embarrassment. "No, but I pick up cash here and there."

Vic narrowed her eyes. "You selling?"

"No, no, I-I don't sell," Valerie admitted truthfully. "I-I just . . ."

"Just what, sweetheart?" A.J. asked softly.

"I make drop-offs from time to time."

Without condemnation, Vic said, "But you crossed over the line and started using. Why?"

"Got depressed. Ain't never had no support at home. My mother wouldn't forgive me for getting pregnant with two 'black bastard' babies. That's what she calls 'em. She threw me out. Didn't have no place to go other than to Scooter's."

Vic drew in a deep breath. "Is Scooter running drugs?"

Valerie's gaze drifted from A.J. to Vic and she pursed her lips.

"Valerie," A.J. reminded her gently, "Vic and I want to help you—and your babies—but we can't do that if you don't help yourself."

"You don't understand the streets, Dr. B. You talk and you end up dead."

"But you're going to slowly kill yourself if you continue living like this," Vic whispered.

"I know," Valerie acknowledged, her voice a mere murmur.

A.J. stood to his feet. "Valerie, Vic and I know someone who could help you."

Valerie's eyes widened. "Who?"

"His name is Lieutenant Zach Tate," A.J. advised.

"B-But he the police," Valerie cried out in fear.

A.J. patted Valerie's shoulder. "He's a friend, first and foremost. He'll help you just like Vic and I are trying to do."

"I-I don't know . . ."

A.J. offered a gentle smile. "What do you want most in the world, Valerie?"

"I-I don't want my babies to end up like me."

Vic made an urgent appeal once again. "Then let us help you, sweetie."

Valerie shook her head, slid down in the bed, and pulled a white sheet up to her chin.

A.J. gathered a blanket at the foot of the bed and pulled it up, tightly tucking it around Valerie's slender body. "Whenever you're ready to talk to me or Vic again, let one of the nurses know. They'll be able to contact us. Okay?"

Valerie nervously glanced between A.J. and Vic. "I-I just don't want nothin' to happen to my babies."

A.J. nodded. "If that's what you truly want, then the power to make certain nothing happens to them is left up to you. You have to make a call to the right people who can help your babies. Do you understand who you need to call?"

Valerie gave a slight nod.

A.J. smiled. "We'll come back and see you tomorrow."

Vic sat in the passenger seat of Baptiste's white BMW X5 as they drove south on Interstate 880. "Baptiste, Valerie knows more than what she's telling us."

A.J. never took his eyes off the road and smiled. "I know that."

"B-But, Baptiste, we need to go back and talk to her some more. Today." She glanced up at his profile, stressing her last word with urgency.

"We'll talk with her again." A.J. took the Twenty-ninth Street exit and pulled into the parking lot of a run-down housing project in East Oakland, circling until he found a parking space. After leaving Valerie's hospital room, he and Vic had gone back to the nurses' station to look at Valerie's chart and locate her address.

"Baptiste—"

"It won't be today, Honey." He steered the vehicle between two faded white lines, then put the gear in park.

Vic sighed heavily and threw her hands in the air. "Why not?"

A.J. cut the engine, turned, and braced his arm along the back of the passenger seat. "Patience, woman." Leaning forward, he kissed the tip of her nose. "That's something you've got to learn." He cut off whatever comeback she was about to make with another quick kiss and opened the driver-side door. "Come on. Let's see if we can find Valerie's babies."

Accepting his hand when he came around to assist her out the car, Vic looked up at him, surprised by his calm reaction and response. "How do you know they're here?"

A.J. shrugged causally. "Valerie told us." He laced their fingers together. "Come on."

After they'd walked the building a couple of times, Vic finally located Valerie's apartment. As she and Baptiste headed to the front door, they saw three Oakland police officers exiting with two small infants. A woman followed behind them.

Vic rushed toward the woman. "Excuse me, ma'am. Is everything okay?" Before the woman could answer, Vic quickly added, "My name's Victoria Bennett. I'm a registered nurse." She looked at Baptiste to introduce him, but he'd already extended his hand.

A.J. smiled. "Gail, it's been a long time."

Gail Bishop, a caseworker with Social Services, slipped her hand inside A.J.'s. "You're right. It has been a long time. How are you, Dr. Baptiste?" She turned and offered Vic a smile. "Dr. Baptiste and I have known each other for quite a few years. Unfortunately, it's because we worked on child abuse cases when he was over at Children's Hospital."

Vic nodded and was glad a relationship existed between Baptiste and Gail. Perhaps she'd be willing to provide more information than she normally would. "One of our patients, Valerie Watkins, lives at this address. Are those her babies?"

Gail nodded sadly. "Yes, they are. We received a call a short time ago from an anonymous source advising that Ms. Watkins's children were at this address unattended."

Vic glanced over her shoulder and saw the police officers strapping the infants into car seats. She turned back to Gail. "Ms. Bishop, their mother was injured earlier this morning and has been admitted to Highland Hospital. She asked us to come here and check on her babies."

"I understand that, Ms. Bennett," Gail said, "but without proper adult supervision, I have no other choice but to remove them and place them in Child Protective Services."

A slight frown creased A.J.'s brow. "What about Valerie's relatives, Gail? Could the children be placed with them?"

Gail nodded. "That's the plan, Dr. Baptiste. It's always best to place children with their biological relatives, if possible. I'll work on that just as soon as I get back to my office."

"Could we just see them before you take them away?" Vic asked and pointed at the police car.

With the social worker's permission, Vic and Baptiste walked over and stared down into the faces of two fraternal twin girls. Vic guessed they were probably about eight months old. Sleeping peacefully, they were totally oblivious to the chaos and uncertainty going on in their lives.

Vic placed her hand against her mouth and turned to look up at Baptiste. "Oh, my God. Look at 'em. They're so precious."

A.J. ran his finger along the sides of their soft, chubby cheeks. "Yes, they certainly are."

Vic walked back to Gail and extended her hand. "Thank you, Gail. Do you think there's any way we can keep in contact with you regarding Valerie's babies?"

CHAPTER 9

"T-One and T-Two ain't here, right?" Zach, A.J.'s brother-in-law, asked the question in a strained but controlled voice as he stood in the vestibule of A.J.'s home later that evening. After listening to A.J. and Vic recount what they'd done after leaving the hospital, he tapped his foot against the hardwood floor, sucked his teeth, and waited for an answer.

Vic stood next to Baptiste. They held hands like two children who had been caught in an act of mischief and shook their heads sideways. She swallowed hard, real hard, before glancing over at Baptiste. Then, she found the courage to answer Zach's question. "Uh . . . Ray has them."

"Umm-hmm," Zach mumbled, nodding stiffly, glancing back and forth between them. "Are y'all crazy?" he yelled at the top of his lungs.

A.J. blew out a soft breath and ran his hand across the top of his head. "Zach, we can—"

"Hush!" Zach snapped and followed the order with a string of oaths.

Vic grimace. "Listen, Zach—"

"You, too!" Zach stalked off toward the dining room.

Vic whispered to Baptiste, "Think he's mad at us?"

A.J. nodded. "Oh, yes."

Seated at the dining room table, Zach yanked his jacket back and reached inside for his notepad and pen, glaring at Vic and A.J. until they settled in their seats. "All right, Starsky and Hutch, roll this back to the beginning for me."

After leaving Valerie's apartment, Vic had called Zach on her cell phone on the way home and asked him to stop by A.J.'s house because they'd uncovered some information about the hit-and-run.

Zach twirled his pen between his fingers. "And you say Valerie referred to the guy who beat her up as Tony?"

Vic sat in the chair next to Zach. "Yeah. That's what she called him at first, but then it was like she suddenly realized she was using his real name and referred to him as, uh . . ." She paused, placing her index finger next to her temple. "Scooter?" she exclaimed, snapping her finger the moment she remembered, positive that was the name Valerie had said. "That's it. Scooter. Zach, Valerie also said he was driving the car that hit me and Nicole."

"Scooter?" Zach drawled, astonished.

Sitting on the opposite side of the table, A. J. frowned. "That's right. Do you know him?"

"Humph, if it's who I think it is, yeah, I know him," Zach snorted with disdain. "He's a wanna-be drug dealer and a high school dropout. Betcha he's barely seen his eighteenth birthday. For the last few months, he's been a drug runner over in East Oakland. Been trying to nab him for a while. Real name's Tony Grice."

"Zach, did you hear what I said?" Vic cried impatiently, placing her hand on his arm. "He was driving the car that hit me and Nicole."

Zach had paused for a moment to jot something in his notepad, but stopped writing and lifted his head. "I heard ya there, Baby Girl. I'ma get to that in a minute." His gaze shifted back to A.J. "Did she say where Scooter was?"

"No," Vic chimed in quickly. "Now what do we need to do to catch him?"

"Victoria." A.J.'s voice was slightly stern.

It was only the second time since she'd known Baptiste that he'd ever called her by her given name. He was upset with her about something then. She knew without a doubt he was mad now. "Baptiste, I'll be careful."

A.J. shook his head. "No, you'll keep out of this. Let Zach and the Oakland police do their job."

"Baby Girl—" Zach nodded at A.J—"I gotta agree with brother-in-law this time. The folks this Scooter character works for is known to blow stuff up, and I ain't talkin' with a Molotov cocktail, either. Understand what I'm tellin' ya?"

Vic's jaw tightened, and she braced her hands on the table. "So, y'all gonna just let Scooter get away with beating that poor child half to death?" Her gaze angrily darted between A.J. and Zach. "She's trying to turn her life around and get away from him."

Zach tucked his pen behind his ear. "Listen up. First of all, y'all gotta remember I'm on ya side in this. I trust ya instincts, all right?" He focused on his notepad, deep in concentration. "Tell ya what, I'll arrange for police protection around the clock as long as Valerie's in the hospital."

"But, Zach," Vic cried out in frustration, "that's only a day or two, at the most."

A.J. walked over to Vic and placed his hands on top of her tightly balled fists. "Listen, I'll contact Cates and Harrison. Maybe between the three of us we can stretch things out for her to stay there the rest of the week."

Vic shook her head, glancing over her shoulder at Baptiste. "Valerie doesn't have health insurance, and you know once the hospital staff gets her halfway stabilized, they're gonna boot her out the door."

"If I can convince Harrison and Cates, her bill will be covered. Don't worry about that," A.J. promised.

Vic sighed. "But she can't stay there forever. What happens after she's released?"

Zach cleared his throat. "Listen, the first thing we need to do is get her to open up to us. If she's got information on Scooter's operation, perhaps the D.A. would be willing to go light on her."

"Do you think that's possible?" Vic asked, hopeful.

Zach sighed. "It's worth a shot. This Scooter's got the brain cells of an ant and likes to front. He's young and wants to climb the meat chain for the folks he's dealin' for. Plus, he talks too much. When ya work the streets, ya have to learn to keep ya mouth closed."

"Zach," Vic said, "I want to go back and talk with Valerie again."

"*Victoria*," A.J. growled in a dangerously soft voice.

"Baptiste, let me finish my thought here before you start in on that 'I'm impatient' speech again." Vic grabbed his right hand and laced their fingers together. "Maybe if the two of us go back and talk to her again, you know, present a united front, she'd open up to us some more." When she noticed the hesitant look on his face, she pleaded, "Come on, Baptiste. Please. She came to the clinic when she didn't have any place else to go. Besides, she told us stuff and didn't know us from Adam. She's scared and alone, and I believe she trusts us." She rubbed her neck with her free hand. "There's something about her, Baptiste. I don't know. It's like . . ."

A.J. moved behind Vic and took over her massaging efforts. "Like what, *mon amour*?"

"It's like she's been placed smack dab in our lives for some reason."

Zach plucked his pen from behind his ear and pulled his notepad closer. "All right, I'ma let y'all slide on this one, but I want ya to be careful, hear me?" He settled back in his chair and flipped to a blank piece of paper. "Let's go back to the night of the accident. Ya say Valerie told ya she was in the car that night?"

A.J. and Vic nodded simultaneously and shared with Zach the information Valerie had told them.

Zach nodded and closed his notepad. "If y'all really want to help her, get her to talk to me." He looked sternly at Vic and A.J. "Do I make myself clear?"

"Yes," they answered in unison.

Valerie?" Vic called out as she opened the door to Valerie's hospital room on Tuesday, a little past noon, with Baptiste right behind her.

"Vic . . . Dr. B. That y'all?" Valerie answered.

Vic and Baptiste walked inside. They'd received a call from one of the nurses on duty that morning who told them Valerie wanted to talk with Zach.

"Hey there, sweetie," Vic replied cheerfully.

"How are you feeling today, sweetheart?" A.J. placed a vase of flowers on the table next to the bed.

Valerie smiled, and her eyes lit up when she saw the huge bouquet. "Better." As she looked at the roses, her eyes became misty. "Thank you."

"You're welcome, baby," Vic replied, swatting away a tear of her own.

"I-I did what you told me to do, Dr. B.," Valerie said, sucking in her breath.

A.J. nodded. He knew Valerie had placed the call to Child Protective Services and told them her children were left alone. He sat on the edge of the bed, lifting her trembling hand inside his. "I'm very proud of you. What you did took a lot of courage."

Valerie choked back tears. "A-Are they okay?"

"They were sleeping when we got there, but they looked good," Vic answered. "Valerie, your baby girls are beautiful. What are their names?"

"Brianna and Chloé," Valerie said proudly.

Pulling up a chair to the side of the bed, Vic asked, "You ready?"

Releasing a long exhale, Valerie nodded.

A.J. left and returned a few moments later with Zach. "Valerie, this is Lieutenant Zach Tate." He glanced over at Zach who stood on the opposite side of the bed. "Zach, this is our friend Valerie Watkins."

Zach extended his hand. "Valerie, pleased to meet ya."

Valerie nodded.

Vic stood and stepped away from the bed. "Dr. B. and I will be right down the hall. Okay?"

"Vic," Valerie uttered in a trembling voice.

Vic walked back over and ran her hand across the top of Valerie's head. "Everything's going to be just fine. Dr. B. and I are here for you."

After leaving Valerie's hospital room, Vic asked Baptiste if they could check in on Nicole, the other hit-and-run victim, while they waited. They took the elevator from the third floor up to the intensive care unit located on the sixth floor. As soon as they rounded the corner, Vic's eyes widened, her spine grew rigid, and she stopped mid-stride.

"What's wrong, *mon amour*?" Concerned, A.J. glanced between Vic and the man exiting the doors of the intensive care unit.

Vic's tone was icy. "Evans, what the hell are you doing here?"

Ron Evans, Vic's ex-husband, stopped and fumbled with the stethoscope in his hands, almost dropping it in the process. "I-I'm here consulting on a patient," he finally managed to stutter.

Vic was so angry at seeing Ron that she didn't say another word. Instead, she stepped backward.

Ron took two steps forward, but halted when A.J. stepped directly in front of him, blocking his path to Vic. He peered around A.J.'s massive frame. "W-What are you doing here, Vic?"

A.J. answered instead. "We came to check on Nicole Broussard."

Ron nodded. "She's the patient I'm here consulting on."

"Baptiste, let's get out of here," Vic shouted angrily, standing in the hallway with her back to him and Ron.

"Doctor?" Ron pointed to the stethoscope draped around A.J.'s neck.

A.J. nodded slightly. "Pediatrician." Then he briefly explained to Ron how he and Vic's path connected to Nicole's.

Vic whirled around and tossed a seething look at Ron, a renowned pediatric neurosurgeon specializing in the treatment of brain tumors. Suddenly her eyes flared, and she knew in addition to the traumatic brain injury Nicole had sustained from the crash she must have a brain mass, too. It was no surprise to her that the physicians at Highland Hospital had flown Ron out from New York. He was one of the best in his field.

"Baptiste." Vic shouted louder this time than she had before as nausea hit her stomach.

Ron moved around A.J. with tentative steps and inched closer to Vic, "Could I talk—"

"Go to hell," Vic shot back and stalked away.

Tears streaked down Vic's face as she tossed her clothes inside an open suitcase on the bed in the guest bedroom at Baptiste's home, not noticing that half of them had landed on the floor. After leaving the intensive care waiting area, Baptiste had checked in on Valerie again, then driven back to his home. Vic had sat in the passenger seat, empty, hurt, and confused. She'd cried softly during the entire drive.

A.J. walked inside and stood behind her. "You don't have to leave."

She didn't bother to turn around. "I-I gotta get out of here."

At that moment, the only thing she could think about was how her heart had gone out to Nicole when she'd visited her the other day; how she'd prayed for her to live, unaware of her condition; and how of all the doctors on the planet, Ron would have to be the one consulting on her case. A heaviness of spirit she hadn't felt in a long time washed over her and her hands shook so badly, the blouse she held almost landed on the floor, too.

A.J. gently wrapped his arms around her waist. "Stay. Let me see you through this."

Vic held on to her tears, determined this time to deal with the situation alone. She refused to let him or anyone else see her pain. "I-I can't."

"Why?"

Her chest grew tight, and she heaved trying to regulate her breathing. "Living here with you is not setting a good example for the girls."

He didn't buy her explanation and knew it was her way of retreating to do what she always did—deal with a painful situation in solitude. Turning her around, he saw such anguish reflected in her eyes that it was almost more than he could bear. "If you want to cry, scream or whatever, go ahead. There's no one here but us."

It took a moment for the meaning of what he'd just told her to register. "W-Where'd they go?"

"I called Pop and asked if the girls could spend the night with him and Mama Z."

A lone tear managed to slip down the slope of her cheek. "Baptiste," she sobbed, "my babies shouldn't have to be uprooted from their home because of me." Wiping her face with the back of her hand, she began to panic. She knew how close Baptiste's family was and how they shared information with one another. "You didn't tell Alcee—"

"No," he interrupted, shaking his head furiously. "I told you before that I'd never betray your confidence." He took the blouse that was balled tightly in her hand and placed it on the bed. "Stay."

"Baptiste, w-why did I have to see Ron now?" she cried out in frustration, slamming her fists against her thighs. "Why?"

"Baby, I don't know. There are a lot of things in life we'll never know the answers to, but you have to believe me when I say time has a way of healing wounds."

"Time?" she shouted back and plopped down on the side of the bed. "I marry a man who ends up sleeping with another man, and just when I'm getting over that pain, he pops back into my life." She shook her head. "You're wrong, Baptiste. Time can't heal that."

"But time will heal the hurt you're feeling now," he said quietly, sitting next to her and folding her trembling hand inside his. "Honey . . ." He paused, searching for the right words. "Like it or not, Ron is the best doctor to treat Nicole's brain tumor, and he's here doing the job he's trained to do."

"I don't care what he's here to do," she blurted with fury, her spirit of compassion as a person and a healthcare professional temporarily lost. "He screwed around with another man and made my life a living hell."

He simply nodded. The raw anguish in her eyes was something he'd never seen before, and despite her strength and determination, it threatened to break her spirit in two. "Honey, you're strong, and in my heart I believe you'll make it through this."

"How?" She wiped the tears from her face. "All right, I'm strong, so you say. You know, you can fight against something when you can see it coming, not something that blindsides you. No one can do that, Baptiste." Pausing, she sucked in a deep breath and released a cynical chuckle. "The bottom line is that the man I married betrayed me. Guess that's my fate in life, loving men who betray."

A.J. stood, taking her with him, and turned her by the shoulders to face him. "Let me ask you this. Are you upset because Ron is one of Nicole's doctors or are you upset because you saw him again for the first time in eight years?"

"Both." She stalked over to the dresser and snatched up her purse and keys.

"Where are you going?" he asked calmly.

"I need to get some air and clear my head."

A.J. took the items from her hands and carefully placed them back on the dresser. "If you think I'm going to let you get behind the wheel of a car this upset, think again. You're too distraught to deal with anything right now."

"Whatcha mean distraught?" A new wave of tears streamed down her face.

"Honey . . ."

She stared at him, releasing an anguish whimper a few seconds later, "Baptiste . . ."

"I know, baby, I know." He placed his finger against her lips when she tried to speak. "Now is not the time to talk to anyone about anything, not even me. Give yourself a few days to get over the hurt of seeing Ron again."

She raised her hands to her face and sobbed. Leaning into Baptiste's chest, she screamed, her shoulders quivering, and was unaware she'd slid to the floor, physically, mentally, and emotionally drained.

A.J. never released her from his embrace and followed, wrapping his arms tighter around her. If he needed to, he'd stay in that very spot with her all night long.

Around midnight, Vic awoke from a fretful slumber and lifted the covers to roll onto her stomach. She hoped the position would help her fall back to sleep, but noticed a figure in the beam of light from the hallway. An unsettling feeling came over her and she sat upright, rubbing her eyes to bring the blurry shadow into focus. At first, she thought it was one of the girls, but suddenly remembered they weren't there.

A.J. stood at the threshold of the door. "Are you okay, *mon amour?*"

She shook her head, but doubted he saw her movements. The tiny nightlight plugged in near her bed did little to brighten the room, but she was able to see something she'd never seen before. Baptiste had freed his ponytail and his hair hung across broad shoulders. He looked primitive, wild, and amazingly sexy. Finally, she found her voice and softly uttered, "No."

His path to her was direct and he climbed atop the bed, crawling to her on all fours, closing the gap between them. "Tell me what you need."

Unable to move or speak, she didn't even think or try to understand why he'd come to her. She opened her arms as well as her heart. The heat from his body scorched her palms as she ran them along his shoulders and back. Without hesitation, she drew his head down, and this time, she was the one who devoured him with a kiss that released all the pent-up desire, lust, and passion for the man who'd given her his strength when she couldn't find her own, who'd shown immeasurable love when she was too afraid to love in return.

Her lips parted and she gloried in the feel and taste of him, arching up closer to bring them chest to chest, thigh to thigh, and soul to soul.

Only the need to breathe made her pull back, and she held his gaze, communicating everything her heart felt but until now hadn't been able to utter aloud. His nearness pulled forth a rumble from the back of her throat.

"Baptiste," she whispered on a strangled sob. "Love the hurt away."

It was a request he wouldn't deny.

"Open these pretty legs for me," he whispered, running his hands along her thighs. This time, he loved with the skillfulness of his fingers and the magic of his tongue. He touched her, tasted her, and blissfully tormented her until she thought she'd lose her mind. Sensations built to a fever pitch, causing her heart to race so that she thought she'd pass out. When he inched his finger inside her, gently probing, in and out, back and forth, up and down until her eyes fluttered, she lost her breath. She stalled, sputtered, and crashed into the depths of love faster than a spiraling jet plunging to earth. Lifting her lips to his, he kissed away every moan she uttered until she stilled.

Afterward, she cuddled next to him, wrapping her arms tightly around his waist. With her head nestled against his chest, she fell into a peaceful slumber.

And before the break of dawn, love claimed her heart.

CHAPTER 10

"Baby Girl ain't here, is she?" Zach whispered the question, peeking around A.J.'s burly frame when he answered the door the next morning.

A.J. stepped to the side to let Zach enter. "No. Why? Is something wrong?"

After his shower that morning, A.J. had almost panicked when he discovered that Vic had left. It wasn't until he noticed her suitcase was in the same spot she'd left it in the night before and read the note she'd taped on the dresser mirror saying she needed to take care of some things—alone—that he settled down.

He decided it was best not to go after her because whatever she had to confront, she had to do it by herself. He took assurance in the fact that she loved him. He'd seen it in her eyes, had felt it in her touch, and had heard it in her voice every time she'd whispered his name the previous night.

"I just got off duty and I'm tired," Zach answered, stretching his neck. "Brother-in-law, I'm gettin' too old to be chasing these bail jumpers all over town. Between that and working with the DEA on some stuff . . . ya know, a brother can only take so much."

They headed down the hallway into the kitchen and Zach slumped in a chair, releasing a loud, weary sigh.

"Pull out my Crown Royal and a glass for me, will ya? I need a drink right about now."

A.J. chuckled. "It's not even noon." He retrieved the bottle Zach always kept in an upper cabinet along with a shot glass and placed them in the center of the table. "Your butt's probably tired because you're trying to keep up with that young sister of mine," he teased, referring to the twelve-year difference between Zach and his twenty-eight-year-old sister, Moni.

Zach chuckled. "Don't hear me complaining, do ya?" He poured the brown liquid into his glass and added, "And you can best bet the bank that ya ain't gonna *never* hear my baby complaining."

A.J. grinned, then bunched his brows together because Zach hadn't touched his drink. "So, what are you waiting for?"

Zach swung his right arm up and tapped the crystal face on his watch. "Noon. Only have one shot, and never before then."

"You need to eat something," A.J. reminded him.

Zach winked. "Thanks for asking. Don't have no problems with leftovers, ya know."

A.J. fingered his moustache and grinned. "How do you know we have leftovers?"

"When Baby Girl cooks, there's always leftovers."

After fixing Zach a plate, A.J. braced himself against the counter near the microwave with his feet crossed at the ankles, waiting for the food to finish heating. "Tough day, I take it."

Zach checked his watch again, picked up the shot glass, and tossed his drink down in one gulp. "Tough," he said, grunting, "ain't exactly the word I'd use to describe it. After I spoke with Valerie at the hospital yesterday, I was able to track down Scooter."

A.J. placed the dish on the table in front of Zach and pulled his chair away, straddling it backward. "What's going on?" The unevenness in his tone did little to mask his own anxiety.

Zach placed a couple of forkfuls of food in his mouth and chewed before he answered. "Started off by asking friend if he knew how his woman ended up beaten to a pulp. Of course, he said he didn't know nothin'. Then I asked him if he knew about the hit-and-run accident." He released a half chuckle. "Partner all of a sudden comes up with a case of temporary amnesia."

"Do you think Valerie was telling the truth about the accident?"

Zach snorted. "Brother-in-law, I know I'm a big old country boy and might look crazy, but trust me, I ain't stupid. She knows that, and then some."

"All right, Zach. Let's hear it."

Zach wiped his mouth with a napkin and pushed his plate away. "Listen here, gotta keep ya mouth shut with what I'ma tell ya. Dis here is between us and the gatepost. Ya hear me?"

"Yeah," A.J. muttered unhappily. He really didn't want to be in the position of having to conceal anything from Vic. In the last few weeks, he'd witnessed firsthand her pain from a man's betrayal, enough to last him a life-time. "So, what did Valerie tell you?"

Staring at his glass, Zach shook his head. "Ain't bit mo' got no business tellin' ya this than a brother walkin' up in a Klan meeting."

"But you're going to, right?"

Zach nodded. "Looks like the night of the accident, Valerie started the chain of events by making a drug drop, but the other party gave her the slip. They got the drugs, and she got zilch."

A.J. looked confused. "Okay, but I don't understand how Scooter got involved."

"When Valerie didn't get the money, she went back and told Scooter. He gets mad, ups and drives back over there with her to collect. Long story short, things went down real funky. Partner gets some of the drugs, but still comes up short—no greenbacks. He panics because he knows whoever he reports to is gonna be real upset. That's the reason he was driving like a bat out of hell."

"Then they hit Nicole and her parents?"

"Yep. Gotta remember, Scooter and Valerie got a trunk load of crack on 'em along with God knows what else, and stayin' around the scene of an accident ain't exactly an option. Baby Girl just ended up in the wrong place at the wrong time. Scooter speeds off from the first crash and *bam*," Zach exclaims, slamming one fist into the other, "runs smack into Baby Girl. Then here you come through the intersection, and that's how she ended up hitting ya."

A.J. frowned. "Okay. I understand all of that. Why can't you arrest Scooter?"

Zach winked. "Never said I wasn't."

"When?"

Zach reached across the table for his bottle and refilled his glass.

"Hey, I thought you said only one shot?"

Zach shrugged. "Tough day." He swirled the liquid in his glass a moment. "The only thing I can nab Scooter on right now is assault and battery, but I want more than that. Need to track down that car he was driving." He drew the glass to his lips. "Aaah," he sighed happily as the smooth liquid slid down his throat. "Finding that car will lock him up real tight."

"Why can't you just go to the D.A. based on Valerie's testimony?"

Zach raised his brow. "Look here, brother-in-law, Valerie ain't exactly been Snow White in all of this. Her word against Scooter's. The more concrete info I can get connecting partner to the accident, the better chances we have of him not worming his way out and finding the folks who are really running the drug operation. Plus, Valerie told me some other stuff that's a little more complicated."

A.J. hitched his brow. "Well . . ."

Zach shook his head. "No comment."

A.J. sighed. There was no doubt in his mind that Zach hadn't told him everything from his conversation with Valerie. As a physician, he understood confidentially, so he decided not to press the issue at the moment, although he didn't like it one bit. "What about Valerie? What happens to her now?"

Zach shook his head wearily, staring intently at his half-empty glass. "That's a good question. Definitely can't go back to where she was before. She'd be dead before sundown."

Deep in concentration, A.J. focused on the wall in front of him. "Zach, there's got to be a way for us to protect her."

"There's one possibility."

A.J. jerked his head around at Zach. "What?"

"The California Witness Protection Program. Problem is, Valerie has to cut all ties to the life she has now. I don't know," Zach drawled, leaning forward and palming his glass with both hands.

A.J. stared. "What?"

"Brother-in-law, Valerie's got them babies. She could take them with her, but I don't think that's the best thing for her to do right now. She needs to get herself together first, then deal with being a mama." Zach looked dead at A.J. "She loves them kids, I can tell ya that much, but when I brought up the Witness Protection Program to her, she got spooked. I don't know if she'll go for it because she ain't got nobody to help her."

"When can you get her into the program?"

"*If*," Zach emphasized. "I'm working on that now."

A.J. nodded. "Is she in any immediate danger?"

"Naw. I still have my men on her 24/7, so she'll be all right. As funny as it may sound, the safest place for her to be right now is at the hospital. But once she's released, we gotta get her the hell out of Dodge." Zach downed the rest of his drink and released a long sigh. "Keeping Valerie safe is the least of my concerns right now."

A.J. frowned. "Why do you say that?"

"Let's just say Scooter's not as dumb as I thought he was."

A.J. shook his head, confused. "I'm not following you."

"Apparently, according to Valerie, friend's kept a record of his drug transactions for the past year and a half."

"You mean like a diary?"

Zach smiled wryly. "Yeah, if ya wanna call it that. The information could be on post-it notes for all I care. I intend to get my hands on it. Waiting on a search warrant right now."

"Listen, Zach, if there's something going on that could bring any harm to Honey or my girls, I need to know about it."

"Naw," Zach drawled fiercely. "Whatcha need to do is take care of ya woman and my nieces. Let me worry about catching the bad guys. Okay?"

A.J. stood and braced his feet apart. "Zach—"

"Brother-in-law, this here is one time ya gonna have to trust me." He nodded at the chair in front of A.J. "Take a load off. I don' told ya mo' than I should've already. We ain't dealing with the neighbors next door. Feelin' me? Whoever is running this drug ring would kill their own mama to keep stuff on the DL. But I promise ya, I'm not gonna knowingly let any harm come to ya family or Valerie."

Begrudgingly, A.J. sat and spoke in a dangerously quiet tone. "Zach, make absolutely certain you don't."

"Hi there." Vic's voice quivered the moment her best friend Caitlyn answered the door at her estate. "Are you by yourself?"

"Yes. What's wrong?" Caitlyn asked, concerned. She pushed her reading glasses on top of her head as soon as she noticed the tears pooling in Vic's eyes.

Vic sniffed. "Just need to be around a friend right now, that's all."

Caitlyn waved Vic inside and ushered her to the living room, then turned to leave.

Vic called out to Caitlyn from behind. "Where're you going?"

"I'll be right back," Caitlyn advised, smiling.

Weary from emotions, Vic plopped down on the long snow-white couch in the spacious room and released a long exhale.

"Close your eyes," Caitlyn announced a few moments later, walking back into the living room.

"Why?"

"Are they closed?"

Vic sighed. "Yes."

Vic heard two soft thuds against the coffee table and opened her eyes. Her gaze fell on the unspoken symbol of communication she and Caitlyn had used with each other for eighteen years, the signal they both knew was the indication for them to discuss anything openly—a pint of Rocky Road ice cream with two spoons stuck in the middle and a box of tissue. She burst into tears.

Caitlyn didn't utter a word. She sat next to Vic and reaching over, grabbed her best friend's hand and held it until her tears finally ceased.

Once Vic regained her composure, she shared with Caitlyn the real reason for her divorce and the circumstances involved in seeing Ron at the hospital the previous day.

"Sweetheart," Caitlyn uttered softly as they shared a sisterly embrace, "why didn't you tell me this before now?"

Vic shrugged. "I don't know. I-I guess I was too ashamed for being a fool for not knowing that I was marrying a man who was gay."

Caitlyn leaned back, placing her hands on Vic's shoulders. "You have absolutely nothing to be ashamed of, and there's no reason to blame yourself."

"Yes, I do."

"No, you don't," Caitlyn said adamantly.

"God, how could I have *not* known," Vic uttered with disgust.

"Vic, when I first met Cole," Caitlyn said, referring to her ex-boyfriend, "I had no why of knowing he'd turn out to be a stalker. I ran from him for three years, but I never let myself feel guilty for his issues."

Vic looked at Caitlyn as the impact of her words sank in, but didn't say anything.

"Does A.J. know?"

Vic nodded.

"That's all that matters," Caitlyn said with assurance.

Vic folded her arms across her chest and focused on the wall straight ahead.

Caitlyn was on her feet in an instant. "Wait here." A few moments later, she returned with a folder and held it out to Vic. "Read this."

Vic leafed through the pages in the binder and met Caitlyn's gaze with her mouth wide open. "You mean . . ."

"Yes," Caitlyn nodded. "Sweetheart, you're not alone in this."

Vic's attention was drawn once again to the file containing a proposal submitted to BF Automotive's philanthropy foundation, which Caitlyn oversaw, from a group seeking funding to form an Oakland-based chapter of a national organization, whose members, like her, had experienced the pain of finding out that their spouse was either gay, lesbian, or bisexual.

"Oh, my God," Vic whispered.

Caitlyn sat next to Vic. "I got their request for support a few weeks ago." She reached out and folded Vic's hand inside hers. "Nothing beats talking to someone who's been in the same situation. Call them."

Vic nodded.

"Finding out about Ron has kept you from loving A.J., hasn't it?"

Vic remained silent for a long time before she nodded.

"Vic, loving the right man can see you through anything."

Vic chuckled lightly. "I am so wonderfully jealous of you, you know that, right?"

Caitlyn chuckled back. "Why?"

"You have a husband who adores you and two beautiful babies, that's why."

"Except for the marriage certificate, you have the same thing."

"Do not."

Caitlyn smiled. "Oh yes you do. You have A.J., Taylor, and Tyler."

"But—"

"A.J. loves you just as much as Marcel loves me. And you have two beautiful girls. So, you see, there's no need to be jealous. We're dead even."

"I'm scared, Caitlyn," Vic whispered.

"Scared of what, sweetheart?"

Tears flowed down Vic's face and she lowered her head. "Scared to risk having my heart broken again."

With her index finger, Caitlyn gently lifted Vic's head up. "Do you remember what you told me one day shortly after I met Marcel?"

Vic wiped her face with a tissue. "No, what'd I say?"

"And I quote, 'Stop trying to analyze everything and figure out where all the pieces will fit. Sometimes you have to step out on nothing but faith. At some point, you've got to learn how to trust again. Understand what I'm saying?' End quote."

Vic chuckled. "Did I say that?"

Caitlyn nodded. "Verbatim. I was just like you, remember? I was scared to death to admit my feelings for

Marcel because of what I'd gone through with Cole, believing that Marcel would end up doing the same thing."

Vic sucked in a long breath and slowly released it. She felt as though a weight had been lifted off her shoulders. All her life, she'd never been one to share her pain with others, but she knew she needed to disclose her hurt to someone who'd been through the same experience. It was a first step in her healing process. She glanced over at the woman who was the sister she'd never had and smiled. Caitlyn hadn't condemned her for the way she felt nor had she denounced Ron for who he was. She'd done exactly what a friend was supposed to do—be there in the time of need. Her eyes drifted to the carton of ice cream. She kicked off her sandals and placed her feet atop the table. "Well . . ."

Caitlyn giggled and replicated Vic's actions as they placed spoonfuls of their favorite treat inside their mouths.

"Stop. You're eating all the marshmallows again," Caitlyn fussed.

"I'm not. Hush and eat." Vic offered a huge grin. "Love you, sweetie."

Caitlyn grinned back. "Love you, too."

Later that afternoon, after Vic left Caitlyn's estate, she drove to her parents' home, arriving shortly after three.

Louise sat at the kitchen table with Vic and pushed aside a cup of herbal tea. "Talk to your mama, baby, and tell me what's wrong. You're mine, and I know when something's bothering you."

Vic shook her head. "What makes you think something's wrong?"

Louise chuckled and nodded at the table. "Since you were a little girl, any time something made you upset, you'd do just what you're doing now."

Vic looked down at the napkin she'd methodically shredded into tiny pieces. It now resembled a mound of confetti. "Sorry."

"Now, what's wrong?"

"Baptiste."

Louise chuckled. "Are the two of y'all still battling like the Hatfields and McCoys?"

"No, and that's the problem."

Louise shook her head. "Perhaps I'm running a little slow here today. I don't understand what the problem is."

Vic sighed. "Mom, as long as Baptiste and I were at each other's throat, I had a chance."

"A chance at what?"

"Not losing my heart to him."

Louise hitched her brow as a smile surfaced. "And now?"

"I'm in deep doggie do."

"Do you love him?"

"After Ron, I didn't think I could love any man again."

"Why not?" Louise replied in a bewildered tone.

"Because . . ." And before she knew it, Vic blurted out the real reason for her divorce from Ron.

"I don't believe that A.J. would ever betray you," Louise said.

Vic could tell her mother was trying to hide her anger, and she opened her arms and cried out, "You don't know that, Mom, and neither do I." She shook her head. "I can't take the chance."

"Sweetheart, look at me." When Vic didn't comply right away, Louise spoke more forcefully. "Victoria Louise Bennett, look at me. A.J. loves you."

"I know," Vic softly confessed.

Louise gathered Vic's hands inside hers. "I'ma ask one more question: Do you love him?"

Blinking back unshed tears, Vic nodded. "But . . ."

"But what, baby?"

"H-How do I get over the hurt, the pain of Ron's betrayal? How do I learn to forgive?"

Louise smiled. "To answer your first question, you pray. You ought to try it sometimes. It really works. And to answer your second question, you pray some more."

Vic sniffed and chuckled. "So you're telling me I need to go to church more often?"

Louise snorted. "Listen, you can move in the church house if you wanna. It won't help. When you're faced with a problem, it's not where you go, it's Who you go to and what you hear from Him that counts."

"I'll never forgive Ron for what he did to me," Vic said bitterly with her head bowed.

Louise clicked her tongue against the top of her mouth. "You're getting things a little mixed up, baby."

Vic's head snapped up. "Why do you say that?"

"There are two issues you're dealing with here: betrayal by one man and your love for another."

Vic shook her head, confused. "I don't understand the point you're trying to make, Mom."

"Didn't you just sit here and tell me that you love A.J.?"

Vic nodded.

"Baby, you're denying yourself a chance at happiness with the man you love by always remembering the circumstances that caused another man's betrayal."

"What?" Vic cried out incredulously. "Ron was the one who got caught in bed with another man, not me. How can I forgive him again after that?"

Louise nodded. "You're right. But you share some responsibility, too."

"What?" Vic cried out.

"Baby, don't you see, you've let *your* sin—the inability to forgive Ron's betrayal—rule your life for the last eight years?"

"Have not."

"Have, too."

Vic whispered back under her breath, "Have not."

Louise chuckled. "Vic, you've got a heart of gold. You'll help anybody—give 'em the shirt off your back— but your downfall has always been learning how to forgive." She chuckled again. "Remember how getting you to turn loose a grudge was the one thing we fought about the most when you were growing up?"

Vic chuckled, too. "I remember. I didn't speak to Harrison for weeks when he broke my favorite doll."

Louise nodded. "Umm-hmm. That poor child begged you for two whole months to forgive him."

"I know," Vic said, smiling as she brushed back a tear.

"Vic, the past is the past. You've got to learn to let go of the hurt, the anger, and move on."

"But I can't," Vic whispered in a choked voice.

"Yes, you can."

Vic brushed her hands across her face. "How?"

"Let me ask you this. Was A.J. mad at you when he found out you were the one who hit him?"

"No."

"Did he forgive you?"

"Yes."

"Case closed."

"B-But Louise, that was an entirely different situation," Vic defended.

Louise inclined her head and braced her finger at her temple. "Tell me how it was different. Tell me how your trespass against A.J. is any different from Ron's sin against you. Go on, tell me. I want to hear this."

"Mom—"

"Child, don't let somebody else's sins make you sin. Besides, you got enough stuff of your own you got to give an account of. Don't need to add someone else's drama to the mix."

"B-But how will I know that I've forgiven Ron for all the pain he caused?"

Louise smiled. "You'll know. Trust me."

"How?"

Louise grabbed Vic's hands in hers. "Baby, when you can look Ron straight in the eye, think back on all the unhappiness he caused, and wish him well, you've forgiven him."

Vic shook her head in amazement.

Louise smiled again. "Listen, I'm not sitting here telling you that A.J.'s a saint—no one is. Hell, if he ever decided to run around on you, it would be with a woman, not a man. But I don't believe you even have to worry about another woman."

"How can you be so sure?" Vic asked between sniffles.

"Anytime a man looks at a woman the way that man looks at you, can't tell me he'd ever stray."

Vic stared at her mother for a long time as the impact of what she'd said slowly sank in and admitted that she hadn't thought about it from that perspective before. For eight years, she'd been scared of another man's betrayal. It had been betrayal, not love, that had kept her from giving her heart to Baptiste.

Vic sighed. "I'm scared, Mom."

"I know you are, baby, and you're also having a tough time moving out of that safety zone of yours."

"But Mom—"

"No buts."

"I can't—"

"Yes, you can."

"What if—"

"Don't worry about it."

Vic giggled. "Mom, you don't even know what I was getting ready to say."

Louise giggled, too. "Okay, what were you going to say?"

"It's been so long since I've been with someone, I don't know . . ."

Louise inched up her brow. "Mean to tell me you been living in the man's house all this time and y'all ain't—"

Even though she and her mother had always openly discussed everything, especially sex, memory of A.J.'s head cradled between her legs as well as the things he'd done while he was there made her blush. He'd evoked feelings within her that made her tighten her thighs together with the agonizing need for him to do it again. "Sort of."

Louise smiled, nodding. "I see. A few appetizers, but no entrée. How's his ribs doing?"

"Much better."

"That's good. He can move around now, right?"

Vic nodded.

Louise winked. "The two of ya'll have been playing. 'Bout time you help the man get on his back, side, or whatever other position you decide to come up with and get to the real thing."

"Mom," Vic shrieked, mortified.

"What?" Louise replied innocently. "I'm telling the truth. Your mama's sixty, not dead." Looking off in the distance, she mumbled, "Lord, I hope that child has taken a CPR refresher course."

Stunned, Vic asked, "Why?"

"Just trying to be sure you got on-the-spot first aid, that's all. From what you telling me, if anything does go down, you gonna need it."

"Mom, I probably wouldn't know passion if it hit me in the face."

"Humph, give the man half a chance, and you just might find out. Baby, you'd be surprised how quickly passion will surface when you're behind closed doors with the right man." She winked. "Ask me how I know."

"I don't know—"

"Well, I do! You gonna stop being scared of loving A.J. and act like you were raised by me."

"How's that?"

"With some sense." Louise tilted Vic's head back to look her square in the eyes. "Baby, A.J. loves you with all his heart."

"I know," Vic admitted.

Vic stood and shared a long embrace with her mother.

Louise stood back and cupped Vic's face. "You've got a good man, child. I can see it in his eyes every time he looks at you. Besides, for a man—and a single man at that—to step up and take care of some other man's children the way A.J. has . . . baby, you can't tell me he wouldn't treat you right. When a man loves a woman the way A.J. loves you, it's no different than opportunity—it comes around once in a lifetime."

CHAPTER 11

"Valerie?" A.J. strolled inside her hospital room with a bright smile on his face around three in the afternoon after receiving clearance from the police officers stationed outside her door.

After Zach left his house that morning, he dressed, dropped off Taylor and Tyler at preschool, and headed over to the clinic. Once he settled in, he received a call from his sister-in-law, Caitlyn, who, without divulging Vic's confidence, assured him that she was all right. He forced himself to be content with that, and in many ways it was enough. For the past three weeks, they'd lived together as partners and friends. No other woman had ever shattered his control the way Vic did. An intense desire, the kind he'd never felt before for any woman, had for months forced him to wait for her. Even now, he knew they were linked in a way that went far beyond love. In every sense of the word, they were soul mates.

Valerie's face lit up. "Hey, Dr. B."

"How's my favorite patient?"

"Good. I talked with that police lieutenant, Zach."

"I know," A.J. replied, smiling as he pulled up a chair next to the bed. "But Zach also told me that you're a little apprehensive about going into the Witness Protection Program."

Agitated, Valerie wound the blanket tightly around her finger. "Ain't got nobody to take care of my babies if I do."

A.J. shook his head in rebuttal. "Yes, you do."

Valerie's eyes grew wide. "Who?"

"Me."

Valerie chuckled. "Dr. B., what you know 'bout babies?"

A.J. chuckled back. "Well, I've been a pediatrician for ten years, so that should count for something. Plus, I have two little girls of my own."

"You do?" Valerie asked, amazed.

A.J. nodded. He stood and pulled a recent family picture from his wallet and handed it to Valerie.

Valerie fingered the photograph. "They're so pretty." She looked up at A.J. "What's their names?"

"This is Taylor," A.J. advised, pointing to his left. Then, he moved his finger a fraction. "And that's Tyler. I met them when they were a little over eighteen months old."

"How?"

"One night they were brought into the emergency room at the hospital where I used to work by Child Protective Services. I was one of the doctors who helped care for them."

"What about their real mother?"

"Unfortunately, she was a drug addict, probably not much older than you. But you're in a different situation than she was."

Valerie looked at A.J., baffled. "How?"

"You're determined to stay clean. She made the choice not to."

"Do you know what happened to her?" she asked with a wobbly voice.

A.J. nodded sadly. "She ended up dead from an overdose about six months later."

Valerie turned her head to hide the tears that were forming. "I'm scared that's gonna happen to me," she uttered, sobbing.

"It doesn't have to be that way."

Valerie wiped her face with the back of her hand. "Why you say that?"

"That decision, and the direction of your life and that of your babies, is in your hands."

"So you think I need to go into that Witness Protection Program?"

"Only you can answer that question, Valerie. Think about the options you have to choose from. You either go back to Scooter and the life you're trying hard to leave behind, or you start a new life away from the streets and free of drugs. Now, what option do you think would be best for Brianna and Chloé?"

"But I ain't got nobody to help me."

A.J. shook his head again in disagreement. "I told you before, sweetheart, you have me."

"You'd really help me?"

"Yes. I would be willing to take care of Brianna and Chloé until you're in a position to do it yourself."

"Really?" she said with excitement.

He nodded, but quickly held his right index finger in front of him. "Only on one condition."

"What's that?"

"That you continue to stay clean and work *really* hard to care for them yourself one day. Understand?"

Valerie nodded.

A.J. scooted his chair closer to the bed. "Okay, now, tell me about your babies."

A.J. spent the next hour discussing Brianna and Chloe with Valerie. He learned about the twin's likes and dislikes, their eating and sleeping habits, asked detailed questions about the medical history, immunizations, and family history. He hoped his offer to Valerie to care for her babies wouldn't scare Vic too much. It wasn't every day that a woman willingly entered into a relationship with a ready-made family. There was absolutely no doubt in his mind that Vic loved Taylor and Tyler as much as he did. But could she accept the responsibility of caring for two other children, too? Caring for children was in his bones, buried deep in the very depth of his existence.

When they finished talking, Valerie leaned back, and for the first time in a long time, felt relieved. "Thank you, Dr. B."

A.J. smiled. "You're welcome, sweetheart."

After leaving her parents' home, Vic drove around for hours, finally arriving at her condominium around nine that night. As soon as she stepped inside, the place she'd called home for the last seven years felt foreign.

She walked straight into her bedroom, grabbed a suitcase from the closet, and packed the remainder of her clothes. After she'd finished, she sat on the edge of her bed as tears stung the back of her eyes. She could no longer deny what she'd fought so hard against for the last ten months. She wasn't sure when it had happened, but knew without a doubt that it had.

She'd fallen in love.

In the last three weeks, Baptiste had completely consumed her mind, her heart, and her soul. But without warning, the past flashed before her, causing her heart to pound, and she broke out into a sweat. She recalled what Caitlyn had told her earlier and relaxed, taking comfort in the knowledge that she wasn't the only woman—or man for that matter—who'd gone through the same experience with a spouse. She released a low laugh as understanding of the prophetic conversation with her mother came to her.

"God, I love him," she whispered, wrapping her arms around her waist. "And I love the girls, too." She panicked. What if Baptiste's patience with her had run its course? He'd done everything humanly possible to try and persuade her to give their love a chance. In hindsight, she had only herself to blame for the hurt she'd suffered. Not finding a way to forgive Ron for all these years had stood in the way of her finding love and happiness.

The past no longer mattered anymore. Being with Baptiste, Taylor, and Tyler mattered. Caring for a family, *her* family, mattered. And for the first time in eight years, the love she felt conquered the fear she'd held on to for too long. Lifting her suitcase off the floor, she headed for the door. There was one other stop she needed to make.

After that, she was going home.

Thirty minutes later, Vic pulled her BMW X5 into Baptiste's garage. She used her key to unlock the door and once inside, eased down the hallway with suitcase in hand. Quietly, she opened the door to his bedroom.

"Baptiste . . ."

From the threshold, she looked at him standing in the center of the candlelit room. With a boldness she didn't even know she had, she walked inside, dropping her purse onto the floor as she passed him, placed her suitcase in the closet, and turned to face him.

"That's where it belongs, and that's where it's gonna stay."

"You're positive?"

"Yes." She proceeded to tell him about the conversations she'd had with her mother and Caitlyn earlier in the day.

"Are you okay?"

She nodded. "Baptiste, I-I discovered something else today."

"What's that, *mon amour*?"

"I love you."

"*Je t'aime,*" A.J. whispered, even though she still hadn't told him the one thing he longed to hear. "How can you be so sure?"

God, he wasn't making this easy for her, she thought. She sucked in a deep breath, releasing it slowly. "Because I'm giving you my heart—"

His mouth swooped down on hers because, besides confessing her love for him, she'd just placed her heart in the safest place within the entire universe—his hands. Lifting his head a few moments later, he muttered against her mouth, "*That's* what I've needed to hear you say."

She clung to him like a vine, her body rolling against him. "*Je t'aime,*" she whispered through trembling lips. "I-I was scared, Baptiste. The harder I tried to run from you, the more I tried to convince myself not to fall in love with you, the more I came up on the short end. I want to be your woman and make babies with you one day."

He rested his head against hers, his breathing labored. "Let me make love to you."

Stooping, she grabbed out of her purse the box of condoms she'd purchased after she left her condominium. She straightened and handed them to him. "I didn't know so many brands were on the market," she managed to say while her fingers dueled with the drawstring of his pajama bottoms. "Let's not play with this, Baptiste. Wrap it up, right now."

He tore the square packet with his teeth. If it had been any other woman, he would have been embarrassed for ripping his pajama bottoms until they hung in two tattered pieces, but he wasn't. Vic was snatching her clothes off just as fast. When her naked body melted against him like wax—warm and soft—he moaned.

She hadn't meant to charge at him as if she was in heat. She simply couldn't help it. It had been so long since she'd made love and felt the warmth of a man's touch, she was about to go stark, raving mad. So what if she sounded like a mugging victim being assaulted in a back alley somewhere? She just prayed her shrill cries of pleasure vibrating off the walls didn't wake up the girls. Shame didn't enter the picture when they hit the bed hard on one side and landed crooked on the other with her straddled on top.

He lifted her hands to his shoulders and settled her on his hips, issuing a one-word command: "Ride."

She clamped her thighs next to his and wrapped her fingers around what felt like a rod of steel encased in velvet. Guiding him inside her, she sank slowly down on his hard, strong length. She gasped from the initial contact, her body stretching painfully at first to accommodate his fullness. Adjusting to the marvelous invasion, she rocked back and forth, setting a pace he soon followed. Every doubt she'd feared faded in an instant; every reservation she'd held on to for years was stripped away as she plunged up and down. The friction against her swollen bud became so profound that her head tumbled back and tears streamed down her face. His name floated like a cloud past her lips. As tiny sparks of pleasure appeared, faded, then suddenly reappeared with intensity, she halted. She wanted to feel the strong waves of glorious sensations course through her, and out of nowhere, her body exploded, and she whimpered his name out on a broken syllable.

"Don't stop," he begged. For ten long, agonizing months, he'd fantasized about this very moment. He'd even rehearsed how they'd make love long and slow the first time. Now he doubted if he'd make it past the tenth stroke the way she was grinding herself against him. God knows, he tried to retain his control, gave it his best shot to hang on to what little dignity he had. Every movement of her hips pushed him closer to the edge.

The musky scent of their love permeated the air and wafted past his nostrils until they flared. The huskiness of her voice calling out his name made him lose all perspective. On the fourth stroke, he felt like a lethal wattage of electricity had surged through him. He stiffened and roared out her name on a ragged plea.

Slumped over his chest, panting from exertion, Vic tried to sit up, but collapsed from the effort. "Oh, God . . ."

"*Mon amour*," he murmured, breathless, his eyes closed, his hands moving up and down her sweat-drenched back. "Baby . . . oh, baby."

"Oh, Jesus," she called out on a slow exhale.

Chuckling, he planted a kiss on the top of her head. "Our first time was supposed to be long and slow."

Her body was still twitching. "It was all right by me."

He rolled them to the side, the connection of their bodies broken, and headed for the bathroom. When he returned moments later, he stretched out on his side, bracing his weight on his elbow. Looking down at her, he glided his hand underneath her hips, caressing them.

She squeezed her thighs together and moaned. Her face twisted in sweet agony as she cupped an ache with her palm that never felt so good, all the while praying he'd make it go away.

"Want me to make it better?" he asked, understanding her dilemma. His open mouth glided down her chest to capture a nipple.

Her hand slid between their bellies, working its way south until she held him. "Depends on how you do it."

He glanced down at her. "Almost . . ."

Her lips parted in a sensual smile, her eyes signaling him, daring him. She thought him more than ready.

"Let me take the wheel," he whispered, accepting the challenge. Cradled between her thighs, he rolled another condom in place. "I don't want to take the curve too fast this time. I might crash and eject too soon," he groaned softly, joining them.

She'd chance a head-on collision with him any day. Closing her eyes, she tightened her legs around his and the movement drew him in deeper. She cried out her pleasure because he felt that good. Over and over, she loved him, freeing all the passion and desire she'd felt for this man from the moment they'd met.

But it wasn't enough.

With her hands locked over her head, she let him ride her, strong hips pumping, and in return, she gave everything she had: her mind, her soul, and her heart.

"Wrap those pretty legs around me," he growled. Taut lines etched across his face as he lost himself in the ecstasy of making love to her. The woman whose body clasped

163

him so tightly pushed him to the brink of insanity once again.

With her legs at his waist, their bodies became inseparable. Ripples of pleasure swept over her as he plunged harder and faster, and with each thrust, she knew she'd never stop loving him. The need to be closer, if that were possible, made her plant her feet flat on the mattress. Lifting her hips and widening her thighs caused him to touch her womb. And just like the first time, they came together, moaning each other's name on a hushed whisper.

Two hearts had finally merged into one, bound by an eternal love.

CHAPTER 12

It was a little past one in the morning when Vic awoke to the squalling cry of a baby. She sat straight up in bed and listened intently. "Baptiste, who's that?"

A.J. had already roused from his sleep and smiled as he looked at his shredded pajama bottoms, which lay in a heap on the floor along with Vic's clothes. "The newest members of the family," he answered and got up. He went to the dresser to retrieve another pair of pajamas.

"Who?" Vic yawned, rubbing her eyes.

He grinned. "Brianna and Chloé."

Vic shot off the mattress and headed straight for the door.

A.J. called out to her from behind. "Honey?"

"What? What?"

"Baby, don't you think you need to put something on?"

Vic looked down at her naked body. "Oh, Lord, I forgot."

A.J. came over and gave her a quick kiss. "Take your time and get dressed. We're just down the hall."

She took the quickest shower of her life and hurried to the room two doors down where she found Baptiste. He'd already gotten the girls' bottles and was just about to feed them when she entered. "How? When?" she ecstatically asked, lifting one of the infants from her crib.

"Hmm . . . late yesterday afternoon." He told her the details of his conversations with Zach and Valerie and also how Gail Bishop, the social worker with Child Protective Services had contacted him after speaking to Valerie's mother, who had absolutely no interest in taking in Brianna and Chloé. At his request, the twins had been placed with him.

"I still can't believe you're a licensed foster parent."

"Well, I am."

Vic finished feeding the baby she held, listened for a burp, and snuggled her against her chest. "Okay, who do I have here?"

A.J. knelt beside Vic who was seated in a rocker. "You've got Brianna, but the girls and I decided to call her Bébé. We call Chloé CeCe."

A.J. lifted CeCe from her crib along with her blanket and sat in a matching rocker next to Vic. "Hey there, sweetheart," he crooned against her ear. He wrapped her tightly inside the soft material, placed her high on his shoulder, and began humming a soft tune.

Vic watched in sheer amazement at their interaction and how quickly CeCe responded to Baptiste. Now she truly understood that being a pediatrician wasn't simply a job for him. It was his calling.

"And Valerie's doing okay?"

"She's doing great. Honey, I believe she's going to make it."

"I pray she does. She's been through so much. I'm going by and see her later today."

"I think she'd like that."

"Baptiste?"

"*Oui, mon amour?*"

"You've always wanted to be a doctor, haven't you?"

"From the time I was six, but it wasn't an easy road getting there."

"I don't understand."

A.J. chuckled. "I could best be described as a militant growing up. I almost gave the sisters at my high school a stroke."

"How?"

"Refusing to cut my hair for one, and being stubborn for another," he admitted, laughing out loud. "Sister Theresa would cringe every day when I entered her class and she saw my hair hanging down my shoulders. Plus, I was known to get into a fight or two in my younger days."

"No," Vic replied mockingly. She'd heard the family stories of him and the fights that had caused him to be suspended from school on more than one occasion. "What happened to make you change?"

"Father David. He became the principal the year I entered high school. One day, he took me inside his office and asked me what I wanted most in life, and I told him."

She chuckled. "So you stopped your Black Panther ways?"

"Not at first. My *mère* had died the year before, and I think one of the ways I dealt with her death was by becoming a rebel. Anyway, Father David must have seen something in me. So, he talked with Pop and asked if he could serve as my mentor. After that, he arranged for me to shadow some physicians he knew at a local hospital a couple of days a week."

"It worked, huh?"

He smiled. "Yes, it did. I saw that in order for me to become what I wanted to be more than anything in the world, I had to change, so I got rid of the hippie look—some of it, at least—buckled down, studied hard, and the rest is history."

"Angelique," Vic said happily, referring to A.J.'s late mother, "would be so proud of you."

A.J. nodded. "I certainly hope so."

Vic chuckled a while later. "See, I always told you, you were stubborn."

"I've never denied that character flaw, but I learned you do what you have to do if it's something you want badly enough."

"Why did you give up your position as chief of pediatrics?"

"Because of T-One and T-Two."

Vic shook her head, confused. "I'm not following you."

"Baby, I'd reached the top of my career when I got that position. Plus, I was swamped with administrative work and wasn't able to do what I became a doctor for in the first place—help little people get well."

"Trust me, I understand what you mean. And you never wanted to be in private practice?"

He shook his head. "Never. After I graduated from medical school and finished my internship and residency,

I practiced a couple of years with the World Health Organization."

"Really?" Vic said in awe. That piece of information was something new to her. "Why?"

"It was a chance for me to give back and use my training to help others." He shrugged. "I doubt I would have ever developed an interest in public health if it hadn't been for the stunt K-Mart and I pulled during our last year of medical school."

She tried to hide her laugh, but failed. "All right, what did you do, Baptiste?"

"We did to a classmate, Ralph Peterson, what I was planning to do to you."

"What's that?"

"Fake a quarantine."

"What?" she said, trying to quiet down her laughter.

"I'm serious," he admitted, laughing just as hard. "Talk about anal retentive. Even as easygoing as K-Mart can be most of the time, Pete managed to get on his nerves, too. So, we decided our friend needed a little distance away from everyone for a few days."

"Baptiste, y'all really didn't do that, did you?"

"Yes, we did. One day after class, K-Mart and I found Pete and told him that he'd tested positive for encephalitis. After that, we locked Pete up in a room and rationed his food, and he ended up eating like one meal a day. He was so messed up by the time it was over with he spent a week in the psych ward."

"Oh, stop. Man, you are lying."

"No, I'm not. If you think I'm making this up, just ask K-Mart."

"Did anyone ever find out?"

"Oh, yes, and as our punishment, the dean made both of us volunteer at a local health clinic until we graduated. That's how I started working with drug-addicted teen mothers and their babies."

After they settled down, Vic lovingly looked over at him. "That's how you met T-One and T-Two, isn't it?"

A.J.'s look of humor fled, and a somber expression took its place. "Yes. They were brought into the emergency room one night. They were the worst cases of child abuse and neglect I've ever seen," he uttered softly, his voice thickening. He glanced at Vic. "But you know what?"

"What?"

"Despite the agony they were going through they held hands and wouldn't let go of each other. Anyway, I stayed at their bedside. I'm not sure how many days now, but I had to be sure they'd make it through."

She lightly stroked the side of Bébé's face, who had drifted off to sleep. "Then what?"

"I left the hospital one day, headed straight down to Social Services, and applied to become a foster parent. Once I looked into their little eyes, I fell in love with those two munchkins. Their mother's parental rights were being terminated anyway, and within six months she was dead. They would have ended up in foster care one way or the other, and I wanted my home to be the one they came to."

"Oh, Baptiste . . ."

"They required a lot of care at first."

"What kind of care?" she asked, curious.

"They'd suffered so much abuse and trauma they hadn't learned to talk."

Tears rolled down Vic's face. "What did you do?"

He blew out a hard breath. "I knew I couldn't give them what they needed and work, too, so I resigned my position the day they were released from the hospital and brought them home with me." He shifted in the rocker until he faced her. "Honey, remember the day we first saw Bébé and CeCe?"

Vic nodded.

A.J. stared down at CeCe, who was now fast asleep, and cradled her closer to his chest. "I felt the same way about them as I did when I first saw Taylor and Tyler. Somehow I knew they'd be a part of my life."

Vic sobbed softly, remembering that she'd felt the exact same way, but hadn't wanted to scare him off by voicing her feelings.

He proceeded to tell her the fear he'd felt when he made the offer to Valerie to care for her babies. "This is my life, Honey. Living and working in the community, trying to help little ones . . . it's who I am. I realize taking care of Taylor and Tyler is a big responsibility, and now we have Bébé and CeCe—"

"Taking care of all of these babies is what I want, too, Baptiste."

"Baptiste, you hear that?" Later, around eight that evening, Vic lay atop Baptiste's bed, staring at the ceiling.

"Yes. It's called quiet." A.J. was stretched out beside her, elbow bent and his head resting on his palm. "They must all be asleep."

After they'd gotten Taylor and Tyler off to school, Vic and A.J. had come back home and spent the morning with Bébé and CeCe, becoming more acquainted with their personalities. In between the girls' feeding and naps, they had become more familiar with each other. Neither of them had a desire to halt their passion. A.J. discovered that if he slid a pillow underneath Vic's hips while he made love to her and nuzzled a particular spot between her ear and neck, she shattered like a pane of glass.

Vic rolled on her side to face him, her eyes roving over him, her hand stroking slowly over his crotch. "You think they'll give us twenty minutes?"

"God, I hope so," he groaned and covered her mouth with his. He deepened the kiss, but was interrupted by the ringing of the doorbell. Pulling away, they both sighed in frustration before A.J. stood and answered the door.

Zach strolled in a few moments later and took a seat at the dining room table. "Did I interrupt somethin'?"

"Yes," Vic chuckled, winking at Baptiste. "We'll resume later." She focused her attention on Zach. "Listen, you hungry?"

Zach patted his stomach. "Naw, just left from over at Alcee's house. Mama Z fed me today, but I could stand some dessert. Whatcha got?"

"Boy, you eat more than Baptiste." Chuckling, Vic shook her head and headed off to the kitchen.

After Vic left, Zach leaned back in his chair and released a frustrated sigh.

"What's wrong?" A.J. asked, concerned.

Zach ran a weary hand across his face. "The boys from the lab came up empty-handed trying to identify the paint chips. Damn, I need to find the car Scooter and Valerie drove that night."

Returning from the kitchen with a slice of homemade apple pie on two plates, Vic had overheard Zach's comment. She gave one plate to Baptiste and the other to Zach. "Zach, I heard what you told Baptiste. Maybe I can help."

Zach didn't stop eating. "Help do what?"

"Help you find the car," Vic replied.

Zach frowned in confusion. "How?"

"Hypnosis."

Zach lifted his brow. "On who?"

"Me."

"Honey—"

"Baptiste, come on now and listen. Hypnosis might help me remember more about the accident or something about the car that Scooter was driving."

"But, Honey, you said yourself you only got a glimpse of the back of the car before it drove off."

"I know, Baptiste, but hypnosis might help me remember something I saw."

A.J. shook his head.

Vic braced her hands on the table with her eyes narrowed. "Baptiste, I know you're not sitting here telling me I can't do something."

"You're right," A.J. retorted and shot to his feet. "I'm not sitting."

"Baptiste," Vic uttered in a warning tone.

A.J. shook his head, again, rubbing at the base of his neck. "I'm sorry, baby, but I'm just not feeling you putting yourself through hypnosis."

Vic glanced over at Zach. "You just said you needed to find the car, right?"

"Yeah," Zach drawled.

"Come on, Baptiste," Vic said with a pleading look. "It wouldn't hurt for me to at least try, right?"

"Honey, you've been through a lot—"

"I know what I've been through, Baptiste, but baby, I made it. And right now, two other people are involved as well. One's fighting for her life and the other is fighting to save it. They've gone through more than I have. They need my help, and I plan on giving it to 'em."

Zach glanced over at A.J. from across the table. "Brother-in-law, Baby Girl might be right on this one. I told ya the other night the missing link to all of this is that car."

Vic looped her arms around Baptiste's neck. "Baby, if you hadn't stood with me, I wouldn't have made it. Stand by me on this one." She cupped his face in her hands. "Please."

"Brother-in-law, if it makes ya feel any better, there's been times when the police have used hypnosis to help victims remember information that their memory suppressed." Staring intently at A.J., Zach added, "Let me at least check into it, okay?"

A.J. released a sigh so inaudible he barely heard it himself and sat heavily. He begrudgingly relented, in part because he knew once Vic made up in her mind to do something, nothing short of death would make her back down. He also knew that she was right. They had to identify the car. He pulled her onto his lap, wrapping his arms around her waist. "Make no mistake, I'll be right there."

"You took it," Tyler yelled from in the bedroom.

"Did not," Taylor shouted back.

Zach shook his head and laughed. "Thought Thelma and Louise would've been asleep by now."

Vic chuckled and gave Baptiste a sultry look. "We hoped so, too."

"So, is this what I have to look forward to?" Zach asked, wiping his mouth with a napkin.

A.J. chuckled as he peeked around Vic and looked over at Zach. "Yes. Just wait until you and Moni add a second one." He caressed Vic's bottom. "Well, I guess I need to go and determine the source of this battle."

"No, stay and finish talking with Zach and listen out for Bébé and CeCe. I'm on this one." Vic left the dining room and headed down the hall. "All right. Now what's the problem here, people?"

Zach watched Vic until she was well out of hearing distance. "Brother-in-law," he whispered, leaning over, "ya don' talked her out of leaving, right?"

A.J.'s eyes twinkled with delight as he sat, recalling the passion and love they'd shared the last several hours. Smiling, he bobbed his head up and down. "Zach, trust me, I don't believe you have to worry about that anymore."

Zach pushed his empty dish away, sighing with satisfaction, and rested his hand on a full stomach. "That's good 'cause ya woman can burn. If ya ever get tired of her cooking, send her my way. Ain't had cooking like this since I left my mama's house."

A.J. chuckled.

Zach's eyes slid shut. "And ya sure she ain't gonna move, right?"

A.J. nodded. "*Oui.*"

Vic stood in the middle of Taylor and Tyler's bedroom with her hands on her hips. "Ladies, what's going on in here?"

The décor of the space was French antique done in multiple shades of pink and white. The walls were sorbet pink, and the elegant floral fabrics and canopy-topped twin beds added an undeniably feminine charm.

Vic studied Taylor intently to be certain the wheezy sound she heard wasn't another asthma attack. Satisfied that all was well, she bit down on her bottom lip to keep from laughing out loud. Taylor and Tyler sat on their beds with their backs to each, arms folded across their little heaving chests.

Vic needed the facts, and she needed them fast. Asking Taylor was not an option because her logical way of thinking would pose a thousand other questions before she even got around to answering the initial one. So, Vic opted to query Tyler first. She'd have the hardcore truth in about two seconds flat. "All right, T-Two," she said, looking at Tyler, "what's going on?"

Tyler looked up at Vic and tossed her thumb over her shoulder. "She started it, Honey. She took my doll."

"Did not," Taylor shouted back.

"Did, too," Tyler countered. "She took it without 'mission, Honey."

Vic chuckled. "It's called *permission*, T-Two." Then she glanced over at Taylor. "T-One, is that true?"

"Uh," Taylor hedged.

"T-One," Vic said, "the answer is simple. It's either yes or no. Did you take T-Two's doll without permission?"

"Honey, she's not playing with it. It was just sitting there, and the baby doll didn't want to sit by herself. The baby doll needs me—"

"All right, T-One, I get the picture." Vic hid a grin behind the back of her hand, then sat on the floor and beckoned both girls to her. She patted her lap and waited for them to settle themselves before turning her attention to Taylor. "T-One, if you want to play with something that belongs to someone else, you ask their permission. Understand?"

Taylor nodded. "Yes, ma'am."

Vic smiled. "Okay, now I want you to tell T-Two you're sorry."

Taylor mumbled under her breath, "Sorry, T-Two."

Vic glanced over at Tyler. "T-Two, do you accept T-One's apology?"

"No." Tyler huffed and turned her head away.

"T-Two . . ." Vic's voice was stern, yet gentle.

"All right, I 'cept—"

"That's *accept*, T-Two," Vic amended.

"I accept your 'pology—"

"It's pronounced *apology*, sweetie," Vic corrected.

Tyler sighed. "I accept your apology, T-One."

"That's more like it." Vic hugged both girls to her chest. "Listen, we are a family now, and that includes Bébé and CeCe, too. I don't care if the world falls down around you, I expect all four of you to grab hands and hold on to one another for dear life. Understand, Honey?"

Smiling, Taylor and Tyler looked up at Vic. "Yes, ma'am."

Taylor looped her arms around Vic's neck. "Love you, Honey."

"Yeah, love you, Honey," Tyler affirmed.

Vic gave both girls a big bear hug. "Love my babies, too."

"Honey?" Taylor said, with a quizzical look.

"What, sweet pea?"

"You not leave us, right?"

Vic blinked back tears as she shook her head. "Nope. Honey's here to stay."

CHAPTER 13

Friday morning, Vic checked in with the police officers assigned to guard Valerie when she went to Highland Hospital to visit her. She brought along a digital camera loaded with several pictures of Brianna and Chloé that she and Baptiste had taken. Afterwards, she took the elevator up to the intensive care unit to see how Nicole, the accident victim, was doing. She didn't learn until she spoke with one the nurses that Ron had performed a difficult but successful surgery to remove Nicole's brain tumor and the chances of Nicole pulling through had dramatically increased. As soon as she opened the door, she spotted Ron talking with Nicole's parents by her bedside and turned to walk away.

Ron caught sight of Vic from the corner of his eye. "Vic?"

Vic halted when she heard Ron call out to her and turned to face him. "How's Nicole doing?"

"She's in a drug-induced coma, but she's stable. I believe she's going to make it."

So much had transpired in the last forty-eight hours that Vic silently admitted she hadn't given much thought to what she would say if she ever saw Ron again. She glanced up at Ron. "How are you doing?"

Ron swept his hand toward the waiting area. Together, he and Vic walked in silence down the corridor.

After Vic settled in a seat, he sat next to her. "I'm okay." He paused and swallowed the lump in his throat. "Vic, I-I just want you to know how sorry I am for the pain I put you through."

As Vic nodded, she couldn't help noticing the dark circles underneath his eyes. "You look tired."

"I am," Ron replied as a loud growl rumbled inside his stomach. He chuckled. "I guess I'm hungry, too. After I grab a bite to eat, I'm going back to my hotel room and get some sleep. My flight leaves later this evening."

"Ron, you're a gifted surgeon," Vic admitted without hesitation, lacing her fingers together to control the trembling. "Thank you for helping Nicole." Fumbling with the strap on her purse, she looped it across her shoulder, and stood. "I-I better head back down to Nicole's room. I want to see how she and her parents are doing."

Ron nodded, rising to his feet and started to speak, then hesitated before he finally asked, "How are you doing, Vic? Are you happy?"

With the thoughts of the family she'd always longed for now in her life via Baptiste, Taylor, and Tyler, along with Brianna and Chloé, a bright smile surfaced. "I'm good, Ron. And yes, I'm very happy."

"You're positive?"

"Absolutely."

"Vic," Ron uttered softly with his head bowed, "I hope one day you'll find it in your heart to forgive me. I was the one who made the mistake for not being honest with you, for not being honest with myself. When we first met, I was in denial about who I was." He glanced up at her. "You deserve to be happy."

Vic reached out and placed her hand atop his. "I am happy, Ron, more than you could ever imagine." She wasn't so naïve that she didn't realize that it would take time to come to terms with the past. Nor had she forgotten that the first step toward the healing process was to open up to other people who'd gone through the same experience as she had. But she was strong enough to know that she had to release herself from the bondage of the past and move on. She held Ron's gaze and it happened. It was just like her mother had said it would be. Looking Ron square in the eyes, remembering all the pain she'd suffered, a peace she thought she'd never feel toward him came over her.

"Ron." Her voice was clear and strong.

"Yes?"

With tears shimmering in her eyes, she said, "I wish you well."

Vic entered Nicole's room a half hour later. After ending her conversation with Ron, she'd headed down to the hospital's accounting department. The night before, she and Baptiste had discussed and agreed to make arrangements for all of Nicole's bills to be forwarded to them.

Once she entered Nicole's room, Vic spoke with her parents and encouraged them to go and grab a bite to eat, assuring them that she'd stay with their daughter until they returned. She settled in the chair next to the bed and spoke to Nicole even though she was in a coma. As a nurse, Vic knew there were different levels of consciousness and she hoped that by speaking to Nicole she'd be able to hear her.

A nurse came in, and seeing Vic talking to Nicole, gave her a curious look, but didn't ask her to leave. As she checked the monitors and noted the information on Nicole's medical chart, she glanced over at Vic, surprised. "Hmm," she murmured, "I think our little patient here is responding to you."

Gently rubbing the top of Nicole's hand, Vic looked up at the nurse and smiled. "You think so?"

The nurse nodded with a smile. "Her heartbeat is stronger, and her respiration settles whenever you speak. Whatever you're saying to her, don't stop."

Vic waited until the nurse left the room and repeated even more forcefully than before what she'd said to Nicole over and over from the moment she walked in. "Live."

"Man, that's the third bowl of cobbler you've eaten," Vic teased later that evening in the dining room after she and Baptiste had settled the girls down for the night.

"I know," A.J. acknowledged. "But nobody makes peach cobbler better than you." He patted his lap and once Vic settled, wrapped his arms around her waist. "How's Nicole doing?"

Vic shared with Baptiste Nicole's reaction to her during her visit. She also told him that she planned to go back every day until Nicole regained consciousness. Finally, she ended by relating her conversation with Ron. She felt as though a weight had been lifted from her shoulders and her heart because she'd finally found the place inside of her to forgive Ron.

A.J. responded by giving her a long, passionate kiss.

Vic chuckled when she was finally able to gather her senses again. She looked at the bowl. "You bet' not tell Zach I make my cobbler with no sugar."

"Really?" A.J. was stunned.

"Umm-hmm. Everything I cook now is either low in fat or sugar-free."

"Why?"

"Child, diabetes runs in my family. Plus, a few years ago, I suffered with high blood pressure from messing around with those crazy people at work. They almost had my pressure up to stroke level." She wiggled her bottom against him. "Besides, with these big hips, I knew I needed to make a lifestyle change and lose some weight."

"You're not big."

"Hey, I fill out a fourteen real good. That's about as far up the ladder as I want to go."

"But you're a good-looking fourteen."

"Yeah, right. You're just saying that because you want me around to feed you."

"No. I want you, period," he answered easily.

Vic glanced at him, clamping her thighs together. The softness in his gaze made her body jerk with desire to be touched by him, soon. "I want you, too."

He stood and grabbed her hand. "Come on, let's clean up the kitchen. It'll probably be thirty more minutes before the girls are really asleep."

With his arms stretched wide on the back of the Jacuzzi, A.J. let Vic settle herself between his legs. "What about you? Did you always want to be a nurse?"

She smiled. "Actually, becoming a nurse was not what I set out to do. Even though I had an excellent example in Mom, it wasn't until I was challenged by one of my teachers at a career-day fair in high school that I decided to take the plunge." She chuckled and glanced around at him. "It's funny how Harrison and I followed after Mom and became healthcare professionals."

"But you ended up in administration. Why?"

"After I graduated from nursing school, I worked in pediatric oncology for a couple of years. Took care of a little guy whose parents were like Nicole's; they didn't have insurance. That's when I started to really understand the disparity between the haves and the have-nots. I literally had to fight tooth and nail to get the hospital to provide the treatment I knew he should receive."

"Did he make it?"

Vic smiled happily. "He did, and to this day I stay in contact with him and his family. After that incident, I knew in order to change the system I had to be at the table where decisions are made."

"Why did you quit?"

She chuckled. "The main reason was to get away from you."

He whispered against her ear and jokingly said, "I never would have guessed that."

She laughed. "Hush, man. No, seriously, I got tired of the cat fighting. This person, that person worried about their next promotion instead of doing their job. Plus, I had a boss who was a closet racist."

"Why do you say that?"

"He about flipped the day I came to work with my dreads."

Lifting them in his hand, A.J. let them fall through his fingers one by one. "I like them. So what was his problem?"

"He told me off the record that my 'look,' " she explained, making quote signs with her fingers, "wasn't conservative. The dumb dickhead wouldn't have known what conservative was if it slapped him upside his head."

"Honey," A.J. said, chuckling, "I'm going to have to wash your mouth out with soap."

"Well, it's the truth." She made the Girl Scout sign. "I promise from now on to watch my language around the girls."

A.J. threw back his head and roared with laughter. "Too late, *mon amour*."

Vic craned her neck so her vision was better aligned with his. "Whatcha mean, too late?"

"The two little women around here who can talk also know how to curse—in French."

"What?" Vic laughed. "Who taught 'em?"

"I haven't figured that out yet. As much as this family gossips, no one owns up to that one."

Vic focused straight ahead, pondering a question she'd been meaning to ask for months. "Baptiste, why'd you put T-One and T-Two in separate classes at school?"

"Because I used to dress them alike and their teacher was having a really difficult time telling them apart."

"Come on now, Baptiste. Yeah, they're identical, but those two munchkins are as different as night and day."

"*We* know that, but I can understand the difficulty someone else would have who doesn't really know them all that well."

Vic nodded. "Yeah, I guess you're right."

"Ready for a shower?" he whispered in a husky tone next to her ear.

The desire in his voice caused a chill to race down her spine. "Mmm-hmm. And I'm ready for what comes after the shower, too."

Upon Baptiste's insistence, Vic slept in late the next morning. When she finally woke up around ten, her breakfast consisted of soggy Cheerios and half-burnt toast, courtesy of Taylor and Tyler. She cringed when she looked down at the breakfast tray Baptiste helped them bring to the bed. She hated Cheerios. But she lovingly ate every single one of them, grateful to her two girls for the gesture. In between eating her breakfast, she fed Bébé and CeCe their breakfast after first insisting they be tucked on each side of her.

Around noon, she walked into the living room with a laundry basket under her arm and noticed Baptiste sitting at the dining room table. Frowning, he stared at the stack of papers spread out in front of him.

Chuckling to herself, she walked over to the table. "Man, what's wrong with you? You look like a bear."

He sighed. "I'm trying to balance my checkbook."

She lifted her brow. "Do you go into hyperventilation this way every month when you reconcile your statement?"

"No. Usually Aimee does it for me."

Vic knew that Aimee, A.J.'s youngest sister, was a Stanford-educated CPA and usually handled all of the family finances. She placed the basket on the floor and pointed at the bank statements. "Here, if you do laundry, I'll balance."

A.J. stood and nodded. "Gladly."

Vic sat and shuffled through the papers. She causally asked, "So, this is your personal checking account, right?"

A.J. picked the laundry basket off the floor. "No. It's the household account, but the personal account needs to be balanced, too, so have at it, if you'd like." He headed off toward the laundry room, but stopped and turned around. "Let me know what day we can go to the bank. I need to add your name to the accounts."

"'Kay," Vic absently mumbled, glancing over the statements. Her eyes bulged at the ending balance. She didn't even recall the numbers in front of the six zeros she'd counted. And this was just the household account? Lord, she was scared to know the amount he had in his personal checking account.

Vic finished reconciling Baptiste's accounts and headed toward the laundry room. Before she reached the door, she heard the sounds of muffled laughter coming from inside. She was just about to open her mouth to fuss at him for joking around and taking two hours to finish a load and a half of laundry when she saw something truly amazing.

Baptiste and the girls were atop the clothes strewn across the floor. He was using something as simple as dirty clothes to teach and observe. Each time he held up a piece of clothing, Taylor and Tyler were able to identify the colors or tell him whether it was big, medium, or small. And whenever he positioned himself behind Bébé and CeCe and made a playful razing sound, they would crawl away as fast as they could while he sat back, observing their gross motor skills.

Vic smiled at the priceless moment being shared between a father and his daughters.

What the heck? The laundry could wait.

Around three that afternoon, Vic walked past the living room and found Baptiste sitting comfortably in an old, tattered recliner, with remote in hand, waiting for the opening pitch of his favorite baseball team, the Oakland A's.

"Baptiste . . ."

A.J. never took his gaze away from the television screen. "Yes, *mon amour*?"

"Man, why did you bring that raggedy chair back inside my living room?"

"Because this is where it belongs," he answered without hesitation.

It had taken her over forty-five minutes to get it out of the living room and into the garage. With her mouth wide open, she stared at him in disbelief. "But I moved it out of here yesterday."

"And I brought it back in today."

"But—"

"No buts," he interrupted.

"Baptiste . . ."

"Listen, woman, you and those other four little bitty women in my life have taken over, and I'm thrilled." He pressed a button on the remote to turn the volume up. "But I'm telling every last one of you right now, this chair stays."

"The leather is split; the springs are about to come through, and even the handle on the side is broken." She hid a giggle.

He pouted, firmly gripping the arms of the recliner. "I don't care. It's mine." He ran his hand along the cracked upholstery. "This recliner and I have traveled around the world together. And we've gone through three World Series together." He jerked his head back, decisively declaring, "And come what may, we're staying *together*."

She leaned over him, whispering next to his ear, "What if I want to watch the game with you one day?"

"Anytime you want, you can snuggle up in my lap."

She straightened and placed her hands back on her hips. "Men . . . sports . . ." She shook her head, completely at a loss to explain how someone with millions in not one, but two bank accounts couldn't—no, correction—wouldn't purchase something as simple as a new lounger.

The chair had to go. She leaned over him again. Her voice dipped to a sultry tone as she ran her fingers up and down the bulge in his jeans, her tongue circling his ear lobe. "What will it take for you to reconsider?"

A.J. closed his eyes and sucked in a deep breath, enjoying the feel of her hands rubbing him this way. He wasn't giving up his chair, though. Breathless, he stuttered, "N-Nothing."

Vic walked away, flashing a wry smile. She'd show him he wasn't the only one who could come up with a crazy scheme.

Vic made one last check on the girls around nine that evening. She went inside their rooms, tucked them securely under the covers, kissed them good night, turned up the volume on the baby monitors, and headed for a shower.

She draped her damp body in a huge towel after a long shower with Baptiste. Standing in front of the dresser, she picked up a bottle of scented lotion.

A.J. walked from the bathroom a few moments later with a towel tucked at his waist. He came up behind her with a box in his hand that he'd retrieved from the top drawer of his nightstand.

"Close your eyes, *mon amour*."

She followed his instructions, and moments later, felt something being placed around her neck.

"Oh, my God, Baptiste," she said in awe once she stared into the mirror at the custom-designed, diamond-and-platinum necklace with the letters *ABW*.

A.J. circled his arms around her waist, nuzzling his mouth up and down the side of her neck. "Now whenever you say it, you'll be telling the truth."

She chuckled with her head back slightly, looking up at him. "What, that I'm an angry black woman?"

"No," he answered, chuckling back. "That you're Alcee Baptiste's woman." Removing her towel, he picked up the lotion, poured a generous amount into his hand, and slowly spread the creamy substance on her body.

"*Je t'aime*." After he finished, he burrowed his nose into the side of her neck.

With her head thrown back, she gasped with pleasure as his lips traveled along the width of her shoulders. "I love you, too." She looked in the mirror at him. "You know I'm supposed to be living in Atlanta now, right?"

"Mmm-hmm," he moaned, and lightly bit down on her neck. "Never made it there, did you?"

Vic chuckled. "Nope, and I'm so happy I didn't." She stared in the mirror at their reflection for a long time. "Baptiste, we really do need to get married."

"We do?" he whispered, never removing his mouth from her scented skin.

Vic chuckled at the irony of it all. She'd vowed never to fall in love with him, and now *she* was the one asking him to marry her.

"Yeah, we really do."

"Why should I marry you, *mon amour*?"

Vic gasped in disbelief until she glanced in the mirror and noticed the wicked grin that made his lips curl upward. "Because we love each other."

"I don't know, *mon amour*," A.J. muttered huskily, cupping her lush breasts together with his hands. With a loving gaze, he looked in the mirror at the woman he loved more than life itself. "You might not be the woman I want to marry," he murmured. Desire and passion swept across her face when he gently rolled her nipples between his fingers.

"What will it take to convince you?" She breathed softly, her eyelids drifting to half-mast. The feel of his roaming hands made her ache for him to take her nipple inside his mouth.

He turned her around by the shoulders to face him and obliged her telepathic request when he circled her nipple with his tongue, then drew it in and sucked hard.

"This . . ." A.J. snatched the towel from his waist. "Turn back around, *mon amour*, and hold on to the dresser for me." With his large hands clamped at her waist, he inclined her forward slightly, nudging her legs apart with his thigh. "Whatever you do, don't close your eyes. Promise me."

"'Kay." Vic clutched the dresser's edge for balance and a not-so-soft moan escaped her lips when he planted open-mouthed kisses along her backbone. He palmed one hand to her stomach while the other caressed her breast. Her arms trembled and her heart raced from the sheer agony of want. She arched her back and waited.

"Don't look away," he rasped, the warmth of his breath searing the area right below her ear. "I need to see you convince me." Bent at the knees, he slid inside her. The feel of being locked in her warmth caused a moan to work its way from deep in his chest.

She watched with passion-laden eyes as he moved inside her with exquisite slowness, thunderous groans escaping from his throat.

"Baptiste," she whispered and dropped her head, knowing she was two heartbeats away from climaxing, "I can't watch anymore."

She felt his powerful arms tighten about her waist. Her flesh felt as though it was about to rip in two. He was relentless and continued to rock against her, each thrust becoming harder, every stroke going deeper until she shut her eyes and blocked out everything but his soft utterance.

"Convince me, Honey," he groaned, his voice rough with passion.

That was when all inhibition fled. Removing her hands away from the dresser, she bent forward until her fingertips touched the floor.

"Baptiste . . ." Her voice rose to a soprano pitch, then dipped to a deep, strangled wail as the slickness of his sweat-drenched belly covered her back. His tone escalated to a mighty roar, and his thrusts became harder, faster, and more urgent until their cries mingled together and finally ebbed on her whispered plea, "Marry me . . ."

CHAPTER 14

"Mom," Vic lifted CeCe over her shoulder, gently patting her on the back as she looked over at her mother. "After she's had her bottle, you need to burp her like this."

The expression on Louise's face indicated she thought Vic's demonstration was ludicrous. "Oh, you mean the same way I did with the three I had when they were babies, right?"

Vic was oblivious to her mother's wisecrack. She frantically searched through the diaper bag and raced over to her father after Louise took CeCe from her arms. "Now, Daddy, this is a Pamper," she noted and held it up. "When you change the babies, use this."

Chuckling, George Vincent peered over his half-rimmed glasses and accepted the disposable diaper. He inspected it from top to bottom. "Yep, looks similar to the ones I used to put on you years ago."

A.J. stood off to the side and chuckled. It was Monday morning, and Taylor and Tyler were at school. Louise and George Vincent were going to baby-sit Bébé and CeCe while he and Vic went down to the Oakland police station. It was the first time since the babies' arrival that Vic had been separated from them. He had never dreamed she'd go through parent withdrawal anxiety this severe. "Honey . . ."

"Uh?" Vic answered hesitantly, but didn't move.

"Come on, *mon amour.*" He placed his arm around Vic's shoulders and guided her toward the front door. "I believe Louise and G.V. know what they're doing."

"Yeah," Louise drawled. "We got this."

Vic stopped and glanced over her shoulder. "But Mom—"

"Sweetheart, your girls are going to be just fine," George Vincent said, with Bébé cradled in his arms. "Why don't you and A.J. go out to dinner and catch a movie since your mother and I are going to pick up T-One and T-Two from school?" He shooed Vic and A.J. forward when Vic nervously glanced up at A.J.

"Mom," Vic stuttered, "you've got our cell phone numbers, right?"

Louise chuckled. "Did they change from twenty minutes ago when you gave them to me for the *third* time?"

Vic shook her head.

Louise smiled. "Then I got 'em. Now please go."

A.J. stood along with Zach and another police officer inside a room with a one-way mirror next to the interrogation room Vic was in. He felt as if the walls were closing in on him. He willed his claustrophobia not to rear its ugly head. Although he wasn't permitted to be with her during the hypnosis session, he'd gladly suffer through this and more if it meant she felt a sense of peace knowing he was nearby.

Zach patted A.J.'s shoulder. "Baby Girl is gonna be just fine." He adjusted his earpiece the moment he heard a voice transit through. He focused straight ahead.

"Vic," a male voice said, extending his hand as he walked into the room. "I'm Officer Arthur McNeil. I'm a police hypnotist with the Oakland Police Department."

Seated inside one of the interrogation rooms at the police station, Vic stood and rubbed a sweaty palm along the side of her dress before she answered. "H-Hi." The single word came out cracked despite her best effort to remain calm and steady her nerves.

She glanced first at the video camera in front of her, then to the tape recorder on the table. Both had been turned on before the officer walked in. She sat again as the officer positioned a chair in front of hers. Listening intently, she nodded occasionally as Officer McNeil explained the process, answered her questions, and dispelled the misconceptions about hypnosis.

"Vic, I want you to close your eyes and breathe deeply . . . relax completely." the hypnotist said. He paused. "Now I want you to count backwards to ten . . . slowly."

"Ten . . . nine . . . eight . . ." Vic counted at a languid pace until she'd reached one.

"Vic, right now I want you to imagine you're inside a movie theater, watching a film. Tell me about every scene that comes up on the screen and describe it . . . just like an investigative reporter would do."

Vic's eyes remained closed. "Ran out of Caitlyn's house and got into my car. Drove round and round Lake Merritt for a long time. Then headed home . . ."

"What route did you take?" the hypnotist asked.

"Grand and Harrison."

"Were other cars around you?"

Vic shook her head.

"All right, Vic," the hypnotist said softly. "What's the next scene you see?"

"Came to a stop light. I missed it twice . . . no, three times."

"Why?"

"I was crying."

"Why were you crying, Vic?"

"Remembered what Ron did to me."

The hypnotist probed again. "What's coming up on the screen now, Vic?"

With her eyes still closed, Vic inclined her head slightly. "Heard a screeching sound and bright lights."

"What did you do, Vic?" the hypnotist asked.

"Tried to move out the way . . . too late." Vic paused. "I hit something . . . then something hit my car."

"Okay, the next scene." the hypnotist said.

"Got out of my car . . ." Silence stretched between Vic and the hypnotist for a moment. "I looked down. It was Baptiste . . ." Vic heaved. "He was very still. Knelt next to him to help . . . couldn't let him die."

The hypnotist jotted notes on the pad resting on his lap. "Describe the car?"

"Red . . . two doors." Vic stopped talking for a moment, then said, "Q . . . U . . . E . . . E . . ." she broke off and shook her head. "Can't see anything else . . . the car is driving off."

"Vic, I'm going to count from one to ten. When I reach the number ten, you will become alert. You'll feel refreshed and relaxed and I want you to open your eyes on ten."

A.J. smiled at Zach and shook his hand the moment Vic recited the partial license plate number to the hypnotist.

Zach glanced over at the officer standing next to him. "Ya get that number?"

The officer nodded. "Yes, sir, Lieutenant."

"Run it through the system. The minute something comes in, notify me."

After they left the police station, Vic and A.J. stopped by the hospital to check on Valerie and Nicole, then drove back to her condominium. At A.J.'s request, Vic spent the rest of the afternoon convincing him to marry her.

Sated, Vic lay snugly in his arms in the middle of her bed.

A.J. placed a kiss at her temple. "I'm proud of what you did today, Honey."

Vic looked up at him with all the love a woman can feel for her man. "I'm glad you were there for me, Baptiste. I just hope Zach can track down the car." She chuckled. "I'll call the realtor tomorrow and put the condo back on the market since I won't need it anymore."

He chuckled back. "Oh, I think we'll need it," he said and circled his tongue on her earlobe. "It's a good hide-away from the girls when we want to get away and be alone and when I need convincing about something."

She playfully punched his shoulder. "Hush, man."

He cleared his throat. "We have a choice."

"What?"

"We can wreck this bed some more—" He broke off to lift his head and look at the clock on the nightstand—"or we can do something really crazy."

"Baptiste, you and me together is crazy enough."

"No, I mean something really, really crazy."

She lifted her brow. "Another one of your outlandish schemes?"

He gave her a roguish grin. "Yes."

CHAPTER 15

After a quick shower, A.J. told Vic she was as beautiful dressed in jeans, t-shirts, and tennis shoes as she was decked out in a designer outfit. It was a little after four in the afternoon as he drove them to the Oakland airport for a flight to Las Vegas.

A couple of hours later, he and Vic walked along the Vegas strip, enjoying the warm desert evening. After losing several rolls of quarters playing slots at one of the casinos on Fremont Street, they viewed a dazzling light show on the five-block strip. Their next stop was the first wedding chapel he found.

"The ring?" the justice of the peace said, smiling.

Vic glanced up at Baptiste before looking back at the gray-haired man. "We don't have a ring."

"Oh, I see," he said.

"Here, woman." Smiling, A.J. took the diamond stud out of his right ear. "Pull your hair back for me," he softly instructed, and then placed the stud in her left ear.

Vic touched her earlobe, smiling again. Suddenly her eyes flared, and she gasped. "Baptiste?"

"What's wrong, *mon amour*?"

"Did you feed Harry and Sally?"

"No."

"Man, it was your day to feed them."

"Listen, woman, if I hadn't had to drag you out of the house earlier when you were giving all those instructions to Louise and G.V., I would have remembered."

Lifting his brow, the justice of the peace cleared his throat. "Uh, excuse me. Are you two sure you're making a wise choice?"

"Umm-hmm," Vic answered with a huge smile.

A.J. beamed. "Absolutely."

"By the power vested in me by the State of Nevada, I hereby pronounce you husband and wife." He looked at A.J. "You may kiss your bride."

Although he'd planned for them to stay in Las Vegas for a couple more days to take in a few of the shows, A.J. grabbed Vic's hand, rushed out the chapel, and hailed a taxi. When the cab came to a stop, he let Vic climb into the backseat first, and heard her mumbling under her breath something about hoping she didn't find two dead fish when they got back home.

"Guess what?" Sunday morning, Vic stood at the kitchen counter and put the finishing touches on a Caesar salad she was preparing.

She and A.J. had invited the Baptiste and Bennett families, along with K-Mart and Alex, over to watch the Oakland A's baseball game that began at noon. After the game, they planned to tell everyone they'd eloped six days earlier.

Brie, Moni, Aimee, Caitlyn, Louise, and Mama Z were seated around the table and lifted their heads to wait for Vic's announcement.

"The girls and I got Baptiste a new recliner."

"What?" they all replied in unison, flabbergasted.

Vic nodded, elated she'd might finally convince Baptiste to give up his worn-out recliner. "It's beautiful. Just wait until you see it."

Aimee made the sign of the cross. "Does he know yet?"

Vic shook her head.

Moni gasped. "Oh, my God. He doesn't?"

"Not yet," Vic said. "I wanted to surprise Baptiste, so I told him he had to watch the game in the family room." She beamed. "I think he's gonna really like it."

Brie chuckled. "Girl, we've tried for years to make him give up that raggedy chair he's lugged around the world and nothing has worked. You'll bury him sitting up in it."

Mama Z slowly shook her head, "That there man ya got is gonna have a heart attack when he finds out."

Louise was out of her seat the second Bébé started to squirm. Shortly afterward, a loud squall came from CeCe. "Naw, you finish what you're doing," she told Vic, who was walking toward the crying infants. "We got this." Louise nodded at Mama Z. "Z, you get CeCe." She lifted Bébé from her high chair. "Come on to your nana, baby," she murmured softly, rubbing the infant's back. "Your mama has lost her mind, moving your daddy's chair like that."

Vic's mouth fell open and she tried desperately to defend her action. "But the new one we got him is really nice." She glanced over at a giggling Caitlyn, who was nursing Nicolas. "What's so funny?"

Caitlyn wiped away tears of mirth. "I just can't wait to see what kind of stunt A.J.'s going to come up with to get his recliner back."

A.J. stared at the huge flat-screen television in the family room and frowned. "You know, I think the picture is much sharper on the one in the living room. Let's move in there." He glanced over at the other men. "Grab everything and hurry."

Marcel, Ray, Alex, Alcee, Harrison, and George Vincent scrambled from their seats.

Ray nudged Alex. "Grab a kid." He tucked Taylor under his arm sideways and headed for the door.

"Unca Ray . . . Unca Ray," Taylor cried out.

Ray halted and looked down at her. "What's the matter?"

Taylor pointed at the floor.

Ray stooped, picked up Taylor's Oakland A's cap, placed it on backward, and rushed toward the living room.

After Alex hoisted Tyler onto his shoulder, she cupped her hand next his ear.

Alex looked at her with his mouth ajar. "Didn't you just go?"

Tyler shook her head. "That was T-One."

Alex headed down the hallway toward the bathroom and shouted over his shoulder, "Pit stop. Save me a seat."

Marcel snatched up a tray nearby and placed everyone's drinks on it. In his haste, one of the glasses tilted over, spilling most of the contents. "Dammit."

Harrison frantically scanned the room until he spotted one of Vic's plants. He quickly grabbed it and sat it over the huge circle of liquid in the center of the table.

Marcel stared at Harrison. "Think Vic will suspect anything?"

Harrison thought for a moment. "If she asks, we'll tell her one of the babies peed on it."

"Tell her they peed out beer?" Marcel exclaimed.

Harrison shrugged. "Yeah. Now, let's go."

Alcee and George Vincent scooped several bowls of snacks off the table, but one of them crashed to the floor before either could catch it. They glanced down at the crumbs and looked at each other. George Vincent swept everything under an area rug. "You didn't see that, right?"

Alcee shook his head. "Didn't see a thing."

A.J. stopped and answered the door on his way to join the others. K-Mart and Chandler entered, followed by Tara and Lincoln.

"Opening pitch in twenty minutes," A.J. quickly advised before disappearing with K-Mart and Lincoln, leaving Tara and Chandler standing alone in the middle of the foyer.

"Dang!" Chandler placed her hands on her hips. "How is it they can love you all night long and before the National Anthem is sung, you get tossed to the wind?"

Tara nodded. "I know. Same thing here." She shook her head. "It's a sad day when a baseball game can make a man move at the speed of light."

A.J. entered the living room a few moments later and carefully stepped over Taylor, who sat near the television. With his eyes glued on the huge screen, he walked backward to the area where his recliner was usually located and lowered his body. He landed on the floor.

Vic walked in and stared at her husband in bewilderment. "Man, why are you sitting on the floor?"

"My chair . . . my chair," A.J. uttered faintly and stared around him at the empty space. "Honey, it's gone."

Vic knelt in front of him. "Baby, the girls and I brought you a brand-new one." She glanced to the other side of the room and pointed to the plush black leather recliner with a huge bow on top of it. "Don't you think it's gorgeous?"

A.J.'s eyes rolled to the back of his head and he lay back on the floor.

K-Mart rushed over to A.J.'s side. "Doc's hyperventilating."

George Vincent rallied to the defense of a half-conscious A.J. "Sweetheart, you just can't move a man's chair up from under him like that. It's too much of a shock on his system. Look at him."

"I hear ya now," Ray shouted from across the room. "It's a shame. Just a doggone shame." Looking around at the other men, he added, "See, I told y'all this was gonna happen. A bunch of sistas done come in and took over *mon frère's* crib."

Chuckling, Zach sipped his beer. "Yeah, and they running it like the White House, too." Then he looked over at Vic. "Baby Girl, it takes years to break a chair in. Process like that is delicate. Takes time. Ya just can't rush it overnight." He nudged Marcel in the side. "Ain't that right, brother-in-law?"

Marcel nodded. "That's right. A man's home is his castle, and *petit frère's* throne has been removed."

A smiling Alcee scooted to the edge of his seat. "Is he still with us?"

Harrison knelt next to K-Mart and placed his finger at A.J.'s wrist. He smiled when A.J. winked at him. "Pulse is faint."

Vic had seen and heard enough. Baptiste had both outsmarted her and found a way to keep his old chair in front of witnesses. She leaned over him, chuckling. "I'm sorry, your majesty. I was wrong. Please forgive me." She stood and waved at Chandler and Tara. "Come on, y'all. Let's hurry and get this man's chair out of the garage before he really does something crazy."

About five minutes later, A.J. was resting comfortably in his old recliner. Sitting on his lap, Vic looped her arms around his neck. "Happy now?"

A.J.'s eyes were riveted to the flat screen television. When the pitcher reared back and tossed out the first pitch, he stood to his feet and shouted, "Strike."

Vic landed on the floor.

After the game, everyone retreated to the spacious patio area in the backyard where Vic had sat up two huge picnic tables. They feasted on grilled chicken, salad, and all the trimmings.

Moni cleared her throat and pointed to her left earlobe. "Vic, I've been here all day and I'm just now noticing it."

Vic fingered the diamond stud in her ear and smiled.

Brie snorted. "Humph, you going blind here, Sharp-Eye Tate. I didn't say nothing, but it's the first thing I noticed when I got here."

Aimee, who sat next to Vic, leaned over for a closer look. "Looks like the mate to the one A.J. wears."

Vic glanced at Baptiste, who snickered and tried to concentrate on the baby monitor she'd placed in front of them to listen out for Bébé and CeCe, who were asleep in their nursery.

Still seated, Moni placed her hands on her hips and looked directly at Vic. "All right, lady, we need to know what's going on around here."

Zach nudged Moni in the side and beckoned her closer. "Ya got two suspects in this, baby. Bring brother-in-law in for questioning, too."

"Oh, yeah, that's right." Moni turned back around and this time she waggled her finger between Vic and A.J. "Well?"

Everyone nodded their approval of Moni's inquiry and shifted their gaze to Vic and A.J., and waited.

Vic nonchalantly shrugged. "I proposed to Baptiste, that's all."

Caitlyn, Moni, Brie, Aimee, and Chandler said in unison, "You did?"

Tara's eyes filled with tears. "Oh, how romantic," she whispered, sobbing quietly.

Lincoln wrapped his arm around Tara's quivering shoulders. "My baby just gets a little emotional, that's all," he defended when everyone stared at Tara, baffled.

Marcel lifted his glass high in the air in a mock salute. "That's the way to go, *petit frère*. Make them come and ask you."

Caitlyn looked at her husband and huffed. "A man is supposed to propose to a woman properly over a candle-light dinner and soft music." She glanced over at Vic. "Right?"

Vic nodded, but didn't say anything.

Caitlyn turned back to Marcel with her eyes narrowed. "And just what do you mean by that last comment, Marcel Xavier Baptiste?"

Zach came to Marcel's aid. "Now hold up, sister-in-law. Y'all women can make a man flat-out tired chasing around after ya."

Moni whipped her head around and tossed her husband a pointed look. "Now you listen here, Zachary Nathaniel Tate. I was the one," she reminded him with her finger jabbed at his chest, "who had to chase after you, remember?"

Zach dragged his lips slowly across Moni's cheek to a spot right below her ear and whispered, "Yeah, but once I did slow down, I made it up to ya. Didn't I, baby?"

Harrison, Vic's older brother, threw back his head, laughing hard. "Oh, now they're sitting over there acting like they're deaf. Don't go there, Vic and A.J."

Lincoln waved his hand in front of him until he got A.J.'s attention. "Man, what did you tell her?"

A.J. took a sip from his bottle of Perrier. "I told her I didn't know if I wanted to marry her."

Stunned, everyone looked over at A.J., then at Vic, before they yelled out at the same time, "What?"

A.J.'s eyes lovingly raked over Vic. "I also told her she needed to convince me."

Alex lifted his brows. "That's a joke, right?"

K-Mart pulled out his cell phone and flipped it open. "What's Cates' number? We need to run another CT scan on you, doc."

Chandler sat next to K-Mart. "That's right, baby. Tell him to make that two, and schedule Vic's first."

"Whatcha mean, *convince*?" Ray shouted loud enough for the neighbors next door to hear him. "Ain't raising four kids persuasion enough? In a minute, ya gonna need a Hummer to transport everybody."

Mama Z sat to the right of Louise and whispered, "Must be waiting on blessings from the church."

Alcee nodded. "That's right. It takes about six months to get approval for a Catholic wedding, you know."

George Vincent lifted his brow. "Well, we Baptists got it down to a three-step process." He gently nudged Louise. "Huh, baby?"

Louise nodded. "That's right. A license, the preacher, and fifty dollars, and it's a done deal."

Zach reached over and grabbed a chicken leg off a platter. "So, Baby Girl, what did brother-in-law tell ya?"

The only thing Vic could do was smile at the memory of how she'd convinced Baptiste to marry her. It was a night she'd never forget. She tossed a sultry wink at him. "Nothing."

"You couldn't talk him into marrying you," Moni gasped, in disbelief.

Vic shook her head. "No, I was able to convince him."

"How?" Moni asked.

Vic smiled. "We eloped."

"Eloped?" everyone shouted.

Vic nodded and tugged at her left earlobe.

Three days later, Vic was happy that Baptiste's sisters, Brie, Moni, and Aimee, along with Chandler and Tara, talked her into having her bridal shower, which was hosted by her new sister-in-law Caitlyn. She loved all of them even more for insisting the event take place at the hospital so that Valerie, Brianna and Chloé's mother, could join in the festivities. Even though Valerie had long recovered from her injuries, Vic was happy that her husband and Zach had somehow arranged for her to remain at the hospital for her own safety while waiting to learn if she qualified for the Witness Protection Program.

After opening Vic's gifts, the women spent the next hour looking at the new pictures and videos of Bébé and

CeCe that Vic had brought along for Valerie to see. Then, Vic turned to Valerie and made an announcement.

"All right," Vic said happily, looking over at Valerie. "Are you ready to receive your presents?"

Valerie's eyes glossed with tears when Vic unwrapped a gift box and lifted out a silk bed jacket. "Thank you, Vic." She ran her hand along the surface of the smooth, turquoise-colored garment and choked back a sob. "I-I ain't had nothing this pretty before."

"Well, that's only one of your gifts," Vic said as she helped Valerie slip into the bed jacket.

Valerie looked up at Vic, baffled. "There's another one?"

Vic nodded and leaned over and whispered in Valerie's ear.

Valerie was speechless for a moment and then stared, stunned, at the smiling faces of everyone in the room. Vic had told her Zach gave his permission and that Bébé and CeCe were downstairs in the lobby with Louise and Mama Z, waiting to see her.

"Are you ready to go?" Vic asked.

Valerie beamed with excitement. "Oh, yes. I can't wait to see my babies again." She looked around the room at Brie, Moni, Aimee, Caitlyn, Tara, and Chandler. "I've had so much fun today. Thank you for having Vic's shower here, and thank you for my presents."

Vic gave Valerie a big hug. "We've had fun, too, sweetie." Vic rolled a wheelchair next to the bed. "Come on and get in."

"Why do I have to go in this?" Valerie asked, frowning, but followed Vic's instructions.

Vic smiled. "Officially, you're still a patient and it's hospital policy that patients be transported in a wheelchair, even if they don't need it."

Valerie nodded. "I can't wait a minute longer," she said gleefully. "Come on, Vic, let's go."

Vic chuckled. "All right, all right. Ready?"

One of the floor nurses walked inside the room and stared at everyone. She shifted her focus dead on Valerie. "And just where do you think you're going, young lady?"

Vic stepped in front of the nurse. "She's on her way to the imaging department downstairs."

The nurse frowned. "I don't recall that request in her chart. Wait right here," she advised and quickly walked out the room.

Valerie glanced up at Vic with a panicked expression on her face. "She's not going to let me go, Vic. What we gonna do?"

Caitlyn nodded in agreement. "Vic, we'll never get Valerie past the nurses' station now."

Vic chuckled. "Child, I've been around Baptiste too long not to get past this. I've also managed to pick up a few tricks of my own," she added. She pulled her cell phone from her purse and made a call.

"Oh, Vic," Tara said fretfully, "we've got to hurry before that nurse comes back."

"Settle down," Vic said with confidence. "Betcha we get Valerie downstairs to see her babies."

Vic noticed how everyone stared at her with their mouths wide open, and she couldn't much blame them. Even she noticed the calmness of her demeanor. Before, she would have walked the nurse up one side and down the other. Patience had never been her greatest virtue, and here she was now calmly waiting, assessing the situation at hand, and contemplating a clever way to get around it.

Chandler quipped, "Lord, have mercy. Yeah, you changed all right. Ain't even worried about the time, either."

Vic chuckled. "Y'all know that man of mine don't rush for nothing." She shrugged. "Guess a little bit of that has rubbed off on me."

The nurse entered the room again with Valerie's chart in her hand and flipped through the pages. "I was right. There are no orders in here for her to go down to imaging."

"Is the patient ready?" Louise asked when she rushed inside the room after receiving a call on her cell phone from Zach, who told her the trouble Vic was having with the nurse on duty. She stopped by the ER to change into a set of scrubs.

The baffled nurse stared blankly at Louise. "Who are you?"

Louise quickly flashed her employee badge. "Imaging department."

Vic's eyes traveled over the nurse as her mind played out the steps of what she'd told Zach she was going to do, and she knew her timing had to be precise. She glanced over at Moni with a knowing look. Moni winked, acknowledging she understood the unspoken request, and eased next to Brie to nudge her in the side. In return, Brie nudged Aimee.

The nurse shook her head and flipped through the sheets once again, starting from the beginning. "But there isn't an order from her doctor for any X rays—"

"What?" Moni cried out. "Let me see this . . ." She plucked the chart from the nurse and began thumbing through the pages.

"You lost our sister's orders," Brie exclaimed.

"Get her doctor on the phone, right now," Aimee shouted.

"No, no," the nurse stuttered with a baffled look and pointed to Valerie's medical chart. "I-I'm sure the orders are in there someplace."

Tapping her foot, Moni handed the chart back to the nurse and tilted her head at it. "Well, start looking."

The nurse looked a second time and briefly raised her head to give Brie a panic-stricken stare.

Brie gestured at the chart. "Don't look at me."

Aimee peered over the nurse's shoulder when she stopped to scan one of the pages. "That's not it. Keep going," she instructed and drew her arm around her back, flashing a thumbs-up to Vic.

While her sister-in-laws had the rattled nurse, who was now mumbling to herself, preoccupied, Vic pushed Valerie's wheelchair to the door and mouthed to Caitlyn, "Open it."

Vic chuckled out loud once they'd all crowded inside the elevator, along with Valerie's police escort, and headed for the lobby. If the nurse got that flustered over not being able to find a medical order, she wondered what would happen once she discovered she was by herself in an empty room.

The next day, A.J. groped for the phone the moment it rang and woke him from a dead sleep. He glanced at the clock on the nightstand. The red illuminated numbers indicated it was three o'clock in the morning.

"Dr. Baptiste," he answered drowsily, pushing himself upright in bed.

Vic stirred and sat up as well, staring intently at Baptiste's face. She mouthed, "Who is it?"

A.J. nodded. "I'll be right there."

"Baptiste, what's wrong?"

He turned to her, the color draining from his face. "That was Zach."

"Baptiste, what's wrong?" she asked anxiously, her heart pounding inside her chest. "Is it Moni? Little Zach?"

A.J. shook his head and sighed. "It's Valerie."

CHAPTER 16

"Oh, Jesus," Vic whispered against the hand covering her mouth. The moment she and Baptiste rounded the nurses' station, she looked at the scene in front of her and grew numb.

Her eyes darted wildly at the swarm of police officers along the hospital corridor. When she noticed the yellow tape used by law enforcement at a crime scene stuck across Valerie's door, her heart lunged out of rhythm.

As soon as Baptiste told her something had happened to Valerie, she'd phoned her parents, Louise and George Vincent. They, along with A.J.'s father, Alcee, arrived within fifteen minutes to care for the girls. Afterwards, she and Baptiste raced over to Highland Hospital.

Vic spotted Zach a few feet away from Valerie's room and ran up to him. "Zach, w-what's wrong? W-What's happened to Valerie?"

Zach, who was talking to a detective named Wallace, faced Vic. "Come on, y'all. Let's go somewhere more private."

Zach, along with Wallace, led A.J. and Vic down the hallway toward the waiting area. He dragged his hand down his face, and blew out a hard breath. "Baby Girl, I-I'm sorry to tell ya this . . ." He paused, staring at the floor. "Valerie's dead."

"D-Dead?" Vic stuttered, in shock. She stepped backwards, her back colliding with Baptiste's chest. "B-But how?"

Zach opened his mouth, and then closed it. Planting a hand at the base of his neck, he tried again. "One of the nurses went to check and found her unresponsive. "He gave A.J. solemn look. "Appears to be a drug overdose."

"How?" A.J. asked, his voice wobbly.

"Had to be an injection, brother-in-law, 'cause we found the syringe next to her."

Vic shook Zach hard by the shoulders as tears began to roll down her cheeks. "*No!* I-I just saw Valerie yesterday. She was happy. She got to see her babies . . . and hold them." She shook him even harder this time. "Zach, no," she whimpered. "*No . . .*"

Zach drew Vic to his chest to comfort her. "It's gonna be okay, Baby Girl." He patted her quivering shoulders. "I know how ya feelin' right now." After several moments, he placed both hands on Vic's shoulders and positioned her upright. "Valerie was under a under a lot of pressure. Guess she just couldn't handle things no mo'."

Stunned, the only thing A.J. could do was rock on his heels. Of all the drug-addicted teenagers he'd treated in the past, he felt Valerie had the best shot of overcoming her addition. Hearing the news that she'd succumbed to her addiction shook him to the core. "Zach . . . when did it happen?"

"A little past one," Zach said. "As soon as the nurse found her, she reported it to the officer on duty at the time. He called me. I got here as soon as I could."

Vic backed away from Zach, her spine rigid, her temper escalating. "Somebody better start talking to me . . . and talk fast," Vic cried out hysterically. "How did Valerie get a hold of drugs in the first place when she's been under 24/7 police protection?"

Zach pursed his lips, and then finally said, "Baby Girl, apparently Valerie was using all along. Found out I gotta a low-life cop on my team, and from what I can gather, he'd been slipping drugs to her on his shift. Don't worry. I know who he is, and I'm gonna arrest him personally."

Vic brushed the tears from her face with both hands. As a nurse, she was familiar with death, but had never received the news that someone close to her had died. Her legs grew numb and she slithered weakly to the chair behind her, bursting into tears again.

"Morgue?" A.J. asked.

Zach nodded. "Got my men contacting Valerie's next of kin now."

Zach sat next to Vic and grabbed her hand, squeezing it tight. "Baby Girl, ain't nothing mo' ya can do now. Let brother-in-law take ya back home, all right?"

Vic shook her head. "I-I want to see her, Zach."

"Honey . . ." A.J. uttered gently, taking his seat on the opposite side of Vic.

"I'm not going anywhere, Baptiste," Vic said in a cracking voice, filled with fierce determination, "not until I see Valerie."

A.J. placed his hands on Vic's shoulders. "Honey, you can't—"

"B-But, Baptiste," Vic cried, even though she knew he was right. Although it had been a while since she'd worked in a clinical setting, she knew the protocol—that when a patient died, their body was taken to the hospital morgue until the next of kin was notified.

"Brother-in-law's right," Zach said. "Listen, I know how tight ya was with Valerie. But ya also know the rules. The coroner is on his way, and after he officially rules on the death he'll release Valerie's body to her next of kin."

Wallace hesitated for a moment before he said, "Lieutenant—"

"Wallace, why don't ya escort Dr. and Mrs. Baptiste back to their car," Zach suggested, jerking his head toward the elevators. "We just 'bout to wrap things up here."

A.J. urged Vic to her feet. Slipping her hand inside his, they followed Wallace toward the elevators. They'd gotten half way down the corridor when he patted the detective on the shoulder. After speaking to him briefly, he placed a light kiss on Vic's cheek and headed back toward Zach.

"Zach, have you been able to locate the car that hit Honey?"

It was the one question A.J. had pondered constantly since Vic had undergone hypnosis nine days earlier. But their elopement to Las Vegas, coupled with Vic's bridal shower, had prevented him from finding out the answer.

Zach turned to face A.J., nodding. "Yeah. Ran the plates before you and Baby Girl left the police station."

"Well?"

"Belongs to a Carmen Jenkins."

"Did she explain how someone else ended up driving it?"

"Nope. She said it was stolen two days before the accident."

With his gazed fixed on the wall, A.J. rubbed the muscles that had started to knot at the back of his neck. *Carmen Jenkins.* Why was this particular name so familiar? Then he remembered there was a nurse Vic had hired from the nursing registry to help out at the clinic for a couple of days after it first opened. But were they one and the same? "Honey told me she'd fired a nurse named Carmen Jenkins the day Valerie came to the clinic."

"Do tell," Zach said, quickly retrieving the notepad from inside his jacket. He jotted down everything A.J. had said.

"So, how did Scooter end up driving her car the night of the accident?"

"Can't answer that for ya right now, brother-in-law. Gimme a couple of hours, though." Pulling back his jacket, he slipped the notepad back inside and tucked his pen behind his ear. "Ya can best believe if I was sporting around in a $250,000 Lamborghini and it came up missing, everybody in the state of California would know about it."

A.J. sighed, frustrated. Nothing that he'd seen or heard in the last thirty minutes made any sense.

Somehow he managed to focus his attention back on the issue at hand. "You do plan to talk to the Carmen Jenkins I'm referring to?"

Zach answered with a wink.

"Have you talked to Scooter yet?"

"Naw, 'cause he don' gone deep undercover. Ain't been able to locate him—yet. But ya can put this on my grandmama's headstone." He inched up to A.J., only inches separating them. "Don't care if I gotta look under every rock in town," he paused, spacing his words out evenly, "I'ma find Tony Grice."

A couple of days later after Valerie's cremation, Marcel and Ray, along with Alcee and K-Mart, hosted a bachelor party for A.J.

After Marcel had made a round of drinks, everyone lifted their glasses up in a toast to the groom. Afterwards, they all retreated to the family room for a game of pool.

"Brother-in-law," Zach shouted out to Marcel, walking in thirty minutes later, after he'd gotten off duty. "Need my . . ." His words stopped when everyone pointed to a bottle of Crown Royal and a shot glass sitting on top of a table.

A.J. walked over to Zach. "What's wrong?

"Been out tryin' to find our friend Scooter." Zach took a big gulp from the drink he'd poured and sighed. "That's the reason I'm late." He glanced around the room. "The women ain't here, are they?"

A.J. shook his head.

Zach sat heavily on a barstool as everyone surrounded him. "Good. They don't need to be hearing none of this no way."

With a hard glitter in his eyes, A.J. softly drawled, "Hear what?"

Zach turned his head sideways toward A.J. "The only reason I'm tellin' ya any of this is 'cause ya clinic is involved."

A.J. lifted his brows. "Exactly what do you mean my clinic is involved?"

Zach palmed his glass. "It was interesting that the nurse ya told me about and the woman the car belonged to had the same name. Thought it might have been a coincidence, at first. Trusted my gut, though, and followed up on the lead. Discovered that *my* Carmen Jenkins and *your* Carmen Jenkins are one and the same. So, I decided to dig a little mo'. Took a peek at her finances while I was at it, too." He tossed the rest of his drink down and sighed again. "She's loaded."

K-Mart sat on the barstool next to Zach. "Perhaps she comes from a wealthy family." He shrugged. "That could explain her money, right?"

Zach snorted at K-Mart. "Ain't nothin' in Jenkins's background to suggest her having that kinda dough." He pointed to his three brother-in-laws. "All of them can justify their bank rolls 'cause they legit. But one and one ain't coming up to two with Jenkins."

A.J. stood behind the bar and leaned forward, bracing his weight on his elbows. "Zach, you never answered me. How's my clinic involved?"

Zach pushed his empty shot glass to the side. "Remembering me tellin' ya that Jenkins said her car was stolen two days before the accident?"

A.J. nodded.

"Well, my antennae went up when I found out she didn't make a report to the police or her insurance company. And it's real strange how the same car was ticketed for a moving violation on the afternoon of the accident. So there's no way it could've been stolen before the crash like she said."

Alcee placed his whiskey next to Zach's empty shot glass. "How did you find out that this Jenkins woman was lying?"

"Father-in-law," Zach replied, "some of the toughest cases I've ever cracked happened because I trusted my gut. I went back and checked my notes 'cause I remembered somethin' Valerie told me."

"And?" Marcel said.

"After talkin' to brother-in-law the other night, took a chance and checked out parking and moving violations," Zach answered. "Bingo. A red Lamborghini belonging to one Carmen Jenkins got a moving violation the same afternoon as the accident."

"Hold up, Zach," Ray said, growing testy. "Who was driving the car when it was ticketed?"

Zach took another sip of his drink and sighed with satisfaction. "Jenkins."

"My clinic," A.J. said again.

"Trust me, brother-in-law. Jenkins, Scooter, and ya clinic are all stirring together in the same pot."

A.J.'s jaw tightened and the muscles along his neck corded. "How?"

Zach shook his head. "Let me worry 'bout that. The only thing I want ya to do is keep Baby Girl away from the clinic for awhile."

"Why?" A.J. asked, although the task wouldn't be hard. Since the day Bébé and CeCe came to live with them, Vic hadn't worked at the clinic. His eyes narrowed. "Is Honey in some sort of danger?"

Zach sighed. "I don't believe so, but I don't wanna take any chances. These hood rats I'm dealin' with don't play."

A.J. sighed softly; he knew Zach wasn't telling him everything. "Zach—"

"Brother-in-law, leave it be."

"I don't believe none of this," Ray snarled, pacing in a circle. "Come on, Zach, let me go get Alex and we'll find this Scooter and tag his ass. Betcha when we finish with him, he'll come running to ya."

"Boy," Zach said, loosening his tie and slipping the top button of his shirt free. "Go sit ya lanky behind down somewhere. Ain't got time to hunt down the bad guys and worry about locking up kinfolk, too."

"So, what if someone could help you find Scooter?" A.J. asked. He casually added, "Like me?"

"What!" Zach stared at A.J. for a moment and shook his head. "Naw, naw. Ya talkin' crazy, brother-in-law."

A.J. smiled mirthlessly. "No, I'm not."

"Whatever crazy scheme that's running through ya mind, forget about it," Zach shot back. He shook his head again. "*I'll* find Scooter."

A.J. responded to Zach's request with an apathetic shrug, his mind already in motion to figure out a way to find the man responsible for a chain of events that had placed his wife in harm's way, supplied drugs to Valerie that ultimately caused her death, and was now threatening the dream that had taken him so long to turn into reality. "So, you're sitting here telling me that if the roles were reversed and Moni was involved, you wouldn't do whatever was necessary to get to the bottom of things?"

"Hell, naw," Zach yelled. "All of y'all know I'd walk to the moon and back for Moni." Slowly, he dragged his hand down his face, releasing a hard breath. "My gut is tellin' me that Jenkins and Grice are mixed up in some shady shit. I wanna lock their asses away as bad as you do."

"Well, with everything you've learned so far, why can't you?" Marcel asked.

"Ain't got enough on either one of them to make a charge stick," Zach blurted out.

A.J.'s eyes were flat. "So let me get this straight." He bent his fingers back as he made his points. "There's a nurse who worked at my clinic, who almost allowed a patient to die, not to mention had a run-in with my wife, and who is obviously involved in some type of drug trafficking with Scooter who, by the way, beat Valerie to the point she had to be hospitalized. Scooter's on the loose and Valerie's dead from drugs that one of *your* officers slipped to her, and there's nothing the police can do anything about it. Is that what you're telling me, Zach?"

Zach turned to face A.J. "Brother-in-law, let the system bring 'em to justice."

"Why can't you arrest Jenkins and Scooter when you find him?" A.J.'s tone was as rigid as a steel beam.

Zach sighed loudly. "'Cause I know how the system works. If I arrest Grice and Jenkins without enough evidence against them, they'll lay down a fat retainer to some big-shot lawyer, along with their sob stories, and I can't get within ten feet of 'em."

Marcel cleared his throat. "Zach, perhaps if you put the word on the street that the D.A. is willing to offer a plea-bargain to Scooter, he'd come out of hiding."

"Hell to the no," Ray shouted. "We ain't got time to be plotting and planning, and waiting on the D.A. to decide jack." He lifted his brows at Marcel. "You wasn't talkin' about no plea bargain when Mazzei nutted up and said the wrong thing to Little Bit," he added, referring to his nickname for Marcel's wife. "Now was ya?"

A.J. glanced at Marcel, remembering how he'd lunged like a madman at his wife's ex-boyfriend after he'd threatened her with physical violence in front of him. A cynical smile touched his lips because what he had in mind to find Scooter would put his older brother's actions to shame.

K-Mart stood next to Ray and nudged him in the side. "What did Marcel do?"

Ray snorted. "If Little Bit hadn't stopped him, *mon frère* was gonna beat his ass to death."

Zach snatched the cell phone clipped at his waist and answered on the second ring. "Tate." He nodded as he listened, then disconnected the call and stood. "That was my wife, and I'm going home to her." He headed for the door, but suddenly whirled around at the graveyard silence in the room. "*You*," he said, staring dead at A.J. "go home to ya wife and babies." Glancing around at the other men, he issued a stern warning. "And if any of y'all get involved with this mess, I'll lock up every single last one of ya. Ya hear me?"

Marcel escorted Zach to the front door. When he returned to the family room, he locked his gaze with A.J.'s. "Go find him, *petit frère.*"

A.J. nodded, then glanced over at K-Mart. "Remember the game of execution we tried out in medical school?"

"*We?*" K-Mart's eyes bulged as he walked backward, colliding with the pool table. "That was your crazy idea. I only came along to watch because I didn't think you'd have the nerve to do it." He paused. "Doc, you're not thinking what I think you're thinking—" He swallowed, and in a strangled voice mumbled, "Are you?"

For reasons he might never get the answer to, his woman, his family, everything he'd worked hard to bring to the community he loved had innocently become tangled in a web of corruption. A.J. offered a smile that would have run chills down the spine of the most hardened criminal.

"B-but, doc, we could lose our medical license if anyone finds out," K-Mart stuttered.

"I know," A.J. softly acknowledged.

"Doc . . ." K-Mart blew out a hard breath.

"Let me ask you this." A.J. walked up to K-Mart and braced his feet apart. "If Chandler was in the middle of all of this would you do anything differently?"

"Same way as before, right?" K-Mart asked without hesitation.

A.J. nodded. "*Oui.*"

Later that night, A.J. sat on the side of the bed with his head down and didn't realize Vic had entered from the bathroom until she touched his shoulders, her fingertips gently kneading the tightness in his muscles.

"Baptiste?" she whispered, kneeling behind him. "Baby, what's wrong?"

"Nothing, *mon amour*," he lied, focusing straight ahead in an effort to collect his thoughts.

"Something's wrong. I can feel it. Come on now."

Slowly, he scooted around to his left in order to curve his arm around her waist, and his gaze locked with hers. The only thing he could think about was how he'd fought for months to win her love and rid her of the pain she'd suffered because of a man's betrayal. His heart said to tell her the thoughts that had dominated his mind most of the evening, but his instincts overruled them. What he needed to do to protect her and their family, he had to do alone. He drew in a breath, let half of it out, and gently pulled her closer to him.

With his hands cupped around her face, he gently moved his thumbs along her cheeks and realized he'd always loved this woman. He loved her strength, her spirit, and her courage. He silently vowed to love, honor, and cherish her until his dying day.

He stood, drawing her with him, and gradually peeled off her robe, which landed at her feet. His kiss was unhurried with a tenderness that had him reeling, and he barely heard his name tumble softly from her lips. He watched her eyes drift close as his hands glided along her arms before traveling languidly across her lush breasts, down the curves of her full hips. Her rising body heat set off his blazing desire.

"Tell me what you want, Honey," he whispered huskily with his lips pressed in the crook of her neck.

She inched her hand between them and gently rubbed his throbbing sex. "This."

He sucked in a deep breath to ward off an ache that had never felt so good. "Where do you want it?"

"Anywhere you put it."

It only took a second for him to slip out of his pajama bottoms and place Vic with her back against the mattress. "Here?" he asked in a whisper, pressing his rigid flesh against her thigh. His tongue traced her lips in unhurried strokes that promised to send them both into a world of heated sensations.

She pulled the band from his ponytail, buried her fingers in his hair and whispered, "No."

When his fingers probed at her center and slipped inside her warmth, a deep ache racked his body. "Right here?"

She nodded and lifted her hips in welcome invitation. "Right there."

Eyes connected again, hearts merged, as man and woman moved together in slow, perfect sync as lovers countless times before them had. Yet he was certain no one had ever loved as deeply, completely, and passionately as they were doing—as they always would.

Blocking out the uncertainty of what he might discover, he concentrated instead on what he'd already found. Halting, he looked down at her, grateful for the opportunity to witness what every man should—the beauty of the woman he loved in the throes of passion with lips parted and eyes half-closed with desire.

"*Je t'aime*," he hoarsely whispered and started his rhythm again. He increased his pace—harder, faster, and deeper than before, wanting a glorious victory with her right at his side. When he felt her body shudder beneath him, he threw back his head to thrust one last time, surrendering to a climax so powerful, his tears mingled with hers.

He'd done nothing in life so far and probably never would to deserve the love of Victoria Louise Bennett Baptiste. Resting his cheek on hers, his eyes slid closed, and all the love any man could ever imagine for one woman penetrated into her sweat-drenched skin.

So much uncertainty was before him, but one thing was for sure. When a man loved a woman, he'd risk his own life in order to save hers.

It was a little past nine when Vic finally got the girls settled in for the night. After turning on the baby monitor and easing the door to Brianna and Chloe's nursery closed, she headed straight for Baptiste's office.

In her heart she'd known for weeks that he was keeping something from her. The sudden late night meetings and the abrupt ending to phone calls whenever she entered the room had made her even more determined tonight to find out exactly what was going on. If there was one thing she knew about her husband, he documented everything, and she wasn't leaving his office until she discovered what he'd been hiding from her. Seated at Baptiste's desk, she opened the bottom drawer where he kept his diary.

"Oh, my God," Vic whispered over and over, carefully reading every entry he'd made for the last six weeks. "How could you do this?"

Slamming the diary shut, she picked up the phone. Listening to the second ring, she mumbled, "Baptiste, whenever I see you again . . . I'm gonna kill you."

CHAPTER 17

"Scooter," A.J. drawled quietly, straddled across his chair backward inside his office at the health clinic. "I'm glad you finally let me meet the rest of the members on your team."

The day after his bachelor party, A.J. hit the streets and found Tony "Scooter" Grice himself. It hadn't been an easy task, though, gaining Scooter's trust under the alias of Andre Rousselle, his paternal grandfather's name. The worry of Carmen Jenkins and Lesea Goldberg discovering his identity didn't trouble him, either. Neither had a clue as to what he looked like. He'd checked the logs Vic kept for the nurses on her staff and both Jenkins and Goldberg had only worked at the clinic twice before being fired. And on each occasion, he'd been away at a conference. Only Chanta, the clinic's receptionist, knew of his relationship with Vic.

He'd gained Scooter's trust by pretending to have met Valerie months earlier as a distributor for the drugs she ran for one of the most sophisticated drug operations in Oakland. With each passing day, he'd learned a great deal of information and drawn one step closer to finding out the truth as to why his clinic had been selected as a site for the distribution of illegal drugs.

"Know what, playa, you right." A wry smile turned Scooter's lips upward as he nodded to Carmen Jenkins and Lesea Goldberg, who stood next to him. "And the people on your side you said could help us move our merchandise, they all squared away, right?"

A.J. nodded. "As a matter of fact they're in the other room." He stood and jerked his head at the door. "Let's go across the hall and meet them."

A few moments later, A.J. Scooter, Carmen and Lesea entered. Marcel, Ray, Alex and K-Mart greeted them.

"Have a seat, Scooter." A.J. nodded at a chair positioned next to a table with a file folder in the center.

Scooter stood in front of the chair, his eyes darting in five different directions once he noticed the set-up in the room. "What the hell kinda shit is this?"

Alex clamped his hand hard on Scooter's shoulder and pushed down. "Sit."

With both palms flat against the table, A.J. leaned forward. "The kind," he hissed softly, "that's guaranteed to make you tell me what I need to know."

Carmen glanced around the room. "W-Who are these people?"

A.J. relaxed and straightened his body, flashing a crafty grin. "My execution team." He walked around the room and introduced everyone, starting at his left. "This is the gentleman who'll argue on your behalf." He nodded at Marcel. He walked down to Ray and tilted his head toward him. "Good to see you, Your Honor." Turning around to face Scooter, he winked. "I'm sure you've spent a lot of time before judges, right?" He glanced behind him at Alex. "You've already been introduced to Bailiff Robinson." He had only one mission now: find out how Carmen Jenkins and Lesea Goldberg were connected to Scooter and why they'd selected his clinic for their drug operation. Shutting out everything, he moved to a chair in the corner and propped his feet atop a small desk.

Scooter turned in his seat and looked over at a smiling K-Mart who sat on top of a hospital gurney with an IV stand attached. "W-Who's he?"

"Oh," A.J. replied, snapping his fingers. "He's the one in charge of executions on my team, but I don't believe you want to meet him." He laced his hands behind his head. "There's only one thing I want to know. Who killed Valerie?"

"Killed?" Scooter snorted. "You got it mixed up, player. Val overdosed."

A.J. shook his head. "That's not what I heard. The word on the streets is that Valerie's death from an overdose was actually murder, and you're the murderer."

Sweat beaded across Scooter's forehead. "I-I ain't heard nothing like that. I don't know whatcha talkin' about."

"Oh, hell naw, *mon frère*," Ray shouted out. "Friend's trying to play us here." He glanced at K-Mart. "G'on head and shoot him up!"

K-Mart lifted a syringe and slowly pushed it in until a tiny stream of liquid was released.

"Don't you say another word, Scooter," Carmen shouted.

A.J. cleared his throat. "Scooter, I'm waiting."

"I ain't tellin' you shit," Scooter nervously chuckled, pointing a finger to his chest. "I got rights, and the only person I talk to is my attorney."

"Shut up," Ray growled and abruptly stood to his feet. "Ya don't know how to spell *right*, let alone know the meaning of it."

"Your Honor, I object." Marcel rose to his feet, smiling. "Could I have a moment to confer with my client?" He pulled up a chair next to Scooter and stretched his arm along the back of it. "Mr. Grice," he uttered smoothly, running his left hand down the length of his silk tie. "I believe it would be in your best interest to cooperate fully with the court."

Scooter snatched his head around at A.J. "Is he supposed to be some kinda lawyer?"

A.J. shook his head.

Marcel flashed a condescending smile. "I do believe I was introduced as the one who'll argue on your behalf."

"Argue against what?" Scooter shouted.

"*Your* death," Marcel replied calmly.

Lesea cried out, "Scooter—"

"Don't listen to her," A.J. warned in a dangerously fierce tone. "Why did you kill Valerie?"

"Man, I'm tellin' you, I don't know whatcha talkin' about," Scooter stuttered.

A.J. stood and walked over to the door and opened it. A few seconds later, Lincoln, Vic's brother walked inside. After a brief nod, they walked back over to Scooter.

Turning to Lincoln with a proffered hand, A.J. smiled. "Prosecutor Bennett, I'm happy you could join us. This is Tony Grice." His gaze connected with Scooter's, who was now on his feet.

Lincoln stilled and his eyes flared when he spotted the huge wet circle on the front of Scooter's pants. Leaning slightly over toward A.J., he whispered, "Do you think this is going to work?"

A.J. nodded and whispered, "Five more minutes is all I need." Picking up the folder on the table, he looked at Scooter and made a tsking sound. "Scooter, you made a terrible mess on the floor."

A.J. shuffled through the folder containing every detail of the conversations he'd documented for the last six weeks. Also, he hoped that if he alleged that Scooter killed Valerie, he'd try and clear himself and possibly offer a piece of information that he normally wouldn't have otherwise. "From what we've discussed, I know you and your team have operated in the big league. I think Prosecutor Bennett's department would be very interested in learning more about how things really work, as well as why you killed Valerie. Right, Prosecutor Bennett?"

Lincoln smiled. "That's right."

A.J. smiled again as he continued to scan over the papers. "You're running cocaine, crack, and I believe you told me a little money laundering is involved, too. This clinic isn't the place you're going to do it. Now, once again, why did you kill Valerie?"

"I-I didn't kill, Val. Honest to God," Scooter stammered and half rose from his seat.

Alex calmly walked over and pointed his empty Glock at Scooter's temple. "Sit down. Court's still in session."

Ray was on his feet in an instant. "Man, you and your folks ain't presented no defense. Guilty as charged. I hereby sentence you to death by lethal injection." He glanced at K-Mart, again. "Stick him!"

"Guilty?" Scooter cried out, squirming as Marcel and Alex strapped him to the hospital gurney.

K-Mart patted Scooter's shoulders. "This won't take long, *if* I can find a nice big vein." He tightened a rubber tourniquet around the upper portion of Scooter's arm. "You'll be gone in less than three minutes."

A.J. pulled back a white sheet covering a tray with three syringes laying on it.

Scooter's eyes grew wide with fear. "W-What you gonna do, man?"

A.J.'s expression was vacant. "You heard the judge. We're going to carry out his order of execution. Now, let me explain the process to you." He picked up a syringe and waved it in the air. "This contains sodium pentothal, a real nice drug . . . it will knock you out fast." He pointed to the second syringe. "Oh, now this one might hurt a little. It's called pancuronium, and it makes your muscles contract. But that's okay." He half-smiled and shifted his gaze to the third syringe. "Aaah, this one is potassium chloride. It will stop your heart in an instant and will make up for any pain you might feel." He looked down at Scooter and fingered his moustache with his free hand. "I think this is an excellent payback for killing Valerie. Don't you?"

"G'on head and take him out here," Ray bellowed.

A.J. lowered the syringe, inserting the tip of the needle into the catheter attached to the I.V. "Nighty-night."

"Wait," Scooter shouted. "I didn't kill Val."

A.J. looked up with narrowed his eyes. "Somebody did."

"I-It wasn't me. And none of this was never suppose to go this far . . . I swear to God," Scooter nervously admitted.

"Don't bring God up in this." A.J. sat on the side of the gurney. "Talk to me."

Because of the restraints, Scooter could only turn his head toward A.J. "Me and Val, w-we was just running for 'em, that's all."

"Shut up!" Carmen ordered.

"Running for who?" A.J. asked with limited patience.

"G-Goldberg . . ." Scooter stammered.

A.J.'s brow lifted slightly and he focused intently on Scooter. "How's Goldberg involved?"

"S-She da one ya want. Been heading up for a couple of years. Had a smooth gig going, too. Nobody suspected her 'cause she's a nurse and all. Cops don't never look at them kind. Just come down hard on a brother working the streets," he added sarcastically.

"You aren't in a position to be making wisecracks, Scooter," A.J. reminded.

"I-I didn't know nothin' about her at first. Nobody did. Always stayed in the background. That's how come she was able to pull it off. Know what I'm saying?"

A.J. shook his head.

Scooter swallowed the lump in his throat. "Man, that's all I know."

"Is that why you beat Valerie up?" A.J. asked.

"Had to. Got a call one day for me to do it. Order came down from the big boss. Plus, Val upped and called 'bout that reward."

"What's the name of the person heading your drug operation?" A.J. drawled.

"I-I don't know the real name," Scooter supplied nervously.

A.J. smiled mirthlessly. "What's the name you know?"

Scooter hesitated.

A.J. began to slowly push down on the syringe.

"Gotti," Scooter yelled out at the top of his lungs.

"Have you ever seen Gotti?" A.J. asked.

Before he got an answer, A.J. snatched his head up at the squeaky sound the door hinges made, indicating someone was entering the room.

Trembling with fear, Vic flung the door open and looked straight ahead. "Baptiste . . ."

"Scooter, this is a set-up," Jenkins shouted as she lunged towards Vic.

Primitive instincts took over and without hesitation, A.J. dropped the syringe and dove in front of Vic the second Goldberg pulled a gun from her purse and pointed it in Vic's direction.

A single shot rang out.

With his body shielding Vic's, A.J. offered a silent prayer of thanks that the shot had missed its intended target.

An hour later, Vic and A.J. stood in the interrogation room with their fingers laced together, along with Zach, Agent Doreen Givens, aka Lesea Goldberg, who worked with the DEA.

Agent Givens sat at the table with her fingers hooked in front of her, shaking her head in welcomed relief and exuberance. "Well, Jenkins, you've certainly made the department work for our paychecks the last couple of years." She smiled. "I didn't ever think I'd ever crack your ring, Gotti."

"What are you talking about?" Jenkins sarcastically asked. "You don't have a bit of evidence against me."

Zach flashed a smile of victory at Agent Givens. "She's got enough to take you and Scooter down, Jenkins."

Agent Givens leaned forward and looked directly at Jenkins. "I have to admit, Gotti, your organization was one of the best I've seen."

Jenkins glared at Vic. "This is your fault."

Vic flinched, but held her composure and remained silent when she felt A.J. give her hand a tight squeeze.

Zach turned to his officer. "Read Ms. Jenkins her—"

"Allow me, Lieutenant," Agent Givens offered, a smile curving the corners of her lips. "I've waited over two years for this moment."

Afterward, Agent Givens stepped aside to allow the uniformed Oakland police officer to escort Carmen Jenkins, alias Gotti, out of the room.

Vic released a long sigh of relief and chuckled the moment the door closed. "Zach, remind me to never get on your bad side." Then she glanced over at Agent Givens. "How were you able to put all of this together?"

"First of all, Mrs. Baptiste," Agent Givens said, "let me apologize for not doing anything to help you with Valerie that day she came to the clinic. It broke my heart to have to stand back and not come to her aid, but if I'd said or done anything, my cover would have been blown."

Vic smiled. "I understand."

Agent Givens smiled back. "But I knew she was in good hands. You're a wonderful nurse. Our department has been investigating this ring for the last twenty-seven months. They had doctors, nurses, attorneys, just about any professional you can think of distributing drugs, and that's the reason why it was so hard to crack. You never think people with respected careers would ever be involved in something like this. After the incident at the clinic I knew we were close to cracking this case. It was just a matter of time to see who would try and cover their tracks. In this case, it was Jenkins. She never counted on her car being involved in the hit-and-run with you and Dr. Baptiste. After that, she ordered Scooter to get rid of Valerie." She shook her head. "I guess he does have some conscience. He told me about the hit. After Valerie stumbled into the clinic, Jenkins was shocked that her orders hadn't been carried out, and that's when she ordered me to kill her instead."

"But how did Valerie know about Jenkins?" A.J. asked, still trying to piece together the maze of information.

"Brother-in-law," Zach drawled, "Valerie didn't know that Jenkins was Gotti. Remember that day I told ya I was working on some stuff with the DEA and couldn't discuss it with ya?"

A.J. nodded as his mind flashed back to that afternoon in his kitchen.

"Well, Valerie mentioned the name Gotti to me," Zach told A.J. "I'd heard the name once when DEA brought Oakland police on the case. I contacted Agent Givens, and we figured the ringleader had to be located somewhere here in Oakland. The problem was figuring out exactly who Gotti was."

Agent Givens nodded. "After Lieutenant Tate informed us of this, it was actually his suggestion to stage Valerie's death, but only if we could guarantee him that she could get into the Witness Protection Program. We pinned our hopes on the fact that if the ringleader found this out, that they'd surface sooner rather than later. Valerie's in the program now and there are only a handful of people outside of this room that know she's still alive."

A.J. chuckled. "But Zach, you didn't find out about Jenkins's car until after you decided to fake Valerie's death, right?"

Zach chuckled and shook his head sideways. "Actually I knew 'bout it before then. Everything you and Baby Girl witnessed that night at the hospital, brother-in-law, was staged. Wouldn't never thought about faking Valerie's death until I found out about ya plan to fake a quarantine with Baby Girl here." His gaze drifted to Vic. "And then y'all decides to up and elope, and Caitlyn ups and wants to host the shower for you, and include Valerie." He shook his head. "Y'all threw my timing off. We'd planned to stage Valerie's death the day after I found out you and brother-in-law had eloped." He chuckled out loud and slipped his thumbs underneath his suspenders. "This here is one time I'm glad my baby talks a lot." He thrust his chest out proudly. "She keeps me informed."

Agent Givens nodded. "I'd already been ordered by Jenkins to kill Valerie and had to stall until your shower was over. After Lieutenant Tate told us you planned to surprise Valerie by bringing her children to see her, I couldn't spoil that reunion. Later that night, we put our plan into action."

"And Valerie," Vic said anxiously, her gaze going back and forth between Zach and Agent Givens, "Valerie's okay, right?"

Agent Givens nodded and smiled. "Mrs. Baptiste, she's wonderful. It took a lot of courage for her to do what she did." She glanced between Vic and A.J. "If the two of you hadn't shown her the support you did, I doubt she would have ever agreed to this plan. But once she knew her babies would be taken care of, she agreed without hesitation."

Vic extended her hand to Agent Givens. "Thank you so much for helping out Valerie."

Agent Givens nodded. "Thank you for helping us crack this case," she replied, winking at Zach, "even if it was a little unorthodox."

"Well, Zach," Vic said, after Agent Givens left the room. A long rush of breath escaped from her mouth. "Baptiste and I are in the wrong profession. Maybe we should come to work for you."

Zach shook his head. "Uh-uh. Right now the only place the two of y'all is going is to a jail cell."

"What?" Vic exclaimed with her hands on her hips.

"Zach," A.J. pleaded.

"Nope," Zach said, shaking his head. "Neither one of y'all is gonna get any pity out of me today." He looked sternly at both Vic and A.J. "Brother-in-law, I warned ya to stay out of this and let me handle it." He tossed a sharp look at Vic. "And you. When ya called me all frantic and told me what ya had discovered brother-in-law was up to, I told ya to stay home and don't move. But do the two of y'all listen to me? *Oh no!* Maybe if you spend a few hours locked up, you'll take me seriously next time I tell ya I got the situation under control."

A.J. chuckled. "Well, Marcel, Ray, Alex, and Lincoln were involved. What about them?"

Zach nodded. "I know, and ya can say hello to 'em when ya see 'em. They locked up, too." He looked over the uniformed police over and cracked a slight smile. "Lock 'em up."

A.J. was headed toward the door when he stopped in mid-stride and turned to Vic. "You did remember to feed Harry and Sally, didn't you?"

Vic chuckled. "Hush, man. I remembered."

EPILOGUE

Eighteen months later

"They're our babies now, right, Honey?" Taylor asked, placing her hand atop Vic's rounded belly.

Vic nodded with tears of joy. "They're ours, sweet pea."

With the court filled with family and friends as witnesses, Vic and A.J. signed the documents making them the legal adopted parents of Brianna and Chloé. After Valerie agreed to the arrangement, Vic and A.J. were more than happy to oblige. For Vic, the feeling was no less different than it was when she became Taylor and Tyler's adoptive mother months earlier.

"And you love this baby, too, right?" Tyler asked.

Vic nodded happily. "The same way I love the four of you," she replied, glancing at her four daughters. "Y'all are the babies of my heart, and this one," she said, rubbing her stomach, "is the baby of my tummy. I love you all the same."

Ray walked up and placed two small, black velvet boxes on the table. He smiled when Vic opened them and gasped at the tiny tea-cut diamond studs and shrugged. "Well, ya got 'em in designer labels. Figured it won't hurt to top it off with a little bling-bling. Can't have Baptiste women running around raggedy, now."

Vic clutched both hands against her stomach and panted as a hard contraction made her belly constrict. Everyone sprang into action with their pre-assigned responsibilities. They swiftly exited the courtroom.

A.J. walked back in moments later and carefully assisted Vic out her chair. "Woman, will you come on here?"

Another sharp contraction hit Vic and literally stole her breath away. "Baptiste, when this is over," she panted, "I'm gonna kill you."

Vic was asleep fourteen hours later, exhausted from a long labor and the C-section that followed when the baby refused to cooperate. A.J. looked down at Vic and thought he hadn't seen a more beautiful sight, despite the dark circles under her eyes. Until the day he died, he'd never forget the moment he placed the results of their belated honeymoon inside Vic's arms.

Walking around the room, A.J. carried his sleeping daughter, who had curly black hair and hazel eyes that he had finally managed to get a glimpse of when he provided her pediatric assessment immediately after birth.

Zach stuck his head in the door. "Brother-in-law," he whispered softly, "how Baby Girl doing there?"

A.J. glanced over at a sleeping Vic. "Tired. She had a tough time."

"Hell, I bet she did." Zach chuckled and nodded at the baby in A.J.'s arms. "Little Mama checked in at ten and some change." He held his arms out. "Here, let me hold her." With expert care, he cradled his niece against his chest. "Got a room full of kinfolk that can't wait to see ya." Glancing back at A.J., he asked, "Does Valerie know she's here, yet?"

A.J. nodded. "Agent Givens arranged for me to talk with her a couple of hours ago, and she's thrilled."

"Ya know, brother-in-law, Valerie is wise beyond her years. As a parent, she made the ultimate sacrifice."

A.J. nodded in agreement. Despite being in the Witness Protection Program, Valerie didn't want to take any chance that her past would somehow come back to haunt her and possibly put Bébé and CeCe in danger. That was the reason he and Vic agreed without hesitation to adopt them. Smiling down at his daughter, he moved in close to Zach. He hated that his brother-in-law had to miss out on the adoption signing, but knew he was across the street at another courthouse for the conclusion of Carmen Jenkins's trial. "How did it go today?" he whispered softly.

Zach smiled back. "We got her. Jury brought back a guilty verdict, and I don't believe friend will ever make it out the jailhouse." He winked. "Seems like me and brother-in-law," he teased, referring to Marcel, "is the only ones making baby boys in the family."

A.J. shrugged. "Hey, it's just my first shot."

"Trust me, you won't get another, either, if they're all this big. All she needs is a backpack and she's ready for kindergarten." Vic grimaced from the pain, but managed to shift up in bed and hold out her arms. "Here, let me have her."

"What's her name?" Zach asked. "Y'all done had us in suspense for months."

Vic trailed her fingers down her daughter's soft cheek and thought back over the past few months, especially of two wonderful women: one she'd come to love, and the other, even though she'd never met, she wanted to honor.

"Valerie Angelique Baptiste."

ABOUT THE AUTHOR

LaConnie Taylor-Jones, a native Memphian, is a health educator consultant and holds advanced degrees in community public health and business administration. Married, she is the mother of four and resides with her family in Antioch, California. She is also an active member of the Contra Costa Alumnae chapter of Delta Sigma Theta Sorority, Inc., the African American Community Health Advisory Committee, Black Women Organized for Political Action, and the San Francisco Area and Black Diamond Chapters of Romance Writers of America.

Coming in May from Genesis Press:

DREAM RUNNER
By Gail McFarland

CHAPTER 1

St. Louis, Missouri:

In the "zone," Marlea Kellogg closed her eyes and let the breath settle through her body. Exhaling slowly, she counted eight beats, then sucked in another big breath and let it course through her long, lean frame. She visualized herself heading for lane four and bending to the blocks, concentrating on what it would feel like to release the power and run, to feel the slap and push of her feet against the track.

Palms flat against the cool tile wall of the field house, her eyes moved behind her closed lids, tracking, seeing herself flashing past the others. Though her feet were still, Marlea could almost feel her body crashing the finish line, and she blew out hard when she imagined the kind of exhilaration that only a win could bring.

"Yeah," she whispered, sliding her hands over her sleek head. Ponytail intact, she almost laughed out loud.

"Libby was right; this mind/body thing has got me so revved up, I can outrun anything and anybody on the track."

She had proven that in the trials. Moving as though she was the only one on the track, Marlea Kellogg kicked it. She had blown past the two girls from Cal State as if they were standing still, never mind that they were from her alma mater. Marlea had done what she had to do, showing them the way it was supposed to be done. Her time on the 400-meter run was an effortless 49.75 seconds. Libby, restricted to trackside with the other coaches and trainers, had gone wild. Six years as Marlea's coach, and she had never seen her protégé come so close to a record time.

"It was a fluke," Marlea said, when Libby finally reached her side. "I've always loved the 400, and this time it just loved me back."

"Shut your mouth, girl! Be humble with somebody who doesn't know you. Honey, you ran the hell out of that track and you know it as well as I do. And you can do it again if you just get your head right."

So Marlea took another deep breath and concentrated on the sound of her heartbeat and the rush of her blood. Opening her eyes, slowly grounding herself, she knew Libby was right. This run, this race, they belonged to her, and nothing about them could be called fluke. Marlea bent into a lunge, felt the balance, shifted her legs, and knew the truth. "This is my destiny."

Raising her arms high over her head when she stood, continuing to stretch as she walked the path back to the track, Marlea struggled to keep her feet on the ground. "This time is gonna be different."

"Talking to yourself?" Libby Belcher spotted Marlea the second she stepped onto the cinder path leading to the track and pushed past other runners to get closer. "All I've got to say is, go on out there and do what you came here to do: run."

Above her head, the tinny loud speaker blared, "400-meter contestants to the staging area, please. 400-meter contestants, please." And Marlea knew it was time to move forward. She felt the edge of her red spandex top separating from her brief shorts and tugged it down. A moment of panic made her drop her hand to check for her hip number. It was there; her fingers found it right where it was supposed to be. No panic, no fear, she reminded herself. "Time to run."

Libby raised both hands in victory. "Do your thing, girl."

"No doubt," Marlea winked. It would have been a privilege to have run in the first heat, but she knew those were for elite runners, runners with higher lifetime marks, but that was okay. She had run in the second heat, and that was okay, too, because her time put her in the finals, easy. *They have to face me now. Now they have to run my race, my way.*

Eyes sweeping the stands, Marlea saw the crowd as one great blur, and loved the busy low roar it made. She heard the final call for the 400-meter run and her blood stirred. Orgasmic anticipation trembled through her, and she looked around to see if anyone had noticed. Not that it mattered; she knew with undeniable certainty what the outcome of this race would be.

Runners, take your mark . . .

Shaking off anything that had nothing to do with the run, she approached the start. Coiling her body, she folded low to fit herself into position. Pressing her heel against the block, she silently called on Jesus and dropped her head.

Get set . . .

Breathe . . . find the rhythm.

. . . go!

The sound of the gunshot was almost a cliché, but Marlea was more than ready for it as her body broke free. Long legs working with hydraulic precision, her feet found their flawless path. Never good at shorter distances, Marlea had no time to worry about it. Knowing that she had enough distance to build, she felt the speed pump through her muscled thighs as she passed someone at 100 meters. Passing the fast-talking Jamaican woman at 200 meters, all Marlea could hear was her own breathing. Rising on the wind, flying the only way a woman can without wings, she barely saw the competition, scarcely felt the break of the ribbon across her chest, and almost cried when she realized her 400-meter dance was done.

Her feet, trained for more years than she could count, continued to run, carrying her another 25 meters before the adrenaline began a slow ebb through her hot-fired body. Her breath pulled tight through her nose and rushed out past her open lips. Her mouth was dry and her lips parched, but her legs felt like she could run for an eternity. As it turned out, that wasn't necessary.

"You did it! You did it!" Libby Belcher screamed, running toward Marlea. Six years together and every win still made the trainer spastic. Libby's short, dark hair stood on end, and her arms flailed the air in delight as she ran toward the fence separating the stands from the track.

Marlea, high on adrenaline, couldn't hear Libby. The sound of the crowd and the slap of her slowing feet filled her ears. Breast rising fast, eyes on the time clock, she feared the seconds might not be enough, might not buy the dream she had wanted for so very long. What was taking them so long to . . .

In lane four . . . Marlea Kellogg . . .

Her knees turned buttery, and her head ached with the effort of trying to hear.

. . . track record . . . time of . . .

"What time?"

. . . 48:52 . . .

"You made it!" The Jamaican runner slapped her back, and Marlea remembered to breathe. Libby finally made it to Marlea's side just as the roar of the crowd confirmed what the runner cherished with her own eyes as her time was posted.

"I qualify," Marlea whispered. "Team trials, and then the Olympics. I qualify." Her eyes closed on the tears she had promised herself she would never shed. She had made that promise back when the "cute" girls teased her for racing boys, and foolishly beating them. And she had promised the tears would never fall back when her back and legs were sore from pounding out the miles, and she still had to make it in to her job at McDonald's, a job that she had to keep to pay for her running shoes.

"I qualify." *I'm finally good enough,* she didn't say, not daring to give voice to the hope that dared to creep around the disappointment she had learned to live with back when she was beaten out of a spot on the 1996 team in Barcelona. Gwen Torrance had blown by her like a force of nature. Marlea had bitten down hard on the hurt back in 2000 when she shortened her distance to 100 meters. The shorter run was nothing like her beloved 400, and all she ever saw of glorious Gail Devers was the back of the girl's head hurdling toward 100 meter glory—and she missed the U.S. team again.

After failing to make the team in Sacramento, she had watched Marion Jones's bright smile televised live from Australia and tried to smile back. Swallowing the bitter taste of ashes, she ignored Jones's flashy speed suit and accumulated medals from 2004. Knowing it was time to get on with her life, Marlea told herself that running didn't matter, but her heart had been promised Olympic gold, and her soul wouldn't rest without it.

When Libby and Hal Belcher decided to move to Atlanta to be close to aging parents, Marlea packed up her special ed degree and followed, as there was nothing left to hold her in Los Angeles. Not a bad move, all things considered. She settled in Marietta, just north of the city, and found a place on the staff of the Runyon Day School. Small and private, Runyon gave her a chance to work with the children she loved, and time to run.

At Runyon, Marlea met the kind of children she longed to teach. Diagnosed autistic, dyslexic, troubled, and otherwise learning disabled, they were children of wealth, privilege, and circumstance. They came from old aristocratic and new money families, and they were of diverse racial backgrounds. But they shared one thing: they all loved their teacher. In part, that love might have come from the fact that she expected the best from each of them and went out of her way to draw out their best efforts.

Her kids were especially proud of her running. There had never been a teacher quite like Marlea at Runyon. Her students thought she was a superhero, kind of like Wonder Woman or something. In each of her races, she had worn something they made for her, and she had won every time. Those gifts were the closest things to good luck charms Marlea Kellogg had ever owned. Today, she wore a band of bright braided thread around her right ankle, a gift from the kids.

And now she had a special gift for them. "I qualify," she said again, just loving the sound of the words.

"Not quite," her coach said. "You're only a couple of points short. A good local race and you're in. This is your year, babe. There's no denying you. Just hit a solid 10K, pick up the points you need, and you're good to go."

"The Peachtree," Marlea said without hesitation. She had already spent a lot of her off time working with her kids and their families on 2, 5, and 10K runs during the school year. Her children, labeled and sometimes limited by their learning disabilities, loved to run. And having them run with her sometimes gave her an advantage in the classroom. A 10K was a longer distance than she pre-ferred to run, but Marlea knew it was absolutely doable.

"If I gotta run one more, then that's a good one." She stopped there. No need telling Libby that she would run through hell in gasoline drawers if it would help get that Olympic gold. One final race to run to qualify for the Olympic Trials and it's the Peachtree Road Race—a piece of cake. Fourth of July in Atlanta would be one hot piece of cake.

Wind sprints were the most irritating thing in the world but . . . if they kept a brother fast enough to stay in the NFL, then he would run wind sprints until he couldn't move. A running back, AJ Yarborough knew he had outlasted a lot of the best, but he also knew that a knee, blown two years earlier, still took some pampering.

"I take care of you, and you take care of me," he bar-gained with his right knee. "It takes two, you know." The knee didn't make an audible reply, but AJ felt it twinge, and slowed to a jog. "No need overdoin' it," he cautioned himself. Four months out of surgery and a contract up for review—this was no time to jam up your knee, espe-cially with new kids out there every year making it harder and harder to compete, particularly when you looked at players like LaDainian Tomlinson, Larry Johnson, and Shaun Alexander.

"The new guys are all so damned young, and not in a refreshing way like the guys who came along with me."

True enough, most of those who started with him were done; except for the rare ones like Ahman Green or Warrick Dunn, most of them were retired warhorses. But these young ones, they were fire-eaters. The boys weren't just young and fast, they were smart, and learning more every time out. They were the competition, the contenders.

They were the future.

The future. "Humph, that used to sound like, 'once upon a time' to me. Now it sounds like a deadline." Truth be told, coming back from injury, it sounded like the end of a lifelong passion. At thirty-four, AJ knew the career wouldn't last forever—but that didn't stop him from wishing and hoping for the best. So he ran harder. Liking the solid sound of his feet against the road, he sniffed cool air and ignored the tiny electrical jolt in his knee. "Doc said I'd feel a little somethin' there," he recalled. "Least I know that my knee is working now."

The click in his knee paced his run and made him analyze his whole body. Taking inventory as he ran, he was pretty sure that everything seemed to work right, but he could practically *hear* his knee. The surgical reminder sounded almost mechanical to AJ's ear. "A machine," he complimented himself, looking for the silver lining and enjoying the free flow of his healthy body as he ran. "This man is a machine."

Following the rolling hills of his southwest Atlanta property, that was easy enough to say, but he sure hadn't felt like a machine during that last game. That was the one where he had been close enough to taste the rushing record. Instead, he had taken the hit—a hard one, right at the knees. It sent him airborne and he had to be helped from the field in anguish.

Still running, he heard the steps of another runner. The pace had a distinctive rhythm, one foot slightly lagging. A hard-breathing man from the sound of it, probably his on-again, off-again house guest. He turned to see who it was. Sure enough, Dench Traylor slugged along, steadily pickin' 'em up and puttin' 'em down. Struggling, the man pulled even with AJ when the bigger man slowed to accommodate him. Puffing, he put out a hand, entreating.

AJ was surprised. Dench had always hated running and he had never made any secret of his dislike for recreational running—not even during their days of scholarship-enforced athletics. Traylor, now a Miami assistant special-team coach, wasn't in bad shape, just not NFL prime. "You running today?"

"Tryin'," Dench puffed.

The player slowed, then stopped. "You might as well know it now, Rissa's not out here with me," he teased. Marissa Yarborough was about the only person in the world that Dench would willingly run behind.

"This is not about your sister, man."

AJ grinned when Dench stopped and sucked wind. AJ circled him, letting his cooling muscles wind themselves down. Dench Traylor shook his lowered head and held out a white envelope. "Whatcha got?" AJ grinned, slitting the envelope's flap with a long thick finger.

"Read it."

Pulling the typewritten sheet from the envelope, AJ was confused by the stiff formal paper. Didn't that make whatever was written official? The letterhead sheet featured his team logo, and for a blank half second, he wondered why anyone from the Miami-based team would be sending him mail. Baffled, he shook the letter completely open and read it. He had to read it twice to make sure of the contents. "They're letting me go? Just like that?" He read it again. "Just like that?"

"Dude," Dench said.

"What's that supposed to mean?" AJ was hard pressed to know whether it was a comment or a criticism. He crushed the letter in his meaty hand and glared at the assistant coach.

Finally able to breathe, Dench stood straighter and stared at the ground. "I thought you ought to know," he said.

Ought to know that his career was over? Know that his numbers were as high as they were ever going to go? That he would never earn a Super Bowl ring to call his own?

Eyes on the sky, it took AJ long seconds to reply. "Yeah, but I thought that when it got to be this time . . ." *What? They would throw me some kind of special big hints? An "over the hill" party? What?* That last play of his last game unwound itself in his head again. The memory was so vivid, he almost felt the searing rip hack its way through his knee when he went down. He could hear the muted voices, as if they thought he couldn't hear . . .

He's had a long run . . .

Could be career ending . . .
More than a setback . . .
What if this time . . .

What could anybody say that would make it any easier? He could go back to his agent, get her to find another team. That was the beauty of hiring your kid sister as your agent. She could ask for some kind of waiver that would give him . . . *a Super Bowl ring? That rushing record I've run my whole life for? Or maybe I should just shut my eyes on the game, the only thing in life that has truly given me pleasure, and move on. Suck it up.*

"I didn't want this to come as any more of a shock than it already is. They won't make the announcement for another couple of weeks, but I wanted you to be ready when it came out." Dench watched AJ circle him, and knew the thoughts that must be running through his mind. He had come so close over the years. Been traded twice, always up, but traded all the same. Every team promised but none fully delivered. AJ was always left hungry.

"I always knew this wouldn't last forever . . ." Even as he said it, AJ couldn't stop himself. A lot of what he thought tended to spill from his lips. It was a bad habit, talking to himself, but it was one he had never been quite able to shake.

Dench crossed his arms over his solid barrel of a chest. "We've been together a long time, man. I know the hurt you're feelin', but this doesn't have to be the end. You've still got power. You can still run."

"An' I'm a thirty-four year old runner in a game played like war by twenty-two year olds. Lasting 'til you reach thirty is a good stretch for a runner. The irony is not lost on me."

"But it's not the only thing you know. You've got other things going for you," Dench suggested. Antoine Jacob Yarborough Jr. was a smart man, smart in a lot of ways. Not a lot of the men gifted enough to play in the NFL had his kind of savvy—even if he did talk to himself. AJ might truly hate his given name, but he was smart enough to have finished the education degree as he had promised his folks. He had gone on to complete the master's degree that got him into physical therapy school during the off-seasons. It's not like he'll ever be hurtin' for money, his friend thought, realizing where the real pain would always come from.

"So, ah, AJ? You got any plans?"

"Not yet," the now ex-player said, pacing. "Maybe I'll go ahead and set up a PT practice on my own. The Lord knows I'll sure have time for it now." Stopping midstep, he looked back the way he had come, then turned and stared out at the road ahead of him. His eyes narrowed, and he wiped his big hands against his sweatpants. "Besides that, I don't know, but I gotta go forward. Got to."

"How you gonna do that, AJ?"

The player began a steady jog up the road. "Only way I know how." He picked up speed, forcing the other man to run harder. "I'm gonna run."

2008 Reprint Mass Market Titles

January

Cautious Heart
Cheris F. Hodges
ISBN-13: 978-1-58571-301-1
ISBN-10: 1-58571-301-5
$6.99

Suddenly You
Crystal Hubbard
ISBN-13: 978-1-58571-302-8
ISBN-10: 1-58571-302-3
$6.99

February

Passion
T. T. Henderson
ISBN-13: 978-1-58571-303-5
ISBN-10: 1-58571-303-1
$6.99

Whispers in the Sand
LaFlorya Gauthier
ISBN-13: 978-1-58571-304-2
ISBN-10: 1-58571-304-x
$6.99

March

Life Is Never As It Seems
J. J. Michael
ISBN-13: 978-1-58571-305-9
ISBN-10: 1-58571-305-8
$6.99

Beyond the Rapture
Beverly Clark
ISBN-13: 978-1-58571-306-6
ISBN-10: 1-58571-306-6
$6.99

April

A Heart's Awakening
Veronica Parker
ISBN-13: 978-1-58571-307-3
ISBN-10: 1-58571-307-4
$6.99

Breeze
Robin Lynette Hampton
ISBN-13: 978-1-58571-308-0
ISBN-10: 1-58571-308-2
$6.99

May

I'll Be Your Shelter
Giselle Carmichael
ISBN-13: 978-1-58571-309-7
ISBN-10: 1-58571-309-0
$6.99

Careless Whispers
Rochelle Alers
ISBN-13: 978-1-58571-310-3
ISBN-10: 1-58571-310-4
$6.99

June

Sin
Crystal Rhodes
ISBN-13: 978-1-58571-311-0
ISBN-10: 1-58571-311-2
$6.99

Dark Storm Rising
Chinelu Moore
ISBN-13: 978-1-58571-312-7
ISBN-10: 1-58571-312-0
$6.99

2008 Reprint Mass Market Titles (continued)

July

Object of His Desire
A.C. Arthur
ISBN-13: 978-1-58571-313-4
ISBN-10: 1-58571-313-9
$6.99

Angel's Paradise
Janice Angelique
ISBN-13: 978-1-58571-314-1
ISBN-10: 1-58571-314-7
$6.99

August

Unbreak My Heart
Dar Tomlinson
ISBN-13: 978-1-58571-315-8
ISBN-10: 1-58571-315-5
$6.99

All I Ask
Barbara Keaton
ISBN-13: 978-1-58571-316-5
ISBN-10: 1-58571-316-3
$6.99

September

Icie
Pamela Leigh Starr
ISBN-13: 978-1-58571-275-5
ISBN-10: 1-58571-275-2
$6.99

At Last
Lisa Riley
ISBN-13: 978-1-58571-276-2
ISBN-10: 1-58571-276-0
$6.99

October

Everlastin' Love
Gay G. Gunn
ISBN-13: 978-1-58571-277-9
ISBN-10: 1-58571-277-9
$6.99

Three Wishes
Seressia Glass
ISBN-13: 978-1-58571-278-6
ISBN-10: 1-58571-278-7
$6.99

November

Yesterday Is Gone
Beverly Clark
ISBN-13: 978-1-58571-279-3
ISBN-10: 1-58571-279-5
$6.99

Again My Love
Kayla Perrin
ISBN-13: 978-1-58571-280-9
ISBN-10: 1-58571-280-9
$6.99

December

Office Policy
A.C. Arthur
ISBN-13: 978-1-58571-281-6
ISBN-10: 1-58571-281-7
$6.99

Rendezvous With Fate
Jeanne Sumerix
ISBN-13: 978-1-58571-283-3
ISBN-10: 1-58571-283-3
$6.99

2008 New Mass Market Titles

January

Where I Want To Be
Maryam Diaab
ISBN-13: 978-1-58571-268-7
ISBN-10: 1-58571-268-X
$6.99

Never Say Never
Michele Cameron
ISBN-13: 978-1-58571-269-4
ISBN-10: 1-58571-269-8
$6.99

February

Stolen Memories
Michele Sudler
ISBN-13: 978-1-58571-270-0
ISBN-10: 1-58571-270-1
$6.99

Dawn's Harbor
Kymberly Hunt
ISBN-13: 978-1-58571-271-7
ISBN-10: 1-58571-271-X
$6.99

March

Undying Love
Renee Alexis
ISBN-13: 978-1-58571-272-4
ISBN-10: 1-58571-272-8
$6.99

Blame It On Paradise
Crystal Hubbard
ISBN-13: 978-1-58571-273-1
ISBN-10: 1-58571-273-6
$6.99

April

When A Man Loves A Woman
La Connie Taylor-Jones
ISBN-13: 978-1-58571-274-8
ISBN-10: 1-58571-274-4
$6.99

Choices
Tammy Williams
ISBN-13: 978-1-58571-300-4
ISBN-10: 1-58571-300-7
$6.99

May

Dream Runner
Gail McFarland
ISBN-13: 978-1-58571-317-2
ISBN-10: 1-58571-317-1
$6.99

Southern Fried Standards
S.R. Maddox
ISBN-13: 978-1-58571-318-9
ISBN-10: 1-58571-318-X
$6.99

June

Looking for Lily
Africa Fine
ISBN-13: 978-1-58571-319-6
ISBN-10: 1-58571-319-8
$6.99

Bliss, Inc.
Chamein Canton
ISBN-13: 978-1-58571-325-7
ISBN-10: 1-58571-325-2
$6.99

2008 New Mass Market Titles (continued)

July

Love's Secrets
Yolanda McVey
ISBN-13: 978-1-58571-321-9
ISBN-10: 1-58571-321-X
$6.99

Things Forbidden
Maryam Diaab
ISBN-13: 978-1-58571-327-1
ISBN-10: 1-58571-327-9
$6.99

August

Storm
Pamela Leigh Starr
ISBN-13: 978-1-58571-323-3
ISBN-10: 1-58571-323-6
$6.99

Passion's Furies
AlTonya Washington
ISBN-13: 978-1-58571-324-0
ISBN-10: 1-58571-324-4
$6.99

September

Three Doors Down
Michele Sudler
ISBN-13: 978-1-58571-332-5
ISBN-10: 1-58571-332-5
$6.99

Mr Fix-It
Crystal Hubbard
ISBN-13: 978-1-58571-326-4
ISBN-10: 1-58571-326-0
$6.99

October

Moments of Clarity
Michele Cameron
ISBN-13: 978-1-58571-330-1
ISBN-10: 1-58571-330-9
$6.99

Lady Preacher
K.T. Richey
ISBN-13: 978-1-58571-333-2
ISBN-10: 1-58571-333-3
$6.99

November

This Life Isn't Perfect Holla
Sandra Foy
ISBN: 978-1-58571-331-8
ISBN-10: 1-58571-331-7
$6.99

Promises Made
Bernice Layton
ISBN-13: 978-1-58571-334-9
ISBN-10: 1-58571-334-1
$6.99

December

A Voice Behind Thunder
Carrie Elizabeth Greene
ISBN-13: 978-1-58571-329-5
ISBN-10: 1-58571-329-5
$6.99

The More Things Change
Chamein Canton
ISBN-13: 978-1-58571-328-8
ISBN-10: 1-58571-328-7
$6.99

Other Genesis Press, Inc. Titles

A Dangerous Deception	J.M. Jeffries	$8.95
A Dangerous Love	J.M. Jeffries	$8.95
A Dangerous Obsession	J.M. Jeffries	$8.95
A Drummer's Beat to Mend	Kei Swanson	$9.95
A Happy Life	Charlotte Harris	$9.95
A Heart's Awakening	Veronica Parker	$9.95
A Lark on the Wing	Phyliss Hamilton	$9.95
A Love of Her Own	Cheris F. Hodges	$9.95
A Love to Cherish	Beverly Clark	$8.95
A Risk of Rain	Dar Tomlinson	$8.95
A Taste of Temptation	Reneé Alexis	$9.95
A Twist of Fate	Beverly Clark	$8.95
A Will to Love	Angie Daniels	$9.95
Acquisitions	Kimberley White	$8.95
Across	Carol Payne	$12.95
After the Vows	Leslie Esdaile	$10.95
(Summer Anthology)	T.T. Henderson	
	Jacqueline Thomas	
Again My Love	Kayla Perrin	$10.95
Against the Wind	Gwynne Forster	$8.95
All I Ask	Barbara Keaton	$8.95
Always You	Crystal Hubbard	$6.99
Ambrosia	T.T. Henderson	$8.95
An Unfinished Love Affair	Barbara Keaton	$8.95
And Then Came You	Dorothy Elizabeth Love	$8.95
Angel's Paradise	Janice Angelique	$9.95
At Last	Lisa G. Riley	$8.95
Best of Friends	Natalie Dunbar	$8.95
Beyond the Rapture	Beverly Clark	$9.95

Other Genesis Press, Inc. Titles (continued)

Other Genesis Press, Inc. Titles (continued)

Daughter of the Wind	Joan Xian	$8.95
Deadly Sacrifice	Jack Kean	$22.95
Designer Passion	Dar Tomlinson	$8.95
	Diana Richeaux	
Do Over	Celya Bowers	$9.95
Dreamtective	Liz Swados	$5.95
Ebony Angel	Deatri King-Bey	$9.95
Ebony Butterfly II	Delilah Dawson	$14.95
Echoes of Yesterday	Beverly Clark	$9.95
Eden's Garden	Elizabeth Rose	$8.95
Eve's Prescription	Edwina Martin Arnold	$8.95
Everlastin' Love	Gay G. Gunn	$8.95
Everlasting Moments	Dorothy Elizabeth Love	$8.95
Everything and More	Sinclair Lebeau	$8.95
Everything but Love	Natalie Dunbar	$8.95
Falling	Natalie Dunbar	$9.95
Fate	Pamela Leigh Starr	$8.95
Finding Isabella	A.J. Garrotto	$8.95
Forbidden Quest	Dar Tomlinson	$10.95
Forever Love	Wanda Y. Thomas	$8.95
From the Ashes	Kathleen Suzanne	$8.95
	Jeanne Sumerix	
Gentle Yearning	Rochelle Alers	$10.95
Glory of Love	Sinclair LeBeau	$10.95
Go Gentle into that Good Night	Malcom Boyd	$12.95
Goldengroove	Mary Beth Craft	$16.95
Groove, Bang, and Jive	Steve Cannon	$8.99
Hand in Glove	Andrea Jackson	$9.95

Other Genesis Press, Inc. Titles (continued)

Hard to Love	Kimberley White	$9.95
Hart & Soul	Angie Daniels	$8.95
Heart of the Phoenix	A.C. Arthur	$9.95
Heartbeat	Stephanie Bedwell-Grime	$8.95
Hearts Remember	M. Loui Quezada	$8.95
Hidden Memories	Robin Allen	$10.95
Higher Ground	Leah Latimer	$19.95
Hitler, the War, and the Pope	Ronald Rychiak	$26.95
How to Write a Romance	Kathryn Falk	$18.95
I Married a Reclining Chair	Lisa M. Fuhs	$8.95
I'll Be Your Shelter	Giselle Carmichael	$8.95
I'll Paint a Sun	A.J. Garrotto	$9.95
Icie	Pamela Leigh Starr	$8.95
Illusions	Pamela Leigh Starr	$8.95
Indigo After Dark Vol. I	Nia Dixon/Angelique	$10.95
Indigo After Dark Vol. II	Dolores Bundy/ Cole Riley	$10.95
Indigo After Dark Vol. III	Montana Blue/ Coco Morena	$10.95
Indigo After Dark Vol. IV	Cassandra Colt/	$14.95
Indigo After Dark Vol. V	Delilah Dawson	$14.95
Indiscretions	Donna Hill	$8.95
Intentional Mistakes	Michele Sudler	$9.95
Interlude	Donna Hill	$8.95
Intimate Intentions	Angie Daniels	$8.95
It's Not Over Yet	J.J. Michael	$9.95
Jolie's Surrender	Edwina Martin-Arnold	$8.95
Kiss or Keep	Debra Phillips	$8.95
Lace	Giselle Carmichael	$9.95

Other Genesis Press, Inc. Titles (continued)

Last Train to Memphis	Elsa Cook	$12.95
Lasting Valor	Ken Olsen	$24.95
Let Us Prey	Hunter Lundy	$25.95
Lies Too Long	Pamela Ridley	$13.95
Life Is Never As It Seems	J.J. Michael	$12.95
Lighter Shade of Brown	Vicki Andrews	$8.95
Love Always	Mildred E. Riley	$10.95
Love Doesn't Come Easy	Charlyne Dickerson	$8.95
Love Unveiled	Gloria Greene	$10.95
Love's Deception	Charlene Berry	$10.95
Love's Destiny	M. Loui Quezada	$8.95
Mae's Promise	Melody Walcott	$8.95
Magnolia Sunset	Giselle Carmichael	$8.95
Many Shades of Gray	Dyanne Davis	$6.99
Matters of Life and Death	Lesego Malepe, Ph.D.	$15.95
Meant to Be	Jeanne Sumerix	$8.95
Midnight Clear (Anthology)	Leslie Esdaile Gwynne Forster Carmen Green Monica Jackson	$10.95
Midnight Magic	Gwynne Forster	$8.95
Midnight Peril	Vicki Andrews	$10.95
Misconceptions	Pamela Leigh Starr	$9.95
Montgomery's Children	Richard Perry	$14.95
My Buffalo Soldier	Barbara B. K. Reeves	$8.95
Naked Soul	Gwynne Forster	$8.95
Next to Last Chance	Louisa Dixon	$24.95
No Apologies	Seressia Glass	$8.95
No Commitment Required	Seressia Glass	$8.95

Other Genesis Press, Inc. Titles (continued)

No Regrets	Mildred E. Riley	$8.95
Not His Type	Chamein Canton	$6.99
Nowhere to Run	Gay G. Gunn	$10.95
O Bed! O Breakfast!	Rob Kuehnle	$14.95
Object of His Desire	A. C. Arthur	$8.95
Office Policy	A. C. Arthur	$9.95
Once in a Blue Moon	Dorianne Cole	$9.95
One Day at a Time	Bella McFarland	$8.95
One in A Million	Barbara Keaton	$6.99
One of These Days	Michele Sudler	$9.95
Outside Chance	Louisa Dixon	$24.95
Passion	T.T. Henderson	$10.95
Passion's Blood	Cherif Fortin	$22.95
Passion's Journey	Wanda Y. Thomas	$8.95
Past Promises	Jahmel West	$8.95
Path of Fire	T.T. Henderson	$8.95
Path of Thorns	Annetta P. Lee	$9.95
Peace Be Still	Colette Haywood	$12.95
Picture Perfect	Reon Carter	$8.95
Playing for Keeps	Stephanie Salinas	$8.95
Pride & Joi	Gay G. Gunn	$15.95
Pride & Joi	Gay G. Gunn	$8.95
Promises to Keep	Alicia Wiggins	$8.95
Quiet Storm	Donna Hill	$10.95
Reckless Surrender	Rochelle Alers	$6.95
Red Polka Dot in a World of Plaid	Varian Johnson	$12.95
Reluctant Captive	Joyce Jackson	$8.95
Rendezvous with Fate	Jeanne Sumerix	$8.95

Other Genesis Press, Inc. Titles (continued)

Revelations	Cheris F. Hodges	$8.95
Rivers of the Soul	Leslie Esdaile	$8.95
Rocky Mountain Romance	Kathleen Suzanne	$8.95
Rooms of the Heart	Donna Hill	$8.95
Rough on Rats and Tough on Cats	Chris Parker	$12.95
Secret Library Vol. 1	Nina Sheridan	$18.95
Secret Library Vol. 2	Cassandra Colt	$8.95
Secret Thunder	Annetta P. Lee	$9.95
Shades of Brown	Denise Becker	$8.95
Shades of Desire	Monica White	$8.95
Shadows in the Moonlight	Jeanne Sumerix	$8.95
Sin	Crystal Rhodes	$8.95
Small Whispers	Annetta P. Lee	$6.99
So Amazing	Sinclair LeBeau	$8.95
Somebody's Someone	Sinclair LeBeau	$8.95
Someone to Love	Alicia Wiggins	$8.95
Song in the Park	Martin Brant	$15.95
Soul Eyes	Wayne L. Wilson	$12.95
Soul to Soul	Donna Hill	$8.95
Southern Comfort	J.M. Jeffries	$8.95
Still the Storm	Sharon Robinson	$8.95
Still Waters Run Deep	Leslie Esdaile	$8.95
Stolen Kisses	Dominiqua Douglas	$9.95
Stories to Excite You	Anna Forrest/Divine	$14.95
Subtle Secrets	Wanda Y. Thomas	$8.95
Suddenly You	Crystal Hubbard	$9.95
Sweet Repercussions	Kimberley White	$9.95
Sweet Sensations	Gwendolyn Bolton	$9.95

Other Genesis Press, Inc. Titles (continued)

Sweet Tomorrows	Kimberly White	$8.95
Taken by You	Dorothy Elizabeth Love	$9.95
Tattooed Tears	T. T. Henderson	$8.95
The Color Line	Lizzette Grayson Carter	$9.95
The Color of Trouble	Dyanne Davis	$8.95
The Disappearance of Allison Jones	Kayla Perrin	$5.95
The Fires Within	Beverly Clark	$9.95
The Foursome	Celya Bowers	$6.99
The Honey Dipper's Legacy	Pannell-Allen	$14.95
The Joker's Love Tune	Sidney Rickman	$15.95
The Little Pretender	Barbara Cartland	$10.95
The Love We Had	Natalie Dunbar	$8.95
The Man Who Could Fly	Bob & Milana Beamon	$18.95
The Missing Link	Charlyne Dickerson	$8.95
The Mission	Pamela Leigh Starr	$6.99
The Perfect Frame	Beverly Clark	$9.95
The Price of Love	Sinclair LeBeau	$8.95
The Smoking Life	Ilene Barth	$29.95
The Words of the Pitcher	Kei Swanson	$8.95
Three Wishes	Seressia Glass	$8.95
Ties That Bind	Kathleen Suzanne	$8.95
Tiger Woods	Libby Hughes	$5.95
Time is of the Essence	Angie Daniels	$9.95
Timeless Devotion	Bella McFarland	$9.95
Tomorrow's Promise	Leslie Esdaile	$8.95
Truly Inseparable	Wanda Y. Thomas	$8.95
Two Sides to Every Story	Dyanne Davis	$9.95
Unbreak My Heart	Dar Tomlinson	$8.95

Other Genesis Press, Inc. Titles (continued)

Uncommon Prayer	Kenneth Swanson	$9.95
Unconditional Love	Alicia Wiggins	$8.95
Unconditional	A.C. Arthur	$9.95
Until Death Do Us Part	Susan Paul	$8.95
Vows of Passion	Bella McFarland	$9.95
Wedding Gown	Dyanne Davis	$8.95
What's Under Benjamin's Bed	Sandra Schaffer	$8.95
When Dreams Float	Dorothy Elizabeth Love	$8.95
When I'm With You	LaConnie Taylor-Jones	$6.99
Whispers in the Night	Dorothy Elizabeth Love	$8.95
Whispers in the Sand	LaFlorya Gauthier	$10.95
Who's That Lady?	Andrea Jackson	$9.95
Wild Ravens	Altonya Washington	$9.95
Yesterday Is Gone	Beverly Clark	$10.95
Yesterday's Dreams, Tomorrow's Promises	Reon Laudat	$8.95
Your Precious Love	Sinclair LeBeau	$8.95

Order Form

Mail to: Genesis Press, Inc.
P.O. Box 101
Columbus, MS 39703

Name _____
Address _____
City/State _____ Zip _____
Telephone _____

Ship to (if different from above)
Name _____
Address _____
City/State _____ Zip _____
Telephone _____

Credit Card Information
Credit Card # _____ ☐ Visa   ☐ Mastercard
Expiration Date (mm/yy) _____ ☐ AmEx   ☐ Discover

Qty.	Author	Title	Price	Total

Use this order form, or call 1-888-INDIGO-1	
Total for books	_____
Shipping and handling: $5 first two books, $1 each additional book	Total S & H _____
Total amount enclosed	_____

Mississippi residents add 7% sales tax